KF
4c

GOODBYE L.A.

BY MURRAY SINCLAIR

Black Lizard Books • 1988

Ben Crandel Mysteries by Murray Sinclair:

TOUGH LUCK L.A.
ONLY IN L.A.
GOODBYE L.A.

Copyright © 1988 by Murray Sinclair

For information contact:
BLACK LIZARD BOOKS
Creative Arts Book Company
833 Bancroft Way
Berkeley, CA 94710

Typography by QuadraType
Cover Design by Charles Fuhrman
Cover Illustration by Jim Kirwan

Library of Congress Cataloging-in-Publication Data

Sinclair, Murray
    Goodbye L.A.

    (A Ben Crandel mystery)
    I. Title. II. Series: Sinclair, Murray. Ben Crandel
mystery.
PS3569.I525G6   1988   813'.54   87-71821
ISBN 0-88739-082-X

Manufactured in the United States of America.

For *Lauren*

· ONE ·

There's a mile and a half stretch of Santa Monica Boulevard, between Robertson and Crescent Heights in West Hollywood, that caters to more needs than most people would ever dream of having. But if you happen to be the sort of guy or gal who would rather buy a few pairs of custom-made silk bikini briefs than take your niece or nephew to Disneyland, it might be just your sort of place. You can get anything along here, from a new Rolls Royce or Mercedes to a remote control vibrator the size of a California Redwood. The boutiques have names like International Male, All American Boy, The Pleasure Chest, or Machismo. There are discos and pickup bars of various persuasions. Step into the wrong one on a hot August night and you'll stand a good chance of getting a beer glass cracked across your puss. It's not a great place to be a tourist taking uneducated guesses, but if you need to get yourself waxed, tanned, massaged, or adjusted; if you'd like to take home a live lobster or eat a steak, burger, chili, chow mein, tacos, pizza, or pancakes; if you wouldn't mind doing a little bargain shopping for your S/M party wear while your poodle is getting groomed; or if you just haven't been able to find anything adult enough to read in the middle of the night, why, then come hither!

For myself, I find it all about as appealing as that smog-on-toast aftertaste you get when you're caught in the right-hand lane following a belching semi, but the Palm Restaurant is on the Beverly Hills side of this circus. It's a small stagey place with sawdust on the floor and cartoon caricatures on the walls depicting nearly the entire living, dying, and dead population of the land of That's Entertainment. For about a hundred bucks per person, you can get yourself a medium size New York, a five pound lobster, drinks, a bottle of house wine, and a cup of coffee, but it's good stuff. The homemade cottage fries and onion rings just melt in your mouth, and the throwaway wall art makes for easy roving eyes. The haut monde of moviedom makes it a point to visit here regularly, and you can gawk at anybody your little heart desires as long as you're pretending to be looking at that cute doodle of Dino just above their head.

I was hoping this might be a good place to take somebody who presently wasn't much for conversation. You see, I was on a mercy mission to pep up my buddy George. Being a cop, he wasn't exactly the Hollywood type, but the Palm Restaurant was close enough to his beat in West Hollywood and I knew he liked a good steak, so I thought it was worth the splurge. I could afford it. I'd been riding high since the last writer's strike. I felt like celebrating. I only wished that George did.

I'd been worried about him. Steifer's a fierce little guy, serious but quick to quip, that is until his recent divorce. I thought his problem had something to do with the possibility that he was still in love with his ex-wife Shirley who had fallen for her marriage counselor, somebody with money who was now showing her a better time than George had, which had something to do with Shirley's guilt over not being able to bear George any children. Getting this vague background out of Steifer was as easy as pulling teeth and took many months. He liked having company, but he didn't like talking about himself. My specialty is filling a void and I had been bullying Steifer, force-feeding him drinks and conversation for as long as I could remember now. But he wasn't loosening up. Tonight, if anything, he was stiffer than usual. I was drinking myself under the table in my effort to get him lubricated; and the drunker I got, the soberer he seemed.

Once or twice in the course of our dull delicious meal, our eyes crossed paths; mine were probing for an opening as I worked hard to keep my concern from turning into consternation; his made me think of our lobster looking up out of the boiling kettle in the kitchen. Nonetheless, I thought I had the ticket when two girls with English accents and sleeveless linen dresses that should have gone with parasols leaned over from the booth across and asked us if the lobster was a good choice. The prettier one had eyes for George. She kept looking at him in that naughty innocent way they have, but George had no idea she wanted him to ruffle her petticoat. He was too busy staring at his plate. I pitched right in and started talking too much and asking too many questions. They didn't live here and yes they were on holiday for a fortnight visiting relatives. They smiled brightly each time I slurred a word, but George brought the whole thing to a close when he asked for the check, then got up and left the table after saying he was sorry he didn't feel well.

I found him outside, leaning up against a parking meter. Yes, he was OK. No, he wasn't feeling sorry for himself, he wasn't trying to avoid new people, and it wasn't Shirley, his ex. It was something else. I told him he was sounding pretty damn mysterious and reminded him that you can bring a horse to water, but you can't make him jump in the Jacuzzi. It's easy to be flip about it now, but my dander was up at the time. I thought Steifer was crying out for a good kick in the butt and I told him so. Sure, we could keep hitting the hot spots, but if George didn't open his mouth or look people in the eye, he was going to fossilize. He just had to get over Shirley.

George nodded along as if he was taking my advice. Full of myself, I ordered him to take a walk with me and gave him more of the same as we made our way through the heart of Boy's Town. Guys rubbed shoulders with us all the way. Two cars, one with a single lonely soul, the other with two, stopped and asked us what we were doing. George kept

quickening the pace and before I knew it we were up past La
Cienega. There was action up ahead of us. Girls in furs and
high heels walked slowly around corners, trying to look as if
they were waiting for the school bus. Young men carried paper bags into Winchell's Donuts and came out empty-
handed. Assorted clusters of skinheads and longhairs, black
dudes in shiny rayon and wide brim hats milled about the
parking lot across from the Starwood Club up at the corner
of Crescent Heights. The Starwood had gone from glitter
rock to punk over the past few years. Evidence of this was to
be found as a slew of spikey-haired demons poured onto the
sidewalk, coming out of the exits. A set had just ended and
they were getting air. George was looking up ahead. He kept
barreling forward. I was getting winded just keeping up
with him.

I was ready to turn around. I wasn't dying to pass
through a youthful crowd of pale sneering faces. I knew the
punk scene firsthand. My boy Pete was on the verge of dropping out of high school so he could dedicate himself to his
"music," as he called it. He was the lead singer in a band
called Claustrophobic, which was just what they did to me.
You wouldn't have to hear them to understand. Take my
word for it.

"George, come on," I said. "I'm not walking through any
jungles without my compass and pith helmet."

I didn't especially feel like bumping into my son tonight
either. He spent half his waking hours hanging out around
here. Truth is, I was feeling a little lonely. What I really
wanted was to drag Steifer back to the Palm before those English sisters finished their steak and lobster.

"George."

I put a hand on Steifer's shoulder. He shrugged me off in
a way that made me raise my eyebrows. Then, straightening
suddenly like a pointer who had just picked up his scent, he
was off running. My mouth agape, I stood there watching as
Steifer broke through the crowd of punks, setting off a chain
reaction that sent their shadowy figures toppling over each
other like a bunch of upended dominoes. They swore like

sailors, yelling after George. I shrugged, then followed suit, getting through the parted sea without incident.

Steifer was chasing a tall wiry white-haired kid in a loose unzipped leather jacket that flapped outwards on both sides of him as he ran. He wore heavy boots with biker chains shackled about the ankles that rattled like maracas and looked to be putting him at a disadvantage as Steifer narrowed the distance, his short legs pumping high, his hands clutching for a hold of any kind.

They flew off the sidewalk, hit the street, then bounded up onto a short triangular patch of grass in the middle of the intersection. The white-haired punk jumped into the crosswalk against a red light, forcing two cars to slam on their brakes and careen up onto the grass island. He cut sharply up the northeast side of Crescent Heights, then back across the street, dodging more oncoming traffic. Steifer followed recklessly.

I made a sharp left at the corner and intersected their approach on the side street. They came running at me. I got ready to roll a body block across the sidewalk when George snagged hold of his prey by the jacket collar. The punk looked back and chopped upwards under Steifer's arm, freeing himself, but then he stumbled. George jumped him and he lunged forward, going flat-out facedown over a short patchy lawn fronting a small apartment building.

Steifer rode the punk's back, using him for a bobsled. He leaned forward, his elbow and forearm going directly to the kid's neck, squishing his face into the ground. Then he got off, kneeled by his shoulders, and switched to a headlock. His face ran with sweat and his khaki suit coat, wet through now, hung limply about his powerful small shoulders. His striped tie had been swept around the back of his neck. He looked like David battling Goliath's kid brother. The punk was bird-boned but tall, long-legged. He looked comical struggling to lift his head, with his butt almost straight up and his legs pumping crazily, like some sort of ostrich that had got stuck. He had black roots at the base of his frizzhead of short white hair. Five or six cold sores framed a long, lipless mouth biting desperately at the bit as he squirmed to free himself. His pasty complexion was reddening and his wide eyes were amazed, but certainly not panicked. He'd been through this sort of thing before.

Steifer tightened the stranglehold and banged the kid's head against the ground.

"You been giving me bum steers, Jimbo," Steifer grunted once he caught his breath.

"I swear to you, I—"

"You swear shit!" Steifer let go suddenly and got to his feet. "Get up," he commanded.

Jimbo stood up. He rubbed some dirt off his mouth with the back of his hand and kept his arm up longer than he needed, to shield himself in case Steifer couldn't keep his temper.

"Man, I been tryin'," he whined, sniffling by habit as he talked. "This is a trial and error sort of situation."

He was shirtless underneath the ratty jacket. A sloppy Maltese cross decorated his clavicle; covered with perspiration, the temporary tattoo was blotting into a large inky blur. Steifer slammed it with the heels of his open hands, making a loud thud against him.

"My ass. Turn me on to a group of eight-year-olds in Altadena. You call that helpful?"

"They keep changin' their names. It's not my fault. I'm tryin', man, I really am."

Steifer slapped Jimbo hard enough to rock him backwards, then followed with a few mean shots to the breadbasket. The kid gulped once, then fell to his knees on the sidewalk, gasping for breath. Steifer kneed him into the street, then pulled him up by his white hair and hit him some more. Lights went on in some apartments across the street. I heard a rumbling from a block away as the music started up again in the Starwood. George winced and put his hand to his mouth after missing the punk's neck and connecting against the side of his head. He sucked on his fist as he kneed Jimbo in the groin and shoved him up against a parked car.

"What's going on?" demanded a gruff old voice from a few stories above.

"Police," George answered.

"It's about time," said the same voice as the lights went out in his apartment.

George grabbed Jimbo by the neck and went up on his tiptoes as he lifted the tall young man and pushed his head back against the car roof.

"I told you this was important," he said harshly. "I'm not asking for miracles. I just wanted you to help me out. I keep you out on the street when you should be doing hard time, and what do I get? Bullshit with a ribbon around it."

George banged the kid's head against the car roof to show how he felt about such presents.

"I'll try harder! I promise," young Avis said meekly, sounding as if he was putting it on.

George choked him. "Give."

"What d'ya mean?"

"You gotta have something."

"There's a group called Dead End. Did I tell you about them?"

Exasperated beyond anger, Steifer let go and pounded the roof with both his fists.

"You're not only slimy, you're stupid," he said, lifting his hands to the dark sky. "You told me about them. I talked to them already. They're high-school kids."

"Man, they're all young. What d'ya expect?"

Steifer turned toward Jimbo. He looked limp and defeated. The fight had been drained out of him.

"Get it together, OK?"

"I'm tryin', man, I'm tryin'," the punk whined self-righteously.

"I don't want to have to fuck up your parole. But push me just a little farther and I will. Understand?"

"Definitely," Jimbo nodded solemnly.

"Don't ever give me the same bad lead twice."

"I wasn't tryin' ta—"

"And call me with something good by tomorrow morning."

Looking distinctly relieved that George had stopped pummeling him, Jimbo nodded like there was nothing he wanted to do more. His mouth relaxed into an easy smile.

"Sure," he said.

"OK."

George gave the kid a light pat on the back, then, quickly, he whipped around, jumped him, and put another headlock on him. Both his feet were momentarily off the ground until the punk bent over from the waist, giving in to the force and weight. George rammed the kid's head into the rolled up driver's window of the parked car at least a half-dozen times. The car rocked and the punk squirmed and tried to yell out.

I was afraid he was going to put the kid's head through the window. Steifer was off his rocker tonight. Something had gotten into him. It seemed like he might be on the road to doing things he was going to be sorry for.

"George," I said abruptly. "Cool it."

I might as well have been trying to cool off a hot iron with a moistened fingertip. Keeping the headlock, Steifer pulled the kid away from the car, then he released the hold and pushed him away with a kick to the hind end.

The punk staggered and fell. Then he got to his feet and started running. His gait was unsure and wobbly. Once he got to the corner, he turned around and yelled something. You could tell it was nasty from the way the mean smile bloomed on him, but he was panting so hard I couldn't make it out. He didn't care. He'd got that last word in edgewise. A small pleasure, but he was the kind of guy who had to take whatever he could get.

• TWO •

Steifer bit his bottom lip and stared dully into space as Jimbo disappeared.

"I'll try him one more time," he told himself. "That's it."

He loosened his tie, pulled off his ready-made khaki coat, checked it over for damage, frowning at the grass stains on the elbows from the beginning of this odd skirmish, then put it back on over his shoulder holster. He turned and gave me a slight, tired grin, knowing that I was going to expect an explanation. I shook my head as we started walking back down the boulevard.

"You don't mess around, do you?" I said for beginners.

"Can't afford to."

"So what's it about?"

Steifer gave me another little grin. "It's involved and I'm tired, but you're gonna report me for police brutality if I don't tell you."

"Not exactly, George, but you did get a little—"

"He's scum, trash," barked Steifer. "Put him out, the garbage men wouldn't take him."

"Still, that's not a very good way to win somebody's cooperation."

"You don't know what you're talking about, Crandel. He's fucked me over so many times I've lost count. Besides, here's a disgusting punk who'll sell drugs to a kindergartner and you're gonna defend him? Please, save your bleeding heart for Boy Scout duty. With guys like Jimbo, you gotta stay rough. That way they keep their cover and once in a while maybe give you something, especially if you arrest them every now and then."

"What's your beef with him? What'd he screw up on?"

"An *L. A. Times* reporter disappeared, about two weeks ago."

"How's that relate to all this?" I said, gesturing toward a smaller slew of punks still loitering on the sidewalk before the Starwood.

"Anybody but a Vassar girl would have enough sense to keep away from this crazy shit," Steifer said, scowling at a few prepubescents practicing their angry-young-men looks. "She had it in her head that this stuff is of some special significance, a comment on our times."

"She was doing a piece on the punk scene?"

Steifer nodded.

"Was she last seen with a punk or something?"

"She was last seen at the *L. A. Times* in her office."

"But you don't have anything else to go on."

"You get smarter every day," Steifer told me without smiling.

"My kid's a punk," I told Steifer for his information. "I hate to break it to you, but I think they're all crazy but harmless."

Steifer gave me a wolfish smile. "You think whatever you want, Benny. It's a free country, for now."

"You're impossible tonight. Is there any chance you're on your period?"

Steifer had stopped in his tracks in front of the Starwood. Cars and sundry punks were jammed about the inside parking lot before the club. George was looking for something, but he didn't know what it was. His eyes bounced back and forth from the loiterers on the inside to those who were hanging out on the street. I couldn't see any difference between them.

"Men have cycles just like women," I added for his edification.

"Let me buy you a drink," said Steifer.

A fine idea, except George turned toward the Starwood, walking ahead of me and making his way toward the entrance before I could so much as nod. He was working overtime and I was along for the ride. The only reason I didn't bail out was that I felt sorry for him. I had to keep reminding myself of that because, as I said, if I hadn't known him better, I would have just assumed this Captain Cold act was his regular style. Whatever was bugging him, Shirley, his job, or an ingrown toenail, I was tired, and the thought of those English sisters going back to Auntie's house without me was sobering indeed. It would have taken much more than a nightcap to get me jolly at this juncture. I decided to make it quick and head on home. I'd sweated through my shirt and my head felt as sore as I thought Jimbo's probably did. I felt like I'd been banging it up against a wall all night

in trying to get through to George. I'd had enough of him
for now.

But when we got inside, he became talkative for the first
time all evening. We pushed through hoards of stumbling
teenagers, some of whom had the fifties styled pomaded jobs
with ducks and white sidewalls, most of whom had either
short wild spiky hair set that way deliberately by perverse
perm, or shaved heads or a combination of both with multi-
colored hair and polka dots like measles painted on their
skulls. Their clothes, for the most part, were tacky and nondescript. The head finery, along with the leather, chains, and
the sleeveless butch look, was the main thing. I found it of-
fensive in the same way the establishment had disdained
long hair and hippiedom in the Nixon years. You couldn't
take it too seriously, but hippie girls had been prettier and
my thought was that light shows and love-ins had been live-
lier fare than this dingy scene that was desecrating nature
rather than reveling in it to excess. We'd been frolicking
puppy dogs. People couldn't tell if we were boys or girls. But
these kids were creatures from another planet.

Steifer ignored them. He was too busy grumbling about
the last week and how godforsaken it had been. The *L. A.
Times* reporter's name was Elise Reilly. She was a twenty-
three-year-old transplanted New Yorker who had done her
undergraduate work at Vassar and finished off at the Colum-
bia School of Journalism. Steifer had been to all of the major
local punk clubs and talked to many of the musicians and
scene people the young reporter had interviewed. He was
working from Reilly's field notes and the rough draft of her
article.

"Not one single lead," Steifer pronounced bitterly.

I knew that the club scene couldn't be covered in a week.
There were joints for these kids all over the city. I told Steifer
he had to give it time, but it doesn't do much good to say
something like that to somebody who's been chewing his
fingernails.

The main room was a dim affair packed solid with young
bodies that undulated in a slow wave as the crazed ones

pogoed up and down and pushed and shoved and slam danced about the front of the stage, sending forth currents that reached the back of the crowd where the celebrants were increasingly less frenzied making with the spastic gyrations. The noise was excruciating. Four skinny kids in jeans and sleeveless t-shirts were making it. One held a mike, two had guitars, and something with a shocking white face, a shaved head black as an eight ball, and breasts beat on a drum set like there was no tomorrow. She made vicious faces at the crowd as her cohorts conspired contrapuntally, baring their teeth with blank predatory smiles and nodding slowly like a trio of dashboard Chihuahuas. Punks hurtled onto the stage, then dove back onto the heads of the crowd before the beefy security men could get their hands on them. I saw one boy who couldn't have been over twelve crawl up onto the stage. His skull was shaved except for a six-inch-high chartreuse Mohawk patch running down the middle. His torn t-shirt said SID LIVES in messy caps and had X's scrawled all over it. He screamed in triumph, brought his hands together, and dove into the crowd as if he was going off a high dive. He missed and landed on the floor, screaming. The crowd moved toward him, stepped over him, meting out some kicks. I hoped he could take it.

Considering that most of these kids were under twenty-one, the bar was the quietest spot in the room. I ordered Jack Daniel's and George got Cutty. We couldn't talk much. It was too noisy. I put a finger in my ear for some respite and tried to imagine why my son Pete would want to be a part of this and couldn't think of a reason. But then it was obvious that these kids looked down their noses at my polo shirt and penny loafers. If I'd said Dylan to them they would have thought I meant Bob and hated him because he was just another aging hippie.

Oh, well, you can't win 'em all. I went to take a leak and met a skinny punk with pimples and a horizontal shaved patch across the center of his head that divided his coiffure into two bristly lawns, one passion pink, the other powder blue. Something was scribbled on the bald part and he

seemed to be studying it in the mirror in addition to popping
a zit on his nose.

Backwards in the mirror, I read aloud, "Eat shit."

This was too much for me. It gave me pause, about two
seconds worth. "Is that tattooed or temporary?" I asked him
as our eyes met in the mirror.

He didn't answer, of course.

"I mean, is it your motto or something? Why do you
wanna go around with that on your head?"

He looked scared. For no reason. I wasn't trying to intim-
idate him. "How about 'Eat at Joe's' or something?" I
asked him. "I mean, 'Eat shit'—why?"

"Because you're fucked!" he hollered, his voice cracking
as he whipped around, expecting me to do something, then
flying out the swing door when all I did was smile at him.

I walked to the urinal and did my business, shaking my
head and remembering how much fun it used to be to be a
bad boy. No matter what they said and did, the goody two-
shoes always knew they were missing something. Things
had changed, but not all that much, or had they?

It wasn't until I stood at the sink, washing my hands as an
excuse to look over the wall graffiti, that I noticed something
truly out of the ordinary. A foot, a scuffed heavy biker boot
with a thick chain about the ankle stuck out sideways onto
the floor beyond the first toilet stall. It was at an odd angle,
sole up with the heel off the ground, and it stayed like that,
didn't move. I couldn't imagine how anybody standing or
sitting at the can had ended up in such a position. After a
minute or so of staring at it, I nudged the foot in question
with my own. It tottered slightly, then skewed back to an
even odder angle.

"Hey, how's it goin'?" I said.

Obviously, somebody had passed out while heaving their
guts into the toilet. I'd done it myself once or twice. I swung
open the door to check on the guy.

It was somebody kneeling in front of the toilet, all right.
His head was down inside the bowl. I reached down, got
him by his scruffy hair, and pulled him out. As I did, I saw

that the water was tinged red. I turned him around and got stared at by a pair of wide button shallow eyes. It was Steifer's informant, Jimbo, and it wasn't until after I slapped his face and saw the small caliber oozing wound at the top of his forehead that I fully realized he was dead. I took his pulse at the neck and wrist to be sure. His gaping jaw gave him a surprised expression, as if he'd been shot straight-on by the last person he ever would have expected. I got him under the arms and pulled him out of the stall, then eased him down onto the tile floor on his back. His knees were still bent and his feet stayed a foot or so off the floor.

My hands were sticky from where they'd touched his hair. I stepped over to the sink and washed them off. The first splash of water turned slightly milky. I looked over my shoulder at Jimbo. His short mousy hair was plastered to his head. The white dye had run.

I yanked a paper towel from the wall dispenser and walked back into the band room to find Steifer. I looked down at my hands and for a moment it surprised me that I was still holding the paper towel. I wasn't sure where it had come from. I was in a little bit of a daze. Finding a dead man does that to you.

I picked my glass up off the bar and finished it, then I turned to George who had barely seen me either leave or return.

"You can come out of the trance now," I yelled above the deafening shriek of sound. "Your informant's lying dead on the bathroom floor."

George faced in the general direction of the stage. His expression was sour. Little tics moved around his mouth and eyes in response to the horrible dissonance. He nodded to me as if he'd heard what I just said, although of course he hadn't. He finished off his Cutty. He nodded at me, then at his glass.

"One more for the road," he said, opening his small mouth wide to project his voice.

I grabbed his arm and pulled him toward me as I leaned down and spoke into his ear. "Jimbo's dead," I practically screamed. "I just found him in the john."

Steifer pulled back and glared at me. He could tell I wasn't kidding. He put his glass down on the bar.

"Show me," he said.

A song was ending as we pushed our way through the crowd. Kids were coming in and going out. Steifer went through them like they weren't there. One, a hulking ex-jock, brushed by me and came back at him, plowing toward his back on a run. George lunged forward, but kept his feet. I grabbed for the kid, but his meaty arm was slippery with sweat and he got by me, lunging back into the mob as the band started making noise again.

The men's room door was open and a crowd of kids spilled out from the inside. Others were pushing their way in.

Steifer stopped in his tracks. He smiled hard, looking like he had a gas pain. "Where's security?" he asked in a high voice that took note of the futility of such a question.

I started to push my way in. Steifer held me back. "Know what we do now?" he said. "Don't laugh," I was admonished as he took out his gun and fired a round into the low ceiling.

They scattered like cockroaches. The john was clear within ten seconds. We went in. George crouched down by Jimbo and stared into his face.

"Small entry, no exit wound. Looks like a peashooter, a .22," he said for my benefit. He closed the kid's eyes and ran a caressing hand down his cheek. "He was nice sometimes, especially when he wanted something from you."

"He must have known something he wasn't saying. Maybe somebody was worried he'd open his mouth."

"Or maybe they got mad at him for the way he cut his nose candy. Lousy stuff if I must say so myself."

George went through Jimbo's pockets quickly, coming up with a pack of matches advertising an adult correspondence school, a small switchblade, and the calling card of a known ambulance chaser. Steifer patted his cheek, stood up, keeping his eyes on the dead punk's face. I looked down at it, too. It didn't tell me anything helpful.

"It's disgusting how meaningless a life can be," Steifer said, shaking his head. "And it frightens me how easy it is to understand. You let it happen to yourself, and you can even check for signs of it, like when you've gotta grasp at straws to think of something that makes you happy."

I nodded along, not saying anything or offering any wisecracks. Sure, it was a weird time to take time out for a coffee break, but George was carrying a lot of weight on those hard little shoulders of his. He needed to get some of it off. But news travels fast when dead boys start cropping up, and a .357 doesn't exactly sound like a cap pistol when you fire it at a low ceiling inside a windowless room. We heard sirens overlapping sirens, a panic-stricken serenade.

George snapped out of it and turned toward the door. "Stay here," he told me, moving quickly outside as tires squealed and car doors opened and slammed. Raspy voices barked orders and heavy feet hustled toward me.

The next moment, a double duo of men-in-blue and khaki-uniformed sheriff's boys bullied their way in and told me I could go. I walked out, found George, saw the punk whom I'd encountered in the john before coming across Jimbo, and watched as George called after him on his way outside.

The kid bolted for the door. George went after him and yelled down to the conclave of cops who were standing before the parking lot entrance and the street, blocking off access and exit.

"I want him!" Steifer yelled.

The patrol boys pulled their guns. A team of highway patrolmen pulled rifles from the gun rack inside their car. The kid went into a panic. He dashed sideways a few feet and jumped onto the hood of a Cadillac limo backed against the sidewall, then he proceeded to hopscotch his way down the line of parked cars. Cops came at him from both ends of the lot. He ended up on the roof of a Porsche Carrera, hands up and crying in a cracked voice. The Christmas lights spinning atop the patrol cars played off the crazy colors of his hair. Sweat glistened over his face and bare arms.

"Stop, don't shoot!" he bawled out.

He sounded convincing, like a self-professed sinner ready to turn over a new leaf. I would have believed him, except we all know, of course, that the real-life threat of a firing squad will put the fear of God in just about anybody—for a minute or two.

• THREE •

They got the punk off the Porsche, a patrol boy patted him down and handed him over to George, and it couldn't have been thirty seconds later that the kid was nastier than ever by a longshot. He had no ID on him and wouldn't even tell anybody his name. They put cuffs on him and pushed him in the back of a black and white. Patrol boys moved in and sat on either side of him. I didn't think he'd shot Jimbo or even knew who Jimbo was, for that matter. He probably hadn't known that somebody a few years his senior had lost his life just a few minutes before he entered the men's room. This kid had been too busy looking himself over in the mirror, checking out his multi-colored hair and popping a few stubborn pimples. But you never know.

I followed George back to the door of the club and told him I was going, but he was so busy calling out orders, he didn't hear. I had to tap him on the shoulder and wave. He nodded to me as he told a patrol cop named Bishop to get the coroner right away. His jaw was bunched up. It tautened his whole face, gave it more definition, and the tension heightened his color. His skin was olive again, not asparagus, and his shoulders had lost their slouch. He wasn't happy about all this, but rather hopeful in a mournful way. He had something to work on. I had just never seen him look so desperate about it.

By the time I walked back to my car, it was past

one-thirty. The Palm Restaurant was closed. My English girls were probably up in one of the canyons by now, taking in the twinkly view out of the picture windows of some boy mogul's mansion. I got in my new leased Alfa, turned left on Robertson Boulevard, and proceeded south past the chi-chi expensive junk displayed in the windows along decorators' row, down to west Pico, the once-Jewish neighborhood that now had soul food take-outs and gospel and Korean churches next door to the kosher butcher and neighborhood delis. The ghettos of the city were breaking down. Disparate cultures and races were intermixing with mixed results. It made some people bitter and gave others hope. Society, more than ever before, was in a state of flux this year, I think was the polite way of putting it. The daily newspaper headlines kept tabs on it with leads like: MURDER RATE IN LOS ANGELES COUNTY INCREASES AT RECORD-BREAKING PACE or LAPD'S PROBLEMS SERIOUS RETIRING OFFICER SAYS. Homicides were up about ten percent for the first part of the year, with the second half expected to be higher, as usual, considering the traditional hot weather effect.

And the average Joe scratches his head and wonders what it all means. Is life getting uglier or is there just more of it? Any time you mention it to somebody who once meditated and listened to sitar music, they'll end up telling you it has something to do with karma, the welfare system, television, the air, and Wonder Bread. That's what it all seems to come down to. And maybe they're right.

I kept my hippie-dippie thoughts to myself, got on the Santa Monica Freeway going west, leaned back and took in the cooling sea air as I cruised toward the beach with the top down. I got off the freeway at Lincoln and headed south down to Washington Boulevard and turned toward the beach. I hadn't been working every second over the last few years, but when I had I'd been taking home good money. That's the way it is in Hollywood. If you're not related to anybody, you have to cultivate your snobbery, make them think you're so precious and refined that, like vintage bubbly, there's only so much of you and they'd be lucky to have some. At least that's what my agent tells me, and he's not in the sort of tax bracket where he has to do his own laundry. Nobody trusts their own instincts in the entertainment world. That's what you bank on, intimidating people. Your talent doesn't matter, it's the way they sell you. Sometimes, it makes you wonder, but not enough to feel you're undeserving of whatever you can get for putting up with the morons you're forced to deal with when you're on an assignment. I didn't have to strain my scruples to feel I was entitled to the two-bedroom bungalow I'd put my twenty percent down on about a year ago. It looked just like the place I'd rented in Laurel Canyon and was barely any bigger, but it was worth three times the price on the real estate market because it was a block from the beach. It was also on one of those short promenades with a sidewalk instead of a street, and it was relatively quiet for Venice, on the far side of the sleazy street scene, closer to the Marina.

I was glad to be out of Hollywood. Trouble comes out of the woodwork in that place. All you have to do is take a walk and look what can happen. Five years in that fur-lined pit had been plenty. It was enough that I made my daily bread in and around the studios; I didn't have to live there. When you can't get a cup of coffee without hearing some clown bitching pig latin about his script, his agent, the producer, the director, or casting, and you feel like you've got emphysema every time you step outside for a breath of fresh air, then you start thinking about a change of scene. Personally, I'm way past the point of thinking the movies are wonderful. Like anything else, writing for them is a living. Sometimes, it works out well and you pat yourself on the back; mostly, you'd rather not be reminded. Hobbies like gardening, cooking, gun collecting, or crocheting doilies can suddenly become interesting overnight.

Lately, I'd taken to bicycling on the boardwalk at the beach. I had a custom-made bicycle, elastic racing shorts, and a collection of striped shirts that go well with a number on the back. I had one of those silly-looking leather helmets, too, that serious enthusiasts like to be seen in. I liked to ride down to Palos Verdes or take a train to Santa Barbara and ride back. I had a volleyball also, but where there's teamwork involved, there's a corollary that says you can always count on finding some know-it-all to tell you how it's done. I'm on the solitary side. Volleyball didn't last with me. Yeah, I'd been getting pretty easygoing and I liked it.

I'd forgotten about George and the grisly scene in Hollywood as I breathed in the medicinal salt air, stretched, and strolled down the path to my house. But it wasn't for long. I started hearing that familiar noise the young punks called music and shook to with such angry ecstasy inside the Starwood and, yeah, of course, it was coming from inside my place.

I stopped in front of my door where the noise was louder, saw the living room light through the shuttered window, and kept walking. I wasn't ready to face the music, as they say, not yet anyway. I went the rest of the way down the block to the sand, walked out to the volleyball net and leaned up against a pole. The sky was hazy. You could see the red landing lights on the jumbo jets going in and out of LAX, but no stars. My kid had an eight o'clock class the next morning. He was taking beginning Algebra for the second time because he'd failed it his first year in high school. Nothing new about problem children. Lots of people have them, though few do so by choice. Mine was adopted. We'd been going at it for four years now; before that, I'd been his Big Brother. The only reason I'd gotten into this mess in the first place was because I'd been excess baggage myself. This sounds lackadaisical on my part, but you get awful tired of pushing a square peg into a round hole, especially when other people tried to do the same thing with you. Lately, Pete had become impossible. He was doing the school thing, so he said, to please me, but what he really wanted to do was drop out and get more into his music so he could make it, whatever that meant. Everybody knows the opposing arguments and I was sick of giving them. If he wanted to make mistakes so badly, I had to let him do it, but it was eating me up standing by and watching. He was pumping gas about twenty-five hours a week and saving his money. A few times in recent arguments, he'd let me know he was thinking about moving out.

I kept seeing the surprised face of that dead jaded punk, Jimbo. At the rate he was going, Pete could be in the same place in a few years, maybe sooner; and I was sure if I told him so, he'd laugh in my face.

I felt too tired to save the world tonight. Making up my mind that now was not the time to squabble, I took a few deep breaths, ambled back to the house, and went in. The volume level went up as I closed the door. The air was so heavy with reefer, I felt stoned just breathing. I gritted my teeth and turned from the short hall into the living room. Pete was up at his shrine, the stereo. He was listening to something familiar. It was a tape of him screaming unintelligible words over a backup track of two out of tune electric guitars that sounded like chain saws on the rampage, and drums that were heavy on the cymbals and individual in that they varied the beat all by themselves without giving a hoot about what the others were doing. The overall effect seemed very much like a squabble among alleycats, with all of the action transpiring within the confines of a single trash can. I'd been hearing this same garbage around the house now for at least a week. I never thought I'd wish for more of it, but by now I found I was almost looking forward to the band's next jam session. It was too much to hope for, but maybe the next batch would be better.

Pete looked up at me and nodded. He had probably stopped jumping up and down and pogoing as I unlocked the front door. His blue eyes were black and wild, his blond hair, which a year ago had trailed down past his shoulders, now was about three inches long and stuck up from his head in an electro-spiko perm which looked like it had resulted from sticking the proverbial finger in the light socket. It was a very now look and I could tell he'd just gotten another haircut that afternoon. He was shirtless in his tight Levis and his skinny chest was crosshatched with Marksalot X's that were running from his sweat. He had a short padlocked chain around his neck. I was too sick and tired of this shit to laugh at him. I just walked over to the stereo and turned the damn thing down to a sensible whisper befitting the hour.

"I want to go to sleep," I said. "Let's not disturb the peace for awhile, OK?"

He was so pissed off, he couldn't handle it sufficiently to talk to me. He simply moved back to the volume knob and cranked it up louder than before. Then, just because he knew I couldn't stand it, he started in on that infernal pogo, jumping up and down like a chimp robot on a trampoline.

Now, it was my turn. "If you're looking for a fight, you're not gonna get one," I said calmly. "I'm too smart to play that game now."

I could just see myself taking that little cassette tape, stomping it to bits, then throwing it out the window; instead, proudly, I turned the volume down again.

Pete stopped his pogoing and came at the volume knob again before my hand was off it. I stayed where I was, with my hand on the knob, and prepared for the showdown.

"You're begging me to throw you out so you can get your own place," I told him.

"Hey, man, I gotta hear this," said the hepcat.

"I'm tired. I don't want to argue. I want to go to bed and sleep. You keep this up any longer and the cops are gonna be out here again."

"Fuck those pigs. They're gestapo mind police controlling the public's thoughts."

I laughed. "You're so full of shit, your eyes are turning brown."

He tried to pry my hand off the volume knob. "Look," he smirked, "ex-hippie power monger. Let me do my own thing." He gave me the peace sign with his free hand. "Peace, man."

"Punks are different than hippies, huh? We were corny and you guys are right on."

"Hey, I'm not sayin' anything," Pete said, waving the peace sign with both hands in a way that made it look like the finger. "Peace, man, the love generation rules. I'm a mellow fellow, flower child."

I shook my head and gave up the stereo. Pete the punk got what he wanted. I stood there and watched him start jumping up and down again. I walked into my bedroom and looked under the bed. Stanley, my basset hound, was up at the head corner, his tongue out, panting in his sleep. This was where he went when Pete played his music. I pretended that I was getting ready to go to bed, brushed my teeth, looked at the paper; then I went back into the living room, pushed the reject button on the stereo cassette player, and took the tape out and held it up in the air.

"I was with our friend George tonight," I began. "Remember him? You used to think he was a nice guy, that is until you learned all about the gestapo police."

"Give it," was all he could say.

"One more step and I take this thing outside and burn it."

"What's the matter, man? You forget to take a Jacuzzi in your hot tub? You need a love-in pretty bad."

"Yeah, yeah, sure," I smiled. "And George was telling me about a case he's on. It seems a naive young lady reporter thought she'd do a newspaper piece on the punk scene because she thought it was an interesting social phenomenon or something stupid like that. She didn't realize she'd have to deal with a bunch of wild animals."

"Man, you're total moral majority," Pete smirked savagely, staring wide-eyed with his stony eyes.

"Now, she's disappeared," I went on, ignoring him. "And you wanna know something else?"

"You lost your love beads?"

"I was at the Starwood, your favorite place, tonight and a kid barely older than you ended up dead on the men's room floor because he may have known something about it."

"No shit," Pete said now with interest. "What was the dude's name?"

"Jimbo."

"Shit. He's in the Rodents."

"Well, the Rodents are gonna just have to keep infesting without him."

"He was an informer," Pete said with a sagelike nod.

"How do you know that?"

"It was obvious, wasn't it? It's George's fault, the cops."

"How do you figure?"

"George must have set him up."

"Why would he do that? George was using Jimbo. He needed Jimbo. If Jimbo went around telling everybody he was working for the law, he set himself up."

"He didn't tell everybody. I just happen to know somebody that knows stuff like that."

"Who's that?"

"I ain't sayin'."

"Just tell me one thing," I said. "Why do you want to be a part of a subculture that's so racist, fascist, and idiotically self-destructive?"

"You learn a lot from *Time* magazine, don't you?" he countered.

"And what's that supposed to mean?"

"The fuckin' media fuckin' distorts everything."

"Oh, fuckin', fuckin', fuckin'."

"But maybe you're right. I mean, the sixties love children were all Mansonites, weren't they?"

"I don't remember the notion ever being suggested. I think it took your original mind to come up with it."

"If I'm fucked up and perverted, it took *your* generation to make it possible. Money talks and bullshit walks, as you say."

"Not everybody today is greedy and without values."

"Man, why do you think these fuckin' kids are so angry? Half of 'em don't have parents. The half that do, their parents are too busy gettin' loaded in the hot tub, gettin' ready for the weekly orgy."

"Is there something wrong with sex?"

"Sex is disgusting, man. I lost my cherry three years ago. Sex don't mean shit to me. I'd rather beat my meat."

"You're confused."

"Of course I'm confused!" he screamed.

"And it's all my fault."

"I'm not sayin' that. You can't help it. You're a victim of the times."

"Nice of you to say."

"I'm serious."

"That's the problem. Where's your sense of humor? You need one, you know."

"That's your prerogative. You go through life making fun of everything so you don't have to think about the state of your condition."

"State of my condition, power monger, gestapo police, mind control. You've memorized all the buzzwords, haven't you?"

He gave me a Nazi salute and said, "Heil, Hitler."

"That's not funny."

"Either are crosses, stars, and police badges. It's absurd to play follow the leader, isn't it?"

I scratched my head. "Pretty heavy for a fifteen-year-old," I decided. "But I don't think you know what you're talking about."

"I'm savin' *my* soul. You worry about yours."

"I'm not worried and I think you're in this over your head."

"Come and see us tomorrow night. We're gonna be playin' the Starwood."

"I'd sooner watch the Merv Griffin Show."

"Hey, that doesn't surprise me."

I took the tape with me into the bedroom, slammed the door, and lay down steaming. I got up and hit an old bottle of cabernet in the kitchen cupboard. It had turned. The light was out in the living room. Pete's light was on underneath his door. I went back outside and took another walk.

"What's the world coming to?" I grumbled to no one, hearing the words resonate, then die their quick death in the light fog.

Old folks used to wonder the same thing about me. Maybe I was becoming one of them. I stopped under a streetlight on the edge of the sand, held my hands out, and looked them over. Wrinkles don't mean a damn thing, but they have a way of creeping up on you. It's the same thing with the way you think. Maybe it was the heavy smell of pot in my house, but somehow I found myself trying to recall the last time I'd taken LSD. It was so long ago now, I couldn't really remember. I didn't want to. That Ben had been crazy. I wouldn't want anything to do with him. I was so much wiser now—or had I just scared myself into being careful? Was I merely surviving as compared to the icono-clastic ideal of living? Pete, who thought he was being so wonderfully original, was beginning to think and grapple with some of the major issues he thought I no longer had time for. Contrary to what he might have thought, I had plenty of time to ponder my lot and I didn't think I minded what I'd become. I was self-employed at doing something I enjoyed; sometimes, it was challenging, rewarding. I didn't have to apologize for my livelihood. Just because I hadn't burned myself out like many of my old friends didn't neces-sarily mean I had sold out either. I just didn't happen to think that dying young and gloriously was so romantic any-more, that's all. I liked jazz, baseball, barbecued ribs, chili dogs, pizza, the drive on Sunset Boulevard from downtown to the beach, wandering around the studios, Beverly Hills, gorgeous women, homely women. I liked taking Stanley to the beach at dusk and watching him romp and try to rescue me as I dived under the waves and swam; and I liked a few of my friends. If I was complacent, well, then so be it. I didn't think my life was so bad I had to jump up and down and kick and shout. Pete had a lot to learn.

• FOUR •

A nd so had I, though I would have been the last to admit it. But wisdom, too, like wrinkles, old age, and senility, creeps up slowly. I had plenty of time for it. I was running too late the next morning to think about anything other than making an eight-thirty breakfast meeting with my agent. It shouldn't have been difficult, but I'd forgotten to set my

alarm and Stanley had woken me up, howling for his morning airing at eight, and I'd trudged into Pete's room to find
him still asleep. After pulling him out of bed, I had to make
breakfast for him and feed Stanley. Then I had to drop him
off at Venice High because he was late again and would have
missed the class altogether if I'd let him ride his bike. I was
sure he hadn't done his homework, but I was still rushing
him to school. It didn't make much sense. I got on the freeway thinking one of us or both needed a therapist, but then I
remembered we'd tried that already and it hadn't worked.
Pete, the guy had said, needed more freedom. He felt la-
beled by being in a special school. His reading scores were
above average now and there was no reason why he
shouldn't go back to public school. Great, so now he was
back in public school and feeling so free he seemed to feel
school was altogether unnecessary, superfluous. He wanted
to learn life on the street like all of his jive-ass friends. That
was all fine and dandy, but he didn't appear to be learning
too much, at least not in my book. I was willing to bet he
rolled a reefer with the best of them, but aside from that he
was covered with chalk dust a hell of a lot lately, and there's
got to be a limit to what you can get out of hanging around
nickel and dime poolrooms.

It was 8:45 by the time I walked into the Velvet Turtle coffee shop in the Beverly Wilshire Hotel. My agent was sitting
in a window booth skimming over the entertainment trades.
He was one of a number there doing the same thing. He was
a successful-looking man, a little chubby, but his eyes were
bright and forthright and his puffy face had that smooth tan
sheen to it that's a by-product of good clean affluence. By
the way he looked at the shapely spry waitress, you could tell
he did his daily best to suppress those devilish little urgings
that pull at family men, whispering, "Go ahead. It's not going to hurt anybody." To the best of my knowledge, Ronny
Rosen didn't look like the sort of guy who fooled around, at
least not often. He had three daughters and related to most
younger men as his imaginary sons. Since I'd never really
had much of a father, this didn't bother me. I liked it, in

fact. It made me feel cared for, although with an agent, of
course, no matter who they are, you can never be sure. You
always feel just a little bit like a piece of meat. It has to be
like that.

We had our conference. It was a pep talk about how nicely
my career was going, but how I still had to be careful not to
let myself slide into thinking I'd reached easy street because
there wasn't such a place and never had been. Show biz was
one big never-ending D day and the only thing that could
stop it was the Big One that would stop us all. The novel was
dead. Ronny said I should stop saying I wanted to write
one, that is unless I had something in mind about Nazis,
spies, ghosts, organized crime, or a period piece. No little
stories, please. I got the message which was that I was supposed to take a handful of meetings to pitch some ideas for
some new television shows. We both knew I had none in my
head, but I had done this sort of thing before and *if* the pilots
had gone on to series, blah, blah, blah, yabba, dabba,
dabba. The guy had represented me for two years, he knew
I had a way of coming up with things when I was nervous
under pressure. It's the sort of thing I'm a sucker for. I took
down the appointments and Ronny reminded me I was having lunch with Jodie, his secretary. It made him hot knowing
Jodie and I were doing a number and that he'd been our
matchmaker. Frustrated good men are like that. They turn
you on to some action and it gives them a vicarious thrill.
They also lose confidence in you eventually if you don't
show your gratitude by offering to settle down and put yourself out of commission. It can make a man overwrought and
nervous when the world tantalizes too much and he's afraid
of what might happen if and when he takes a bite he's not
supposed to.

Well, I took my meetings, including the one with Jodie.
None of them was very successful. Meetings one through
three were in production offices at MGM in Culver City, four
and five were at Fox, six was in Jodie's apartment. One
through five are pretty unclear to me now. A few had to do
with staff writing for existent shows, a few pumped me for

ideas, one never got started because I admitted to being unfamiliar with the producer's past and present credits and he, feeling unsure about being a boy mogul, dismissed me, saying there must have been some mistake—I was obviously too inexperienced. He was right. There are some experiences you can do without, even in this day and age. You don't have to do everything, except when it comes to women, which was sort of the theme of my sixth and final meet taken with Jodie. She made us a nice lunch and we got around to it after attending to our more urgent appetites. We ate the shrimp salad in our underwear; after that, I was helping her clean up so she could get back to work, when she tried Door #3. We'd both been winning and she had to go for Door #3.

"Benny?"

I thought she was getting in the mood again, so I put down the plates I was carrying and put my arms around her waist. She was standing at the sink, running the water over the dishes. Her blond hair was real, which was astounding in itself, and the rest of her wasn't exactly hard to look at, but she just wasn't the sort of gal you dreamed of growing old with. That's an old line of goods they stopped manufacturing at around the time kids started doing the fox-trot. It made life a hell of a lot easier if you accepted certain things as a given. One, there's no such thing as a small ego. So, don't pretend. Two, you can trust most people as far as you can throw them. So, don't try. Three, romance is out. It just doesn't happen anymore. So, don't be a dreamer. Thinking otherwise on these big questions can lead to what I call a rude awakening. I don't like rude awakenings. They interfere with my general well-being.

And so this lovely piece, this hot hot number with slightly distant eyes and an underdeveloped laugh that hardly went with the rest of her, wiggled out of my grasp.

"That tickles," so she said.

"That's the idea," leered I, moving inside, tying her up in a clinch.

"Don't you ever think about settling down?"

By the tone of her voice, she wasn't piqued or angry, not

in any way. She sounded entirely inquisitive. This was a rhetorical question and she looked at me with an almost bookish concentration, waiting to see what I would say.

"Yeah, sure. And thinking about it gets you very unsettled."

"My parents think I should marry somebody."

"They're still married?"

"Forty years."

"That's nice."

"Maybe I should try it, you know."

"Marriage, my dear, is something you have to enter into with a sense of conviction."

"It's weird to think of being with just one person, isn't it?"

"Nearly impossible. I suggest we drop the whole subject."

"OK. I just wondered what it was like."

The girl was twenty-three years old, a year out of college, you see, and she hadn't been all the way around the block yet. I liked that about her, even if she was already jaded, talking about true love like it was a course in ancient history. She'd almost surprised me there for a minute, almost. I wished she hadn't. It was a little upsetting. I wasn't sure why.

"Romance is out," I said summarily. "It just isn't in anymore. Nobody's doing it."

She seemed to see what I meant. And I did too, except there was something missing when we kissed good-bye. Now, it occurs to me.

• FIVE •

I came back to Venice and rode my bike until the early evening. Pete didn't come home and I remembered what he'd said about playing at the Starwood. I grabbed a nice sushi combination at this little place I like on Sawtelle, then I took a walk down Rodeo Drive, for lack of anything better to do. I enjoy browsing with the looky-lous and tourists, watching them react to the opulence. It's the writer in me or the sadist, seeing how people look at what they can't have or would give an arm or leg for.

When it was dark, I drove on to the Starwood. Sure enough, the marquee said CLAUSTROPHOBIC and THE SCAPEGOATS. Lovely. I already knew what Pete's band sounded like. I could just imagine the other. Seemed like a great way to spend the evening. I parked close to where George had jumped Jimbo the night before, walked down to the Starwood, plunked down my five-fifty, and went in.

The place was a rat's nest of depravity. I hated the punk scene and I hated the kids. The only reason I was there was because Pete had dared me. This wasn't his first gig. There had been others, and I hadn't showed up before. There wasn't any reason to expect me to begin now. It was something else. Aside from wanting to surprise the kid, I was worried about him. What I'd seen with George the previous evening had sobered me into seeing that this whole punk thing wasn't a joke. There was something desperate going on here. These kids were playing with fire. Not only could they get hurt by the scene they were making, but they seemed to realize this. They were so bored, they were dangerous, and they knew it. They liked it that way. Why else would they belt each other for fun?

You could see them on the dance floor, jarring each other with their elbows, pushing, shoving, bobbing to the music. There were scowls and frowns among them, but most seemed to take a maniacal delight in playing bumper car with each other. I didn't see anything the least bit sensual in it either. They didn't even look at each other. Girls were butted from the front ranks. They spat upon one another with disdain. When the noise stopped between songs, they stood limp and motionless like marionettes who couldn't pull their own strings.

I looked long enough at the group on stage to see that Pete wasn't with them, then I moved away from the dance floor and went over to the bar on the side wall.

I had a few beers and scratched my head. I'd been worried about George, so I'd taken him out to dinner. I'd gotten into a habit of having rotten evenings with him. Now, I was worried about Pete, so I had come down to this abysmal place I didn't like to see him make noise that drove me crazy. Christ, maybe I was bored with myself. What the hell was wrong with me? If you spent all your free time meddling in other people's business, you didn't have any left over for your own. George and Pete were great guys and they were both of the utmost importance to me, but I was trying to make up my mind to let them fend for themselves. I didn't think either of them was doing famously at the moment, but they didn't exactly appear to be begging for my advice. You had to let people sink or swim if they were stubborn and wanted it that way, even your son and a good friend. And there was always the possibility that it wasn't a matter of not wanting a helpful hint or two. Maybe it was what I was saying; maybe it was my style; maybe they didn't respect me.

That last bit pushed my heart right up into my throat. Doubts of this nature seemed to call for something liquid and sweet; succor. I ordered a rum punch to think it all over. When that didn't work, I tried to just watch the mob cavorting in front of The Scapegoats who were still on stage. They looked like real nice kids, that is if you got used to the idea that they'd soon be incarcerated. The lead singer was a black kid with a white Afro, shirtless with chrome slave bracelets running up and down his arms. The other three looked as pale as albinos in comparison and had their coiffures done up like tabby cats, with concentric bands of brown, black, and gold orbiting their heads.

"Where's Jimbo?" one punk asked another beside me.

My first impulse was to turn to the kid and tell him that Jimbo would pogo and slam dance no more, but instead I held back and tried to eavesdrop on the conversation. The noise was overpowering, it was hard to pick up a thing. I turned away from them and tried to muss myself up a little. My hair, far from the little-dab'll-do-ya variety, was still too neat and mannered for this society and I wished it were shorter, too, but I mauled it over and did my best to get it mangy. Then I buttoned my shirt to the collar and pulled up the collar the way you do when you're putting on a tie, except I left it like that. It was the best I could do. I just hoped they didn't see my cowboy boots. There's nothing a punk hates more than a disco-cowboy ex-hippie.

I leaned back against the bar and looked the kids over, keeping my fingers crossed that they wouldn't laugh at me. They both looked to be in their early twenties. One, in black leather pants, vest, and cap, looked more like a gay parade biker boy than a punk. The other one, who had asked about Jimbo, was the spectacle of the evening. I was surprised I hadn't noticed him before. Over baggy jeans, he was wearing a heavy white canvas article that looked like a Judo robe until you saw the metal clasps and ties that identified it as a straitjacket. His hairstyle went beyond the decorous or extreme into a rococo ostentation that boggled my mind. I just couldn't comprehend how anyone would want to look like that. He wasn't raving mad, he was carrying on a conversation. It was artifice. I could see his head was shaved in the back, there was some hair on top that made a wild diagonal pattern; some of it stood up in a red Mohawk. Everything that was shaved was covered with blood red polka dots. What he looked like was a six-foot balding cockatiel with measles, if you can even begin to conjure such an image. I couldn't. I blinked my eyes at him, thinking he'd disappear. But he didn't.

I couldn't compete with him. I put my collar down and undid the top button. I patted my hair down and tucked in my shirt.

"I overheard you guys talkin' about Jimbo," I said finally in their general direction.

They didn't hear me or see that I was addressing them. I tapped the cockatiel on the shoulder.

"I heard you mentionin' Jimbo," I tried again.

"What?"

"Jimbo!" I yelled over the deafening electric death rattle.

"No!" the idiot cockatiel yelled back at me, thinking I was confusing him with somebody whom I knew was dead.

I looked at the leather boy, trying to ascertain whether he

was suffering from the same disease. His head was big for his body, there was a lot between his ears. It gave me some encouragement, even if he had the bad habit of standing with his mouth open.

"Weren't you talkin' about Jimbo?" I shouted at him hoarsely.

"Jimbo ain't here, man."

He was dumber than he looked. Such an irrefutable truth was just a little too obvious.

I smiled condolingly as I nodded at him. Either of them might be Jimbo's friends. "Hey, I know, man. I found him on the bathroom floor."

Neither of them said anything. They traded scowls and turned toward the melee on the dance floor. Kids were jumping each other out there, arms flailing about, fists pummeling. They piled up in clusters over different areas of the floor. Good clean fun, football to music.

I moved up to them. "Why would somebody off Jimbo?"

The leather boy had fat cheeks that went with his fat head. His tiny hole of a mouth was sour and petulant. He didn't like the taste of what I was giving him. "What's your problem?" he asked me, his raised voice getting squeaky.

"I'm just talking," I told him.

"If you're a cop, why don't you say so?" he whined at me.

" 'Cause I'm not."

"That guy you were with, he hung out here just like you."

"He's helping me try to find my sister."

"Fuck your sister."

The cockatiel looked offended. "I think you're crude," he told the biker boy.

"My sister interviewed Jimbo and some other people. She's disappeared."

Biker boy wasn't listening. "Fuck *your* sister, Pinky," he told the cockatiel with a dumb grin.

Pinky's straitjacket flapped a little as his hand went down into his pocket. There was a click, the kind that goes with the weighted flick of a blade, and the open stiletto came up in his hand. He didn't say anything, but just stood there holding the short thick blade against the biker boy's leather-sheathed abdomen. Biker boy looked about five years old all of a sudden, like he'd just woken from a bad dream and found the babysitter instead of his mother. Sweat glistened on his chubby cheeks.

"Take it easy. Joke," he said, squirming backwards and pulling in his gut to get away from the blade.

Pinky smiled vaguely as he leaned forward and slit the top buttons off his friend's vest. He paused then and his face got stony. His hand shook a little like it had a will of its own. Biker boy kept backing away. His belly was as white as Ivory soap and Pinky's hand looked like it was going to carve a bath toy out of it.

"I'm upset too. Jimbo was a good dude," he pleaded.

Pinky was in front of me as I heard the stiletto flick its metal tongue back into its metal mouth. He turned his back then as if he'd forgotten Biker boy was there. Biker boy bolted. In a second, he was lost in the crowd.

Pinky put his knife away and nodded at me. "I don't like him," he said.

"I could see that," I offered.

"I thought the reporter was nice," he said, his brows knitting as he phrased the simple sentence. His words were rounded, he gave a lot of weight to each of them and took pleasure in speaking correctly because it probably went with his new hairstyle, although you could tell it put a terrific strain on him.

"You met her?"

"Yes, I did," he said with a cautious polite smile. "I've also read about her disappearance. It's unfortunate."

I held myself back from laughing in the guy's face. The first band had stopped playing and Pete's band was beginning to set up. I had nothing better to do for now, so, thinking I might pick up something for George, I decided to shine the guy on and talk to him. Pete hadn't seen me either. I liked that because I wanted to observe him in his element.

"You must be concerned," the jackass cockatiel was saying to me.

"Of course I'm concerned. Why do you think I'm here?" I grumbled, getting piqued by his inanity.

He didn't like me suddenly. His face got expressionless the way it had when he'd been holding the knife. Seeing that this tack wasn't going to do one little bit of good, I subdued myself immediately.

"My apologies. I'm a little overwrought," I explained.

Pinky looked like he'd sprouted a few more measles on his head, but then he gave me the nod again. "That's understandable," he said. "My sister disappeared, too," he added obscurely.

"Were you able to find her?"

"I'm not sure."

"How do you mean?"

"She's not the same."

"*Invasion of the Body Snatchers* is one of my favorite movies, too," I told him. "But mine *really* is missing."

He gave me his knife thrower's look all over again. Then he smiled at me for the first time. I'd never seen a kid trying so hard to be weird. It was pretty obvious. Some kids get a feeling of prestige or differentness; a distinction out of acting bizarre.

I looked at the punk with a pious hangdog expression and kept this doleful gaze on him until he wiped the grin off. Then I poured it on just to see where it would get me. "Can't you help me?" I asked pleadingly.

"I would like to," he said in that inimitable phony way of his.

"I have to find her."

"Would she feel the same—that is, if the situation were reversed?"

"Yeah," I nodded, gritting my teeth. "Just help me, won't you?"

"I'd like to," he said with disinterest.

"Is Jimbo involved in this?"

"Jimbo is dead. I knew that before," he said, gesturing over his shoulder to describe the position once occupied by the biker boy.

"Then why did you approach him?"

"For the same reason you're approaching me."

"Can we cut the bull crap or are you enjoying this?" He looked at me like he had no idea what I was talking about, so I just said, "All right, I don't care. I got all night if you do. So then let me interpret: You're trying to find out what happened to Jimbo."

"Yes. I wouldn't mind that."

"You're not positive."

"He was my drummer in the Rodents," he said, as if he was reminding me of something I really should have known already.

"Oh, sure," I told him. "You guys were like this," I said, crossing my fingers. "Why would anybody want to kill him?"

"They didn't like him."

"Who's they?"

"Many of them."

"Because of what?"

"He did it for fun."

"What?"

"You know."

I looked over at the bandstand. This guy was driving me up the wall. I couldn't stand too much more of him. Pete was saying, "Test, one, two, three," into the mike. His voice was a put-on monotone. His blue jeans were tucked into paratrooper boots and he was shirtless with a thick leather choker around his neck and matching leather bands around his wrists and upper arms, all of it with spiky metal studs protruding. His hair was the same, only black. He had dyed it. His oversized wraparound shades gave him insect eyes. It all went with the mutant image the punks loved to cultivate. Space-age outlaws. Modern apemen. The other guys were dressed the same way, except they were even skinnier than Pete. No matter how hard he tried, he couldn't hide the fact that he'd started developing muscles. It wasn't more than a year ago that he'd been pitching All Star Pony League and working diligently on his brown belt in karate. All of that was now old hat.

It came to me what Pinky had been saying. I turned back to him and watched as he lit a cigarette. He had to pull up his straitjacket to do it. "He snitched for fun, you mean," I said.

"I suppose you could say that."

"Quite so."

"I'm not English," he frowned. "Just cultivated. I hope you understand."

"Of course, but could you elaborate?"

"About Jimbo?"

"As you were saying?"

"He enjoyed it. I think that's important."

"In what sense?"

"It explains why many may have had motives. Do you know a private detective?"

"No. Why?"

Pinky sucked hard on his cigarette and frowned at the space above my head as he worked on a series of pro-quality smoke rings. "It might be needed."

"Really?" I started snidely, then stopped short and concentrated on my melancholy brother act with a vengeance. I tugged on Pinky's straitjacket and squeezed his arm the way distraught people do when they think you're their last hope. "We just gotta find her. You thought she was nice. Have some compassion."

My eyes had moistened. I'm good at worming my way into people, especially fools. Pinky dropped his half-smoked cigarette and removed my hand.

"I worship Onan," he said with a completely straight face. "I believe in being self-sufficient."

I nodded like I understood and kept prodding him. "About Jimbo."

"Merely, he snitched on those he didn't like. He liked to tell me."

"He bragged to his friends, then he screwed them behind their backs when he didn't like them anymore."

"I suppose."

"Who were his friends?"

Pinky gave me his knife thrower face. It was too easy to know what he was thinking.

"Were Jimbo's friends your friends?"

"No, I didn't like them. Rodents are my only friends."

Cute. He was polishing his persona, practicing for a new wave talk show. I let it ride. "Good. We know everybody Jimbo didn't like. What we're missing are Jimbo's friends. Maybe they know."

Pinky frowned. His hand went for the knife. "They wouldn't kill Jimbo."

I let him take it out. I was willing to bet this kid hadn't ever stabbed anything more living than a walnut tree. He held the knife away from him, waiting to decide when the time was right to give it the flick. I watched his wrist.

"How do you know?" I asked him.

"Because, why would they?"

"Why does it make you so nervous? I thought you only liked Rodents?"

"Some of the smaller creatures are our pets."

I smirked. "You're trying too hard," I told him. He raised his brow in question. I bobbed mine back at him. "To be weird," I said.

"And when's your sister's birthday?" he hit me with suddenly.

"What does that have to do with anything?"

He smiled craftily and flicked the knife.

"Put on that dime-store Indian scowl, or did you forget?" I asked him.

The knife inched toward me. I waited another moment, then I threw my ice cubes in his face and grabbed it away from him. "You could hurt yourself," I said.

Pete was howling up on stage now. The noise was even worse live than on tape, but it seemed like everybody loved it. My eye caught Biker boy. He'd drifted back toward the bar, but he was still wary of setting foot into Pinky's territory.

I poked Pinky's middle with the tip of his blade and nodded toward Biker boy. "Tell me all of 'em you can think of or

I'll hand him the knife. He might know what to do with it. You never know."

"What?"

I poked at the thick cotton of the straitjacket. Just a little harder and I'd pierce through to the skin. "I could slip," I warned him.

"Guys in a few groups," he said calmly, though one of his eyes had gone into a little twitch.

"Tell me about them."

"I don't know their names."

"Afraid you'll end up like Jimbo? I'm not gonna tell anybody. I'm just doing a favor for a friend. That's the God's honest truth."

"What good does it do you if she didn't know them?"

"Ooo, not bad. Not bad. But how would you know who she came across? Were you with her on her assignment? No? Now, give."

"He hung out with the Bad Boys. That's a group. But they're friends of mine and—"

"Who else?"

"That's all. But they wouldn't a done it."

"You never know, do you? Nice boys turn weird, decide they'd rather be punks or rodents or street queens or pimps or pushers or macho bully biker boys like your friend here. You just never know. It's a strange world, ain't it, Pinky?"

Pinky said nothing. His left eye talked to me, blinking signals about the worry underneath the cool.

"What's your real name?" I asked him. "Don, Harold, Bernard, or Bill? Listen, Bernard, I'm goin' over to your friend and ask him who Jimbo's friends were. If he gives me any more than you did or tells me you're lyin', I'll just hand him this vegetable slicer-dicer. That simple enough for ya?"

I started walking away.

As it turned out, the kid gave me a few more names.

· SIX ·

I walked to the end of the bar and stopped in front of Biker boy. I knew he wouldn't give me a damn thing, but I asked him anyway. When he snarled at me, he looked kind of like Elvis in his fat period. I flicked the stiletto at him and he seemed surprised at first, then he got all whimpery again. Kids around us, I realized, were looking on in admiration. I think they were hoping something would happen so they could say they'd been there.

"Now what?" I said.

He swallowed the frog in his throat, then swore he hardly even knew Jimbo. He just knew somebody who knew him. I could tell he was telling the truth. I folded the knife up and asked him why it took a blade to make him civil to people. I said I wasn't a cop and even if I was, he was still out of line. Somebody's life was endangered and he didn't have to be an asshole about it. I turned back toward Pinky and threw him his knife.

"I'd keep it," I told him, "except you'd go out tomorrow and buy two more."

He looked at me with so much hate in his eyes it made me feel sorry for him. There's nothing more dangerous or pitiful than a youth martyr who feels he's misunderstood. I know. I was one myself and I wasted too much time in juvenile halls and youth authority work camps. You forget about it, except with a teenager in the house and being around kids, you can't help but remember.

I turned back to Biker boy. "See ya."

"You know what, man?"

"I know. Fuck you, too, OK?"

That caught him off guard so much, he almost smiled before he turned away.

I moved onto the main floor and mingled with the crowd. Everybody was sweaty and panting. The kids in the back nodded in time with the wall of noise bouncing off our heads. Then, after they caught their breath, they fought their way forward and slipped back into the mad free-for-all up front where everybody jumped up and down and sideways, their loose heads and shoulders bobbing wildly about and ricocheting from body to body as they rammed each other like a carload of seizuring epileptics. There were a few pockets of holdouts hanging back who were either too luded to fight it out or just a little too old for such antics, although they probably hadn't quite come to grips with why they didn't want to be in the center of the fray.

I squeezed forward. Before I knew it, I was pogoing to stay on my feet as masses of skinny, fat, tall, and small bodies pushed, shoved, and battered me every which way. It took about five minutes to reach the front of the stage.

Pete had taken the mike off its stand and was jumping up and down with it against his lips, screaming hoarsely about all the fuckers who lived in hot tubs and worshipped the plastic fantastic and ate, drank, and talked the phony-baloney. I'd installed a hot tub in my backyard just six months ago; suddenly, I had this vision of stepping into a hot vat of swirling acid some fine evening. My boy was definitely down on leisure. Sweat ran down my forehead as I thought about building a locked room around my hot tub. That way I could have a steam room too.

Pete couldn't see me. His glasses were so dark he couldn't find the mike stand; at least I hoped it was his glasses that were making him trip around like that. Maybe not. By the time the noise stopped and the set was over, I didn't even want to see him. I was too mad. I wanted to grab him by the hair, drag him home, and lock the little bastard in his room. It seemed to be the only thing I could do to keep him out of trouble. I walked back to the bar and sat down there after I saw that Pinky and Biker boy were gone.

I had two double shots of J.D. before the noise started again. I looked back at the stage area. The crowd had doubled on the main floor. It was the other band again, The Scapegoats. I kept looking around for Pete. He had disappeared after his set. Just as well, I thought. I ordered another drink. The bartender had plenty of time for me. There were only two other people at the bar. Two guys in their late twenties, smoking fat cigars that didn't go with their boyish faces, were sitting close together talking. One was wearing a dark blue, satin warm-up jacket with white stitched lettering over the back. I couldn't read it, but it was obviously either the title of a movie or a rock album. The other guy wore one of those fashionably wrinkled linen suits that were the current rage for summer. They both had styled longish hair and one of them was probably a record exec.

The bartender looked like the struggling young playwright type or an aspiring folk-singer, some anachronism. He had that gentle look with soft eyes, wispy beard, slouchy shoulders, and round wire-rimmed granny glasses sliding down his nose.

"How do you put up with this shit?" I asked him. "The music, the people—doesn't it just piss you off?"

He leaned forward, turned an ear at me, and pulled back the coarse hair that covered it. A tuft of cotton fiber protruded.

"Works pretty good," he said. "Not good enough. You look the other way a lot, when people draw blades and such."

I smiled at him. "Keep your nose clean, don't you?"

"Got to," he said after I repeated it.

I got up to go and I should have gone home then, but I didn't for a number of reasons that came to me later. At the time, I just felt like doing something and seeing the spiffy-looking characters at the other end of the bar had given me an idea.

I walked out of the main room, cruised through the front area of the club, and went outside and headed toward the closest liquor store a block away. I picked up *Billboard, Cashbox,* and *Record World* magazines and asked the counterman for the fattest cigar he had. I paid for them, got a pack of matches, took the cigar out of its aluminum humidor, and lit up. After that, I unbuttoned my shirt to the navel, then I walked back to the Starwood, carrying the magazines under my arm and trying not to cough as I got the stogie smoking. I didn't know what I looked like, but I was modeling myself after the two young execs at the bar, guys a little bit on the insecure side about the responsibilities of their big new position, guys who compensate for it with a little quiet swagger.

I walked up to the ticket window, blew some smoke through the talk hole in the glass, and told a blond girl in a leopard-spotted dress that I wanted to speak to the manager. She fanned the smoke out of her eyes and looked at me like she wanted to cut my cigar off.

"Thanks," she said, showing her braces.

"Oh, hey, excuse me." I looked at my watch like I was in a hurry and let my fingers do a nervous musical tap dance on the formica.

"He's busy."

"I won't take but a moment of his time. I'm from M and A Records. Where is he?"

I said this like she didn't have a choice and gave her a conspiratorial smile that I hoped would make her feel there might be something in it for her.

It worked. She got off her stool and opened up the outside door by the side of the ticket window.

"Have you heard of The Lost Generation?" she asked me.

"Yeah, sure. Gertrude Stein's band."

"Who's she?"

"Never mind."

"This is four guys. My boyfriend's in it. They're really good. You wouldn't believe it. Do you think you—"

"Have him call my office. Albie Toklas. That's T-O-K-L-A-S at M and A. We're listed."

That's one thing you can always depend upon in this town, whether you're talking to a high-school girl, the gas station attendant, the waiter, or your dentist, at least one out of two of everybody I meet wants to deliver their message to the world in a song or a story, in person or on celluloid, and if you act like you know something that might help them, you can open a lot of doors for yourself. The only problem is that most of the time you'll wish you'd left them closed.

So she showed me to the manager's office. It was a cluttered, windowless little room that you entered from inside the ticket booth. A battered, black metal desk strewn with a mass of papers and Styrofoam cups served as a fortress for a slight little fellow who cowered behind it, facing the blank side wall in a swivel chair. The writing table was extended. He had both his elbows on it and he was holding the phone to his ear in a delicate manner, the way a child does listening to the ocean in a seashell. He looked like he was praying to it, and the sea across the chest of his floppy Hawaiian print shirt was sopping wet. All of him was—his fingertips were dripping.

"He's talking to the apartment owners association," the ticket girl told me.

"I know," he was pleading. "I'm not denying that. Not for a minute." He nodded and winced along for a few more minutes, interjecting occasional buts and yeses. The nods got ferocious; then, in a quavery voice that opened his mouth wide: "We'll have full security here tomorrow, I promise you. I don't like roughnecks and roughhousing any more than you do." There was a pause. "We didn't have them before because we didn't need them. Next to this *hozzerai*, rock 'n' roll was ballroom dancing. Please, trust me. I've made all the arrangements . . . Yes, I promise. Take care now. Please call me tomorrow if there's any problems. . . . We all appreciate what you're trying to do . . . Yes, and it's just as important to us."

He cradled the receiver gently like it was packed with nitroglycerin, then he turned toward us and took a handkerchief from his shirt pocket and mopped his face. I've seen happier people in my life.

His deep-set, red-rimmed eyes sought me out. "How'd I do?" he asked me.

I couldn't answer him. I'd never met him before and didn't have much of an idea what he'd been talking about. Whatever it was, I thought he'd done pretty bad, but I wasn't going to say so. He looked desperate and sounded desperate. But maybe that wasn't so bad, for him, that is.

Maybe he could be worse. If I'd known the guy, I might have been able to tell.

The girl was nodding at him. "Real good," she said.

"They suspended my license twice," he told us. "The next time they put me out of business. These punk kids are ruining the neighborhood, says their lawyer. But we spend thousands of dollars on security, and they'll complain anyway just having to look at these kids. They're a threat. No more vandalism, they'll still complain. See what I mean? How do ya win?"

I puffed on the stogie and nodded along, letting him work out the kinks.

"This is Mister Toklas," the girl told the guy. "He's with M and A Records."

"Mister *Tuchis*, it's a pleasure," the man smiled.

"Toklas, not *Tuchis*," I said sternly, as if this mispronunciation were a familiar insult to the family honor.

"My apologies. I don't hear so good. I thought you said *Tuchis*. In Yiddish, that means rear end. That's why I smiled. I don't get much of a chance to do that anymore around here. I might be looking to make a joke. Music's some tough business, wouldn't you say?"

"Sure is."

He seemed to want to be my pal, so I told him I was in the process of scouting out a few groups and wanted to see if I could get in touch with them.

The noise of the club was coming at us through the thin walls. It sounded like we were in the hull of a ship cutting through an iceberg. He gestured at it, sweeping both his arms. "You think this is art," he said, not a little hysterically. "You want to record it for posterity?"

Even playacting a young music sharpie, I had trouble coming up with an answer to that one. I thought it best to say nothing aloofly and let him fill in the silence.

"Who am I to say? I go home and listen to Glenn Miller. Don't ask me how I got into this."

"It can't be that bad," I ventured.

"That's what you think. But a dollar's a dollar, isn't it?"

Yeah, sure, a dollar's always a dollar. That's what pimps and whores say, that's what they say all the way from Wall Street to Warsaw, from the Vatican to Vegas. Everybody genuflects before the almighty dollar, everybody does things they feel are crazy, stupid, unmerciful, and contrary to human principle, to make a fast buck, to hustle the green. Pimp and whore and not a whole lot more. The sing-song came into my head. I opened my mouth and almost said it aloud, but it wasn't worth the effort; besides, I wasn't here to argue ethics with the man. If he wanted to screw up his dreams, that was his business. Just as long as he stayed out of mine.

"Right," I said to keep him jolly. Then I asked him if he had any idea how I might get ahold of a few bands by the names of the Bad Boys, Ricky Retardo, and Camp David.

The phone rang and the harried little man had the teeny-bopper answer. Silence reigned as she spoke into the phone, then cupped her hand over the mouthpiece. "It's the apartment association again," she said.

The top of the little man's bald head colored and the cords in his neck looked tight enough to break through the skin. His mouth formed itself into grotesque shapes as he lip sang to the plethora of obscenities thundering in his head. His fists pounded the air and stopped inches above the desk top. Finally, he waved a wild index finger at the girl.

"Tell him to go up and see Mindy."

I went up and saw Mindy in a small office on the second floor. She wasn't a hell of a lot to look at, really, and by the nervous way she had about her, even if she hadn't been wearing a matching Aloha shirt with the same beach scene and outrigger canoes, you might have guessed that she and the little bald-headed guy had something in common. A portable TV and the family photo gallery barricaded her desk. The children all had her mouth, which wasn't something to brag about. It was small but thick, like the lip of a balloon, and her sputtery laugh went with the image. At the moment, she was using it to appreciate a Johnny Carson wisecrack in his opening monologue. Rival network ABC

had come up with a solution to the moral majority's censor-
ship threats against sexploitation. Henceforth, announced a
hopeful programming executive to the press, the risqué
shows in question would shun their moral shiftlessness and
"Jiggle for Jesus."

"Ha-ha-ha. Jiggle for Jesus."

Maybe she wouldn't have seemed so gross if she hadn't
been so diminutive. Her laugh was just too big for her body.
She looked up at me like she wouldn't be sure it was a good
joke until I opened my yap too. So I gave it a couple of chuckles and her little eyes brightened like she'd just downed a shot
of whiskey. That put me on her good side. Once I gave her
my line about being the record producer, she took up where
her husband had left off and voiced her incredulity that presently people were paying money to listen to this type of music. She liked it as much as doing dishes, she told me in thick
Brooklynese, but because of the location of the club, they had
to either keep with the current trends or go out of business. It
took me about ten minutes of telling her how I understood
her dilemma before she thumbed through a little Rolodex and
got me some addresses.

"These kids, they change their damn names every week,"
she said while I was jotting the info down on one of my magazines. "Trade 'em, change 'em, and throw 'em away. You
can never get in touch with them."

"We'll just have to try our best," I said, backing toward
the door.

At that moment, Johnny called for the first commercial
break of the evening. On the office window, I saw Brooke
Shields bend over and launch into one of her naughty
Calvins commercials.

"I have ten pairs of Calvins in my closet," cooed Brooke,
with her child's voice and woman's face and infant's body,
"and if they could talk . . ."

Mindy wasn't amused. "Sometimes, don't ya gotta wonder what the world's comin' to?"

Familiar words. "Or what it came to," I said before I
knew it.

"Well, them moral seniorities or whatever, maybe they got a point," said Marvelous Mindy of Brooklyn, late of Crescent Heights and Santa Monica Boulevards in West Hollywood, sometimes known as just L.A., just Hollywood, just Tinseltown, Boys Town, or as George had once said, Vaseline Alley.

"Yeah, maybe so," I thought aloud.

"Is something wrong?"

"No. Thank you."

My eyes had popped wide, I suppose. Sometimes, you can shock yourself with what you're thinking.

• SEVEN •

I had two addresses. One was in Hollywood, the other a hotel downtown. Nighttime downtown L.A. is ugly and dull. You don't go there unless you have to. So, I got in my car and drove up to Sunset, turned right, and headed toward the empty heart of Hollywood, passing all of the familiar landmarks I'd been trying to forget: Schwab's, home to the hapless, hardy hustlers of Hollywood; Greenblatt's, my old neighborhood deli that first made me famous by displaying my bounced checks in their front window; the gas stations and car washes where you could pick up any extra service you desired and have it by the time they were done with your car. It went like that around here. The pace was frantic. Adult motels and massage parlors were right across the street from Hollywood High School. The kids here didn't have to go looking for work to pick up pocket money. It came to them *fast*. Today, in this neck of the woods, you couldn't afford to be young and impressionable. If you didn't have a firm idea of what you wanted, it was all over for you: poof, just like that, your destiny would be out of your hands. I knew it. I'd seen it. When I was younger, I'd made a lot of mistakes, but it had been easier to get away

with them then, in the Midwest, and you had to try real
hard to make them anything big. Steal a candy bar or a car,
fight a lot, cuss a cop. Christ, that was chicken feed compared to what kids could get into now. And without even
trying.

I looked at my map and got to where I was going in a sort
of daze, thinking about the past and present and trying to
put it together as it related to me and Pete. I passed by the
Hollywood Y on Hudson and turned right on Selma Avenue, stopping before a four-story, thirty—forty unit apartment hotel. It was only then I realized that what I was doing
didn't have too much to do with George. I was trying to figure something out. I just wasn't sure what. One thing I was
sure of was that George wasn't in any state to be dealing
with these kids. The way he was now, he was bound to get
himself into trouble. These kids were monsters, the rudest
motherfuckers anybody could meet. You had to have pa-
tience; otherwise, you broke heads, maybe your own.

I had to remind myself as I came up to the place. Trash
cans were on the sidewalk in front of the lobby window which
had a hairline diagonal crack starting from a fist-sized hole in
one corner. Glaring light from the entry was the only source
of illumination. I could make out a couple of beanbag chairs
and a mangy-looking German shepherd curled up in the
doorway leading to the lighted hall. I looked up at the windows of the rooms. Almost all of them were lighted. Some
were covered by venetian blinds with bent or missing slats;
some had sheets or towels tucked over curtain rods or the top
of the sill; others had ratty-looking houseplants or small electric fans for camouflage; many had nothing at all. At one of
these, a pale blubbery man took off his shirt, rolled up his
second-floor window, and spit out onto the sidewalk about ten
feet away from me. His window shut with a bang and then
suffused with the frigid blue light that comes only from television. Mariachi music came from the floor above him. My eye
followed the sound and came to rest on a sill ringed with
blinking red Christmas lights. The lights and the music had
just gone on. Someone up there thought they were talking my

language. I didn't want to give them any ideas, so I turned away and chugged up the short steps to the entrance.

You went through a short empty vestibule, the walls of which were scrawled over with gang names in black marker, then the front desk came up on your left. I was half-afraid that the switchboard would be buzzing with a message tuned to my arrival from the red window upstairs, but then I saw I didn't have much to worry about. The switchboard had dried flowers sticking out of the plugs, and the deskman sat before me with his head down, snoring. The elevator had signs on it in English and Spanish, saying it was OUT OF ORDER, permanently. The words were spray painted over the doors in white.

Not that I didn't get the usual royal welcome treatment. I tapped the guy on the shoulder, said hi to him, then I gave the desk bell a ping, and the German shepherd roused himself from the lobby and came in and growled at me like he hadn't had dinner. I'm not one to throw caution to the winds in situations such as this. I hoisted my butt onto the counter, then I got up the rest of the way and just stood there on top of the desk. The ceiling was low. I had to bend my head. The dog's yap opened wider and he started snapping at my ankles. I skipped rope over his fangs to avoid him.

The desk clerk chose to wake up around then. He looked at the dog, told him to shut up without seeing me, and put his head back down. I hit the bell with my toe a dozen more times, and he looked up again and saw me. He was a greasier version of the dead punk Jimbo; nineteen, skinny, white as a sheet, with slimy blond hair slicked straight back, wearing a sheepskin jacket collar-up and buttoned to the neck. His cheeks were pitted with acne and there was a large abscess on the side of his neck. His meaningless eyes went with the rest of it. He nodded at me calmly. Nothing could surprise him.

"What do you want?" he said.

"Call this damn dog off me," I told him for starters.

He smiled, showing what was left of a mouthful of rotted teeth. "What's it worth to ya?"

"I don't like your attitude," I said pointlessly.

The dog kept giving me the hotfoot and I kept jumping. The kid just sat there and grinned with his eyes closed, going back into his nod. I stopped jumping away finally, planted my feet, stomped hard and bellowed loud enough to bring the cows home and scared the bejesus out of the animal. He shrieked like somebody had just stepped on his tail and ran out of the room.

The greasy junkie opened his eyes and looked at me like he was seeing me for the first time. I got down off the desk.

"You need help," I told him.

He gave me a twisted smile. "You got anything?"

I thought he was going to OD on me before I could find out if I was in the right place, but then something happened to his eyes and he was suddenly standing alert and bowing from the waist.

"Not bad, eh?" He showed me his teeth and rubbed some gunk off them so I'd see they weren't as bad as they'd looked. The abscess, pallor, and pitted cheeks stayed. "I'm working on a scene," he told me proudly. "From *A Hatful Of Rain*. I'm getting into the character."

What's worse, a young drug addict or a young aspiring actor? It's got to be a toss-up. "Oscar, Oscar. Just don't get in there too far," I told him. "Otherwise, I'm sure it'll get ya places."

He decided to take that for a compliment. "Thanks," he said.

"Play an instrument, write songs or anything?"

"No. Why?"

"I'm in the music business. I could help you out," I said. "You got talent, though, really, it's pretty obvious. I *could* talk to Francis."

"As in Coppola?"

"Show biz is show biz." I made a bridge out of my hands and interlaced the fingers. "Everybody knows everybody. You know."

"It's all related," offered the junior sage.

"Some people call it nepotism."

"The ones on the outside looking in."

"You got it. But to the rest of us, it's one big, everlasting party—natch?"

"Natch. Wow."

"What's your name?"

"Paul."

"Paul." I motioned for his surname.

"Gerard."

"Paul Gerard. It's got that certain ring to it, don't it?" I nodded to myself, acknowledging the incontrovertible truth, then shook my head as if recalling the less impressive duty at hand. "Anyway, Paul, what brings me here is I've just got to find this punk group called Ricky Retardo. They're supposed to live here."

He laughed a little affectedly, the sort of laugh that went with ascots and cigarette holders. If you'd laughed like that when I was growing up, your peer group would have mopped the floor with you. Today, it heralded the beginning of a career; but, of course, this was Hollywood. "You've got to be kidding," he enthused.

I'd hardly known this kid two minutes and he was already very old to me. I got a ten-spot out of my wallet to speed things up a bit.

"No, I'm serious. I'm not sure what Desi Arnaz would think, but I've got to find them. They're young people in their late teens. You wouldn't have any way of knowing, would you?"

A true aesthete, he pushed the ten away. "It's not necessary. Let's see." He stepped back and opened a drawer in the front counter, riffling through a small stack of carbon rent receipts till he pulled one out. "This room is registered to a punky-looking kid. Memorable in his appearance."

"Aren't they all? What'd he have, green hair or blue?"

"Chartreuse and he wears a black glove on his right hand—don't ask me why."

"I wasn't going to. Are there any more you can think of who might be living here?"

"Others come in and go to his room. They might be

living there." He got apologetic at his vagueness, adding, "I've just been here about a week."

"And what's the kid's name?"

"Daniel Shades. Sounds phony, doesn't it?"

"Look who's talking."

His pallor colored for a moment as he smiled his quick embarrassment. I thanked him before he recovered, got the room number off the receipt slip, and went up to the second floor after promising we'd pick up where we'd left off in a little while.

The place was ugly but solid as a cell block. The noise came at you through the open transoms above the doors. Naked bulbs, one on each end of the hall, threw cruel light on the stained carpet. Shreds of stickum-backed floral wallpaper hung off some of the light brown walls. There were more of the gang names, signatures and numbers in black marker, pen, and spray paint. In green crayon, a child's hand had roughed out a small forest of pine trees by a few of the doors. I got to the room I wanted and knocked on the door. I heard the glib monotone of a local TV newscaster. I thought I could hear somebody brushing their teeth.

"What d'ya want?" asked a hoarse cranky voice.

"You Danny Shades?"

"Ain't here."

"Is he coming back?"

"Never heard of um."

"I have this as his room number from the front desk."

No answer. I repeated myself.

"Must be some mistake."

"You're sure you never heard of him."

The door swung open. It was the fat man I'd seen from down below. He had a toothbrush in his mouth. The bottom half of his pot belly hung out over his dirty, striped, small size pj's, which were at least six inches short on all the cuffs.

"I'm positive," he said with a grim smile and joyful hate in his eyes, then he slammed the door in my face.

I started knocking again and I persisted to the point of making him swing the door open a second time.

"That hurt my feelings," I told him.

He told me what I could do with my feelings. Then I offered him the ten I'd offered the thespian at the front desk and he chewed on his toothbrush and swallowed; then he laughed at the ten through his nose.

"I saw the car you drove up in," he scoffed.

I got my wallet out and handed him a twin to match what he was holding. "How's that?"

He grabbed the cash and took the toothbrush out and pointed with it to the left. "Next door," he said with a triumphant closemouthed leer.

I grabbed the bills out of his other hand before he knew what hit him. "You're an asshole," I told him. "That's a minus factor."

"Why you—"

He came at me. I gave him a sideblock that sent him back into the room, then I slammed the door on him and held onto the knob. After a minute or so, he gave up trying to break it down. I moved away as I heard him starting to gargle.

I knocked on the next door and got an old black lady in a hair net whose face was barred by two chained night latches that allowed a four-inch crack opening. She gave me hell for waking her at such a disrespectful hour; but when I agreed with her and apologized, she felt vindicated enough to tell me she had traded rooms with the Danny Shades in question no more than two days ago. Her old room was on the fourth floor on the left side at the far end. She said that the manager had arranged it. She couldn't stand the stairs and the rest of the tenants couldn't stand "tha' boy's noise." She claimed her old room was the quietest one in the building. She must have repeated herself at least twenty times and I was glad she did. Her teeth were out and I had to decipher each syllable. She must have had some idea of the difficulty involved because it gave her a kick when she heard me try to tell her back what I thought she was saying. Whatever, she was a sweet old thing and I'd gotten her out of bed. I gave her the two ten-spots when it was all over. It was the least I could do.

She studied the bills up close and thanked me, but by the tone of her voice it seemed like she thought they were counterfeit. I didn't feel that either of us was up to the strain of any further discussion, so I nodded my head at her and thanked her some more, then I headed for the stairs, thinking that twenty bucks is like two hundred or two thousand to somebody like that; people always get suspicious when you give them something for nothing. I guessed she hadn't thought the kid was worth the bother, that is, unless he was wanted for something. And most cops don't give out greenbacks for a reward, especially to little old toothless ladies in hair nets. She'd been thinking I was fuzz and I'd confused her.

The fourth floor had a heady distinctive odor of fermented underwear and it wasn't pleasant to be savoring it deep through the nostrils as I tried to catch my breath. The wallpaper hadn't been removed here. The lights were out. A half-moon, augmented by the steady glow of streetlights, lit the passage eerily like an underground tunnel you didn't dwell in, but passed through. But I was curious by now just to know if my twenty bucks was going to buy me anything worthwhile, so I walked down toward the last door on the left side, stepping softly.

It was strangely quiet up there. It made me jumpy suddenly, like something not so funny was going to happen and I was waltzing my way into it. You couldn't hear a thing aside from the light traffic on Selma Avenue. I got up to the door, saw its transom was closed, and leaned my ear against it and heard two or three voices engaged in a lazy argument. Then I could smell tomato sauce and I heard some silverware clatter against a plate, with the whir-purr of a small fan for background. I lifted my ear an inch, knocked, then listened again as the voices hushed each other and it got dead inside. Somebody turned the fan off. I knocked again and waited. I stared at the flaked black paint before my face.

"I know you're in there," I said finally. "Nobody's gonna hurt you. I'm by myself. I just want to talk to you."

"We're atheists, man," blurted somebody in a squeaky voice.

"I'm not a Jehovah's Witness. I'm with M and A Records and I really like your stuff and I'd like to talk to you about recording for us."

"What's the name of one of our songs?"

That stumped me right off the line. "Offhand, you know it's funny, I'm blanking on that."

"You like how we added the trumpet and sax?"

"Definitely. That's what really turned me on about you guys. You're diff—"

"There ain't no brass, man."

"Really?"

"You're full of clam juice, really, man, really," the young voice mocked me.

"I need to talk to you about Jimbo."

"We don't know no Jimbo."

"Don't you care to find out what happened to your friend?"

"What's it to you?" said the same voice.

"Open the door and I'll tell you."

"Get a warrant."

"I'm not a cop."

"Then put your hands up. I'm standin' six inches from you. I could blow you away."

I heard feet scrambling over an uncarpeted floor, a loud gun cock, the mating call of a sawed-off shotgun. I put my hands up.

• EIGHT •

It was a sawed-off, alright, but the last time it had been fired was underwater. The trigger was missing, the barrel was orange with rust, and it could go without saying that the squirrelly little guy pointing the damn thing up my nose had hair to match the color of crème de menthe, underneath which he wore the dark glasses that gave him his name. He wasn't wearing a black glove.

My heart slowed considerably, but there's something about a gun being pointed at you. I don't care if it squirts water, farts air, or sprouts a flag. Your imagination won't relax until you get it out of the way. And that's just what I did. I lifted my arm and pushed it gently off to the side.

"It's not polite to point," I said.

There were four others, three boys and a girl, none of whom could have been over sixteen. The one with the gun could have passed for eighteen, but he was just a little mature for his age. His face had a rugged squarish jaw and was covered with a thick stubble. He looked just as scared as the rest of them, and he latched onto the sawed-off with two hands, ready to try to bean me with it if I rushed him. Most of the floor was covered with thin stained mattresses; a section from one close to the door had been cut off so the door could open in and out. Duffel bags were stuffed into the corners with loose clothes piled over them. The whole place was about ten by fifteen, I guess, and the five of them would have had to practically sleep on top of each other.

"You shouldn't have opened the door, Danny," the girl whined. She was standing at a little hot plate atop a small raised table, holding a soupspoon over a tin saucepan. Steam rose from a pot on the other burner.

The three other boys were sitting side by side on a mattress with their backs against the wall. They held paper plates of watery spaghetti across their laps. One put his down, took out a pocketknife, and snapped it open.

"Yeah, well, he heard us, didn't he?" Danny sneered over his shoulder, keeping his shaded eyes on me. "Should I have just waited till he broke in here?" the kid added as a rather pleading afterthought.

"Relax. Eat your spaghetti. Put the gun down. Relax," I said.

Danny Shades held onto his gun and offered his chin to

me in a pugnacious attitude. "What's there to relax about?"

"Not much," I admitted. "But you don't have anything to worry about from me."

The girl must have believed me; either that, or she was too defeated to care. Ignoring me, she took the tin saucepan off the hot plate, brought it over to the three boys against the wall, and heaped on the thin sauce. She was wearing a black-and-white checkered jersey over a pleated black miniskirt. Her sloppy, shoulder length, dark brown hair was streaked with gray. Her high heels wobbled as she walked; her hands were tiny. She had barely entered puberty. She might as well have been dressing up in her sister's ridiculous old clothes; except her sister wouldn't have had dirty ankles. Her sister wouldn't have been caught dead in a joint like this.

"We're just mindin' our own business," said the boy with the pocketknife. His eyes were small and glassy, scared shitless.

The best thing I could do was to ignore him before he martyred himself by attempting something brave, which can happen in tense situations. I kept my eye on him, but all I did was nod.

"So am I," I said. "I'm just trying to find out something, and I thought maybe you guys could help me."

"What makes you think that?" said another kid against the wall.

"Pinky told me."

"Pinky's a scumbag," sneered Danny Shades. "He tell you to come here?"

"He and a friend—"

"What's the friend's name?" asked Danny.

"Didn't get it, but I heard them talking about Jimbo. I was at the Starwood tonight, you see."

"On your way to the disco," sneered Danny.

The kids, except for the girl, gave the big cheese a backup round of chuckles.

"Yeah," I smiled. "I hang out there all the time."

"Like hell," said the blade.

"Pinky said you guys were good friends of Jimbo's. Then you know he squealed for the police."

"He never gave 'em a fuckin' thing," Danny said self-righteously. "He had to pretend to 'cause otherwise he'd a been in jail."

"I can see that," I nodded. "But then why would somebody have killed him?"

Danny had an answer for that one, too. "People get paranoid. He shouldn't a told anybody he had somethin' to do with cops."

"OK, maybe, but there's also the possibility he knew something."

"About what?" a few of them said at once.

"There's a reporter who disappeared. She happens to be my sister," I lied.

That got the girl's attention. She turned around and looked at me as she licked off the spoon. "What's that got to do with Jimbo?" she asked indifferently.

"Jimbo was supposed to be working on it."

"What makes you so sure?" Danny wanted to know.

"My family's been working closely with the police."

"He's a cop," sneered the blade, looking up at Danny.

This only exasperated his ringleader. "So what are we gonna do about it?"

"Ya wanna clean his fingernails?" said the boy next to the blade, looking pleased with himself for the line, then scratching his burr head with a little bit of a worried look as the blade poked at him with his miniature weapon.

"Maybe I should clean your fingernails," the blade said.

The room got quiet for a minute.

"Don't act so stupid, Bob," the go-go girl said, her small mouth pouting with disapproval.

"The voice of reason," sneered the tough boy, seeming embarrassed all of a sudden. He pocketed the knife, took a new wave comic book out of his back pocket, and began reading as he started in on his spaghetti. Definitely a poseur. Each one, including the one who hadn't talked or eaten as of yet, was trying to strike up an attitude, rummaging for a personality that would feel right and stick.

But I could tell that Danny and the girl were interested. Danny was nodding to himself. He took off his shades and squinted at me as he pinched the bridge of his nose where the glasses had pressed.

"Jimbo was supposed to of been workin' on the reporter's disappearance, huh?"

"Right," I told him. "And since you're friends of his and he never tattled on people like you, I thought I'd like to ask you if he might have said anything."

"Pinky's gonna pay for this," said the blade from behind his magazine.

"It wasn't Pinky's fault," I told him. "I overheard him, then coerced him. I got your address from the club manager."

"Who gives a fuck about Pinky anyway?" Danny was saying.

"So did Jimbo tell you anything?" I went on.

Danny shook his head. "Nah."

"Did you ever meet Elise Reilly?"

A pause. Silence.

"You're not suspects. She interviewed most of the local bands."

"She was here once," the girl said finally.

"Recently?"

"Two weeks ago, about," she shrugged.

"Can you think of any reason why somebody would want to kidnap her or hurt her?"

Bob the Blade slammed his comic book facedown, dumped his plate off his lap, and stood up and glared at me. I hadn't noticed that he'd put on reading glasses, but the horn-rims looked out of place with the dagger tattoo inside his forearm.

"Just one thing I wanna know," he hollered. "This what's her name—"

"Elise Reilly," I said solemnly.

"So she interviewed a bunch of punks. Big deal. That

don't for one minute mean we're responsible or that any punks had jack shit to do with it."

"Get off your high horse," I told him. "Somebody's life's endangered. I'm not saying *you've* got anything to do with it. We're just trying to think. Any objection?"

He shut up.

"Your buddy Jimbo's no more. I'm saying there might be a connection. He's told to find out about her and he's got a big mouth. He gets loaded and talks to people. He's a punk. The people he knows are punks. He might have said something that set him up—in *your* network."

"You could be setting us up by comin' over here," said the smart ass with the burr head.

"I doubt it, but it's only gonna get worse if we let this go."

"And they should pay, I mean it," said Bob the Blade. "Nobody gets away with that shit. Jimbo, shit, he's *dead*." His neck craned side to side as he looked to his friends for confirmation.

"I'm glad you guys see it that way."

"Sure, man," said Danny.

The quiet boy had tears in his eyes. He got up and left the room before I could really get a look at him. He was on the short side, but his arms and legs were long and ready for a big growing spurt. The girl went after him.

"That's Jimbo's brother," Danny said, looking me in the eye.

• NINE •

It got quiet. Bobby the Blade sat down and started eating. For the next few minutes, nobody said anything. I walked to the window and looked down at the street. It was past midnight now and the air outside had cooled down. The girl and Jimbo's brother came back. She went back to the hot plate. He sat down in the same place. She asked me if I'd

like something to eat and I accepted. She fished some noo-
dles out of the hot water in the pot with a big spoon, then
picked up the saucepan and poured what was left on top of
it. I thanked her and sat down on a mattress in the center of
the room. Danny Shades and Bobby Blade made polite
overtures to Jimbo's brother, whose name was Jerry. His answer to everything was "I'm OK," but his fork hand was
shaking as he tried to eat; in a moment or so, he gave it up.
Nobody said anything to me until the girl sat down against
the wall by Jerry, told me her name was Suzi, and asked if I
lived in the area. I gave her Reilly for my last name and said
that I used to, but lived by the beach now. I felt guilty for lying. My only consolation was that I felt confident it had
been better that I talked to them instead of George. I kept
telling myself that and cringed inwardly at the blood-and-
guts images flying about inside my head as I imagined how
Steifer would have reacted to a dummy sawed-off shotgun
and a small blade. Not too much of a threat, but in his condition, from what I'd seen as of late, it might not have been
good. I ate a little bit of the offering to be nice, then I asked
if anybody had heard of Pete's group, Claustrophobic.

"Yeah," shrugged Danny. "So what?"

"What do you think of them?"

"They're pussies."

"What's that mean?"

He just shrugged.

"They didn't do nothin'," scoffed Bobby the Blade.

"They couldn't do nothin'," offered the boy with the burr
head.

"You think they're in on this?" Danny asked me.

"Maybe," I lied to give myself a reason for the probe.

Bobby the Blade's eyes got wide. He started to get up
again. "I told you—"

"Shut up, Bobby," Danny told him. "You're givin' us all
a headache. I don't need it."

Bobby was the sort of kid who seemed to expect to be
brought into line. He took his medicine and sulked quietly
after scattering a few choice epithets.

The girl, Suzi, had an idea here. "They could have dealt with Jimbo, but they wouldn't off him."

"Why not? You know them?"

"Not real good."

"They into dealing?"

"I doubt it."

"Listen, they're OK," said Danny. "We just don't love them 'cause we lost a couple a gigs to them."

"Their lead singer's a faggot," said Bobby.

"Really?"

"He thinks he's God." He used his fork as a pretend mike and mimicked Pete's style, shaking it in front of his big mouth which he opened overwide into a howling expression. All of them got a kick out of this. For the first time, there was laughter.

"He's really that full of himself?"

"Yeah," said most of the boys.

"I think he's kind of cute," said Suzi.

None of them liked that.

"You would," the burr-headed boy told her.

"What does he shoot?" I asked casually.

Danny Shades frowned at me and put his sunglasses back on. "We didn't say he was a drug addict, mister."

"I saw him tonight at the Starwood."

"We ain't his doctor, man," sneered Bobby. "We wouldn't know."

I held up my hands, surrendering an apology. "Just asking, that's all."

"Seems to me, you're *just* asking an awful lot of questions," observed Suzi.

I got up to go. "And it seems to me that you're all up past your bedtime; but that's another matter that has nothing to do with me."

"Yeah," Danny nodded. He patted his mouth, faking a yawn, then gave me a slow smile as the burr-headed boy broke into a horselaugh.

"Well, so long, and thanks for trying to help," I told them.

My eye caught Jimbo's brother. He was staring at the opposite wall, trying to keep a stiff upper lip, I suppose; but there was no reason for it. I wanted to tell him something, but I had no idea what to say.

• TEN •

On my way out, I stopped by the desk clerk and thanked him for the three-leg detour he'd sent me on; he reminded me about putting in the good word for him with Francis, so I gave him a short lecture on how to make his own luck without waiting for things to happen. That took the wind out of his sails so bad, though, I finally gave him the phone number of an actor friend of mine, popular in TV, who I hoped might be able to talk some sense into his head on the subject of this demoralizing profession.

I got in the Alfa, turned back to La Brea, and headed down to the Santa Monica Freeway; except when I got there, instead of getting on the west on ramp and cruising home, I went east toward downtown. Don't ask me why. I was restless and bored and, even though it was one AM, I just didn't feel like going home. Freeways are made for moods like this. They speed you up enough so you can get places before you lose the impulse. That's how many of us end up doing what we shouldn't. The telephone can do the same thing; sometimes, it's even better. Just imagine all the rash things you might have been prevented from doing if you hadn't had a car or phone; it was a hell of a lot easier to be rational when you had to write a letter or walk a ways to see somebody.

I was sure that George would be tickled I'd done a little of his homework for him; but that wasn't what was making me drive out of my way. Pete had been nagging at my conscience from the moment I'd found that sorry lost soul Jimbo saying his last prayers at the bottom of a toilet bowl. I didn't want Pete to end up like that, and from what I'd been seeing in the past few nights, it seemed much easier than I'd suspected. Not that I was going to learn a whole lot from B.S.ing with his peers. You couldn't expect to get a straight answer out of them, especially when you weren't quite sure what you were asking. I knew Pete wasn't a drug addict or a lost cause. I just wanted to know if he had whatever fatal flaw it took to become one. And who could tell me if I couldn't see it myself?

One thing for certain: I was drilling down into the gray area that separated Pete's youth from mine. Life was faster now. Maybe the only way to get on top of things was to grow up quicker so you could get a head start. That was one way of explaining why so many ten-year-olds felt compelled to wear designer labels and lose their virginity before the onset of adolescence. And kids have always run away; but in the past, in my day, it seemed that the scales had been tipped slightly in the direction of wanting to fight off "bein' sivilized," as old Huck Finn would say, more than wanting so desperately to be grown-up and saddled with responsibility. From what I could see, this was a type of defense against adult tyranny, becoming one as the only recourse for keeping them at bay. Many kids today weren't bursting with respect for their parents. They wanted to leave home, make money, and live on their own without interference. What was the big hurry? Were Mom and Dad that repulsive?

The Sixth Street exit came up on me before I could box my head into a corner any further. Main Street and Broadway and the rest were dead to any action but an occasional stumbling drunk at this time. The Greyhound bus station was the only place alive. As I passed it, a platoon of soldiers was exiting the terminal. They all had skinheads and carried duffel bags. They didn't realize it, but they would have made good punks, although they were too neat to qualify. Wall Street was just a few blocks from there. It's the financial center of the city, that is, if you're fond of calling venerable places like the Hard Rock Cafe or the Ace-Hi Bar institutions of high finance. In L.A., Wall Street is Skid Row. It's the city's armpit. They built the downtown police station right there to keep it under control, not because it's dangerous, but because it's a sight for sore eyes, a public nuisance that people don't want to hear about or see, especially when big business is doing its damnedest to revitalize this part of town. I should have thought I had the wrong address, but somehow I didn't think so.

Halfway to Fifth, in between two other dilapidated four-story brick buildings, I found an abandoned-looking dump that was Hotel Excelsior. Two bums, one black, one white, were perched ornamentally at the ends of the twin cement balustrades bordering the stairs on the front stoop. They both looked as if they were chewing tobacco, but that may have been because they didn't have any teeth. Their legs dangled over the short front wall. They'd been staring the void in the face for a long time; you could see it by the way their shoulders slouched and their stubbly double chins fit so snugly against their chests. More like them, only the moving kind, staggered about in front of the two bars up at the corner. A dark blue paddy wagon was double-parked up there; momentarily, a black man with wooly gray hair emerged from the joint facing me; he had a crutch under his right arm. Two dark-haired white men and a Mexican came after him with two cops. The gray-haired black man climbed up into the back of the van, and the Mexican and one of the other dark-haired men went with him, but one of the cops held the other man back and wouldn't let him climb on. I couldn't hear him, but he appeared to be begging them to take him to jail. That's got to be the bottom, when the county can offer you better lodging than the flophouses you've been crashing in.

The whole block was a glare of strobe intensity street-lights. The police station garage was directly across the street. Still, I didn't think twice about putting my top up and locking the car before I left it in front.

I walked up to the doormen, wished them good evening, getting no direct answer in return, and went in, praying I'd find a dry desk man who talked to people other than himself. The front desk was directly before the door, just a few feet inside, so nobody could slip by; it was one of those little bamboo jobs, a portable bar, really, that belonged in a Chinese restaurant with Tahitian decor, not a transient hotel. Behind it sat a tiny Mexican fellow who was dressed in gray work pants with a white shirt and a skinny black tie. He couldn't have been more than twenty and I figured he was probably fresh from South America or some place where a crap hole like this would seem like a first class operation. He was dry, he talked to me, but it wasn't in our language. He smiled, put out an open hand, and parroted "Seven dollars a night" to everything I said. I tried out my fractured Spanish on him and suddenly he was laughing really hard. Just as suddenly, he apologized profusely. I couldn't figure it out, and none of the handprinted signs above his head were any help to me: CHECK OUT BEFORE NOON, PAY RENT ON TIME, NO COOKING IN ROOMS, ONE MAN PER ROOM. There were a dozen of them, they made three rows of four, and if you had any brains, you knew the whole story just by looking at the dump from the outside.

After a few more tries, I was ready to give up and walk around to see if I could find somebody, when he came around from behind the bar and motioned for me to follow. We went up a narrow flight of rickety wood stairs covered with center strips of ribbed rubber. He walked out into the hall on the third floor and I tagged along. A third of the way down, we had to step over a dark figure of a man who was sprawled face down across the narrow passage, snoring into the threadbare carpet. He reeked of vomit and the desk boy nudged him with his foot to no avail, then cursed him quietly as he knocked lightly on a door a little further down.

"Yes?" said a woman from behind the door.

"Tengo un hombre aquí quien lesgustan malcriados."

"What?"

"I want to talk to the Bad Boys," I told her.

"Do I know you?"

"I'm with M and A Records. We've been looking for them for weeks."

"There's no such label."

"We're new."

"Doesn't matter anyway. We signed with somebody else last month."

"Are you one of them?"

"Their manager."

"I'd like to talk to them about another matter."

"I'm afraid it's a little late."

"I'm sorry. It's an emergency."

"Of course."

"This is life or death."

"Isn't everything?"

"I like that. A sense of humor."

"What do you want?"

"I need your help."

The door opened. I'd expected to find a nice big fat girl, the kind who develops wits of lightning and a great line of sex patter to fill in for all the sweet romance she thinks she's missing; but you could have blown this gorgeous slight twig of a thing away with a sneeze. She was as skinny as they come without being bedridden—the anorectic type. I'd take a fat girl any day; at least you're not going to break her ribs when you squeeze her, though this one was lovely enough in her way, blond, with cheekbones like handles, and a large soft mouth that could have done things to you if it cared. For now, it studied me, along with the dark eyes that didn't go with the messy short blond mop straggling her head. She wore a thin silk number blocked out with rectangles in red, white, blue, and orange, and it made her nonfigure look all the more beamlike.

"Esta bien?" the desk boy asked her, looking back and forth between us.

Her lips parted and she laughed quickly. "People come here and ask for the Bad Boys, and he brings them up to me," she told me. "I tried to tell him they're a group, but he's got it in his head I'm a madam for a bunch of queers. He thinks you want them for your twisted pleasures."

"I see."

The three of us smiled at each other.

"He's waiting for you to give him a tip."

"Oh, yeah, sure."

I got my wallet out, gave the kid a five, and he thanked us both and went back down the hall, nudging the snoring drunk once more as he stepped over his prostrate body.

"Can I come in?"

She moved aside and I stepped into a small stuffy room dominated by a bowed and lumpy iron-frame bed. The dark wood floor creaked and the walls and woodwork were smudged and filthy, gray. A revolving fan on a chair fluttered a yellow blanket hanging over the curtain rod on the one window facing the police station; it did a poor job of keeping the bright light out from the street. Aside from this basic setup, there was a lot of expensive paraphernalia: a tiny color TV, cameras, tape recorders, jewelry, and chic clothes dumped about haphazardly on the bureau, the bed, and the floor. The TV was on the windowsill. Tom Snyder was interviewing a female transsexual. We both looked toward the TV as the transsexual said something about its newfound happiness. The thin woman bolted the door, then she moved to the TV, and flicked it off, mimicking the guest's affected gestures as she turned around.

"Wouldn't it be nice if that was all it took?"

"A sex change operation, you mean?"

"Maybe that's what's wrong with me. I oughta have my sex changed."

"I doubt it, but tell me one thing."

"Yes?"

"Why are you camped out in this dive if you can afford something better?"

It must have been the wrong question because her hand reached behind her and came up with a serious little surprise from the back of her waistband. It wasn't so little, really. It was a snubnosed .38, chrome-plated with a pearl grip.

"I ask the questions," she said. "What do you want?"

"People have been asking me that a lot tonight," I told her. "I've had two knives, a rusty sawed-off, and now this dainty delight pulled on me so far. You wouldn't believe that a few hours ago I was bored."

"You're boring me," she said, putting her left hand over her right to steady her aim.

"Don't worry. I don't think you'll miss," I told her. "I don't think I'm boring, though."

"Why not?"

"First off, I've got a charming way about me, which you'd know, of course, if you just gave me a chance. Second, I don't think you'd be holding that on me if I were putting you to sleep."

"Let's just walk across the street."

"To the police. Sure, if you feel it's necessary."

She jerked her head toward the door. "Please," she said.

"Have a permit for that?"

"As a matter of fact, I do."

"As a matter of fact, I don't think I've done anything wrong."

"You're a liar," she said calmly.

"Because I said I was with a record company? I can explain, if you'll let me."

She gave me the nod to keep snapping my yap, and I told her the truth because, off the top of my head, I couldn't think of any reason why I shouldn't. When, for the most part, I was finished, she wanted to know why the Bad Boys would have anything to do with it.

"Hey, I don't know the Bad Boys from Adam," I told her. "But I doubt if they do, too, and you seem straight enough to me for a dilettante who needs to fix on a little sleaze and decadence every now and then—otherwise, what excuse would you have to tote that pearl-handled jobbie?"

"Boredom makes us do weird things, doesn't it?"

"At least I had a little bit of a reason."

"Playing goody two-shoes for your police pal and curious about your dear, dear son."

"He is."

"Touching."

I moved over to the bed, took three or four of the Nikons and Hasselblads out of my way, and plopped down, sitting with my feet up and my head against the wall.

"What are you doing?"

"Getting comfortable."

"I don't think you're cute."

"You're not exactly my type either, but my feet are sore."

"I asked what my clients could possibly have to do with this reporter's disappearance."

"And I've been trying to tell you I doubt if there's any relationship, but Jimbo protected his friends, you see, and I've been thinking that since it's possible Ms. Reilly interviewed the Bad Boys for background on her piece, and equally possible that Jimbo wouldn't have told the cops about them even if they were involved, on a long shot, I thought I'd try to have a chat with them."

"That is the most ridiculous, asinine reasoning I've ever heard," she said.

"You're probably right," I confessed. "So let's forget all about it."

I got up, tucked in my shirt, and backed to the door with my hands up. The thin woman looked down at her hands as if she'd forgotten she had a gun in them. She put it down on top of the TV and gave me a little smile.

"That's nice," I said.

"What?"

"That little smile of yours, like you're too cool and civilized to give a big grin. I like that, it's sexy, like how you're real calm when you're angry."

"But I'm not your type, remember."

"And I'm not cute."

We didn't exactly run into each other's arms, but inside of a few seconds, we came in for a close-up. She kissed in that hungry way like some skinny women do; and, when you got right down to it, she felt like she had a lot more shape to her than I would have thought.

• ELEVEN •

S he pulled away before I could find out for sure. I don't think either of us was too disappointed. For me, it might have had something to do with the drunk in the hall changing his campsite to a spot just outside the door. I could hear him slouching down against the other side of the wall; he grunted as his head thumped against the floor. You could smell him, and it wasn't the sort of fragrance that mixed with budding romance or even a quick fling. Not that my newfound acquaintance was interested. For her, a long sloppy smooch meant about as much as a handshake; it was her way of saying, OK, let's bury the hatchet. Or maybe I didn't read her right. If Freud could admit he didn't understand women, so can I. Whatever, she grabbed an alligator handbag off the bureau, opened it, and offered me a ski trip in the Bavarian Alps. I let her go without me and she stoked her furnace with enough nose candy to make her eyes light up like a couple of hot coals. She decided she was worried about her boyfriend who should have been back by now and asked me if I'd mind escorting her to a building nearby. I volunteered my services.

She put her hand to her mouth and gave a little cry when she opened the door and found the sleeping drunk in front of her, though she recovered quickly and went back into the room and returned with one of her cameras to take the poor bastard's picture. She explained this by saying she was doing a study. Some study. You had to really strain your imagination to see what was so fascinating about the subject. He was filthy beyond description, wearing a thermal undershirt, slacks, and laceless shoes. He had just peed himself in his sleep and pieces of regurgitated food decorated his chest. His face, ankles, and hands were covered in grime so thick, you could barely make out the color of his skin; the full head of matted gray-brown hair placed him at anywhere from forty-five to sixty-five. He was a testament, barely breathing, to suffering and poverty, and by the time his photograph hung in a gallery or somebody's home, he was sure to be dead. Love, money, food, none of it could have done any good for him now; it was too late. Maybe it had always been that way. Some of us are born to be cursed lost souls. It's not fascinating, it's sickening. And if you think you can do anything about it, you're a fool; and if you think you can't do anything about it, you're a worse fool.

"Look at the light on his face," she told me.

I couldn't appreciate the aesthetics, but I nodded. I didn't want to bring her down off that high snowy peak.

We got outside without incident. My car was still there. We got in it and she directed me to a three-story warehouse on Figueroa by Pico, a few blocks away from the L.A. Convention Center. She took an electric eye gizmo from her purse, pushed the gizmo, and a two-story corrugated metal panel moved up from the ground. I turned into the narrow driveway and entered. It was around five thousand square feet, big enough for a baseball diamond and then some. The whole place reeked of fresh paint. I drove toward some lights in the far corner. Voices yelled at me to stop. The floor had just been painted. I backed to the entrance, parked, and the two of us walked across the long expanse of cement floor, reaching the lighted area where a half-dozen punks were standing around a white fin-tailed '59 Cadillac.

Everything was a fashionable industrial gray. One step above the loading dock, offices beyond the immediate area were being transformed into living quarters. One room, ablaze with track lighting, had been made over into a kitchen. Its glass front wall faced the main floor. It was no doubt an expensive proposition. Some of my questions were answered readily by the sleeveless t-shirts the six young men were wearing, black with BAD BOYS in uniformly messy white caps across the front and back. They looked the same as the kids I'd been seeing around the Starwood, a little older though; all of them had the short spiky hair; a few had chains. They looked skinny and harmless. The thin woman went up to one of them and kissed him the way she'd done me. I was the only one watching. The rest kept talking about the car. After listening in for a few minutes, I realized they were debating how to destroy it in an upcoming concert. One wanted to torch it, another wanted to do a number with electric chain saws, a third wanted to beat the dickens out of it with crowbars and sledgehammers. The two others vacillated somewhere in between the torch job and driving into the audience. They were all serious, swigging beer and whiskey from the bottle and yelling at each other to stress their points. They didn't seem to notice me; either that or they didn't want to.

My skinny lady and her beau broke off their smooch.

"Hey, we're gonna do all a that shit," he bellowed at the five others. "Let's just not hurt ourselves like we did last time."

Most of them grunted and swore their agreement. "Fuckin' A" seemed to be the general consensus.

"'Cept Darby don't get no chain saw," demanded one of the tallest and skinniest.

"Why, man?" squealed the one who must have been Darby.

"'Cause you get just too out of control, Darby," the skinny tall boy said with embarrassment.

"Pussy," Darby catcalled with a crazy sneering smile.

"You do get a little wild, Darby," said the skinny woman.

"Meow, meow," he answered, adding, "Hi, Michelle. What's new on Rodeo Drive?"

"Fuck you."

"Who's your friend?" a few asked.

"Hi," I waved.

Michelle gave the straight spiel that I'd been turned on to them by Pinky and wanted to know if they knew anything about dear old Jimbo who might have had the inside dope on the missing reporter. Par for the course, they gave Pinky's name a generous thrashing and took great pride in promising him the reddest of red raspberries. Michelle took out her powder and offered it around. Her boyfriend was the first to sample the toot.

"Jimbo sure had great shit," he said, tapping a few thick lines out of the vial onto the mirror of Michelle's open compact, then snorting them up with a hundred-dollar bill she handed him.

"Is that all you can say for him?"

He finished and passed the apparatus on. "What else do you want me to say?" he said nasally, pinching his nostrils and sniffling to get the dregs. "We always bought from him. He'd hang around. Lots of people hang around."

"Did you know he was an informant?"

"No. Was he?"

"Yeah."

"For how long?"

"I don't know exactly," I admitted. "But it seems like just about everybody knew. I'm surprised he didn't tell you guys."

"Why?"

"It gave him a charge. He used to brag about it. He thought it was funny. He fucked over his competition, fucked the police, and meanwhile managed to get out of jail all at the same time."

"I don't get it," said the boyfriend.

"They're trying to figure out why he was killed," Michelle said coolly. "Whether it was drug related or if he got silenced for knowing something related to this police investigation."

The boyfriend shrugged. "I didn't even know he was an informant."

"So be it," I said. "And none of you guys knew him well enough to have any idea whether he had any enemies."

They shook their heads.

"Then let's forget about Jimbo. Seen any weirdos lately?"

They gave me blank looks like they weren't sure whether or not I was trying to be insulting.

"Huh?" said one.

"I know you guys aren't as stupid as you look."

"He a cop?" asked Darby.

"You got something to hide?" I asked him.

"We don't like cops," said Darby.

"I know that's standard policy, but just because I'm not wearing the uniform—punk, I mean—doesn't mean I'm the man-in-blue."

"You're awful anxious to help them out," said Michelle.

I turned toward her. "I came to your place wanting information about the Bad Boys. You told me I was on a wild-goose chase, then you asked me to drive you somewhere because you wanted to know why he wasn't home." I pointed to the boyfriend. "I didn't ask to come here. It was your idea."

She didn't say anything.

"We're just talking," I went on. "I'm just asking you if you've come across anything weird."

"You're very out of it," Michelle told me.

"And you aren't putting on an act?" I countered.

"I don't take this seriously," she said without a smile, gesturing at the Bad Boys. "They know it. They don't either, although they'll be the last to tell you."

"Yeah, we're poseurs," said Darby.

"Everybody's a poseur," said the boyfriend. "Let's change our name to the Poseurs."

"Capital," said one of them.

"Don't you understand that everybody's object is to be as weird as possible?" Michelle said irately with cool malice.

I nodded. "Punk's answer to conformity."

"Mutate or die," sneered Darby.

I raised my hand. "I've had enough bullshit for one evening. I'm not doubting for a second that each and every one of you is making a tremendously valid statement which modern civilization, as we know it, simply cannot do without. And I know you can't relate to what I'm saying, but is there anything you sense to be going on?"

"A lot's goin' on, man," Darby insisted. "Just the other day, some fuck—"

"I know, I know, I know—injustice is rampant—but have you seen anybody weird lately?!"

They were quiet for a moment. Darby pointed at me. "Man, *you*. *You* are weird."

"Thank you," I smiled. "Coming from you, Darby, that's a compliment."

"You want some coke, man?" squeaked the kid next to me.

"Sure," I said, surprising them all.

Nobody trusts you unless you do their drugs with them, that's a cardinal rule which influences everything and nothing. Ten minutes later, I was sitting on the hood of the Caddie, sharing a joint with Darby and answering his inquiries about the approximate cost of condos in the Marina. He was interested, but he wasn't sure if he was ready to buy. Maybe after the next concert tour. It was for his parents, not himself, though he could use the write-off. He wasn't really such a Bad Boy, after all. The gang had spread out. Michelle and her boyfriend had disappeared. A few of the other guys were sitting on the Caddie's rear bumper. The coke came around again as Darby and I were talking over the upcoming Leonard–Hearns welterweight bout. Darby had Leonard for style and speed, I had Hearns simply because he had *weird* incensed eyes that reflected death by KO. Darby wanted to bet me. I got up and shadowboxed myself, horsing around.

"I'm Leonard," I said, hamming it up. "Hearns looks at me with them weird eyes, *bam,* I lie down just praying he's gonna go *away!*"

I laid myself down to illustrate the point, then popped back onto my feet. "The guy's scary, the guy's weird," I insisted.

Getting loaded makes everything free association time, which can be helpful as long as you can keep ahold of a full deck and keep shuffling it till your partner gets a wee bit dizzy and loses some of his. You segue back and forth from past to present, dropping arcane references in and out of the patter like sleight of hand. Weird was the key word. It took us back instead of forward, like I'd been hoping.

"Ever heard of Young Hitlers?"

"Huh?"

"You were askin' about weirdness, if we seen any weirdos."

"Yeah."

"You want weird, man, they're weird."

"Who are they?"

"A band. Jimbo and Pinky shoulda told ya. Jimbo was tight with them, least recently. They cut a demo and he gave it to me to listen to. He was hopin' to get a cut if we turned them onto our label."

"What's so weird about them?"

"I dunno. Sometimes you get the feeling they ain't kidding."

"They're supposed to be weird, aren't they? You guys kill Caddies, they play the gestapo. It's symbolic, I'm sure they say. Americans are fascist pigs. Look what we've become, de-da, de-da, de-da."

"They keep to themselves."

"It's part of the mystique."

"Maybe. If I was you, I'd look into it."

"You think they're really Nazis?"

"They're capable of some kinky shit. Take it or leave it."

"What about you and the chain saw?"

"There's a difference."

"Yeah?"

"I know what I'm doing."

I didn't really know the guy, but the way he said it, I had to believe him; of course, I was so stoned right then, I would have believed just about anything.

• TWELVE •

Things can come to you without even trying: euphoria, found money, overheard conversation, wrong numbers, obscene phone calls, clap, headaches, heartburn, cancer, or a pane of glass out of a forty-story window—the more you think about it, most of what happens to you by chance ain't really so good. So when somebody gives me something I haven't asked for, I don't trust it, which was how I felt about the lead from Bad Boy Darby once I was back in my car, driving home with the top down. I nearly forgot about it by the time I stopped by to see Jodie. I was sure it was past three, closer to four, but what did I care? I was coked to the gills. I leaned on the bell. She opened the door wearing something white and satiny that covered her about as well as a postage stamp. She didn't want to go for a ride and I don't know how I talked her into it, but I did. Leaving should have been the last thing on my mind, of course, but you could hear some guy snoring in the bedroom as plain as day. We didn't even talk about it. She got her work clothes and came along. A little later, she woke me up in my hot tub and suggested we go to bed. When I woke up again, she was gone and, at first, I couldn't remember if I'd made love to her. Then it came back to me. Nice, everything, especially the way we put up with each other. Someone else might have been put off by hearing a stranger's snores from his lover's bed; and then again, someone else might have told me to get lost on more than one occasion. We put up with each other nicely.

Pete was gone. I hoped he'd left early for school, but I doubted it. He'd been home last night. It looked like he'd had a few guys from the band over. Cigarette butts, beer and coke bottles were littered about. I found Stanley in the back, sunning himself on the deck. He'd had breakfast. There was food left in his bowl. I had a cocaine hangover. I moved slow and I felt like I wasn't all there, like my fine-tuning was screwed up and I was chugging along on some but not all of my gunky cylinders.

The phone rang. I went to answer it, saw my phone number on the dial ring. It didn't look right. I didn't answer. I waited till it stopped ringing, unplugged it, and went to take a shower. Then, after numerous cups of coffee, homemade French toast, bacon, and a leftover turkey leg, I went out front, picked up the paper, and came back and read it inside out. Halfway through, I plugged the phone in. To try myself out for the day, I wanted to call somebody before somebody called me, so I called my agent to see if anybody had taken a bite out of yesterday's meetings. I doubted it. If anything's going to happen, you're usually told on the spot in the course of the meeting or your sixth sense feels real itchy with the promise of all the things money can buy. I was right, but not to worry. He was working on something he'd know more about tomorrow. Fine. I wasn't dying to take any meetings, I was just dying. A few weeks rest wouldn't kill me. I had things I could do, sleep, for one. I went back to bed to practice. The phone rang. I'd forgotten to unplug it again. I answered it after the twentieth ring. It was Steifer.

"You're home."

"What's left of me."

"Cold?"

"No."

"Big night?"

"Nah."

"I've got a search warrant for your nose."

I did my best to summon up a laugh which tricked me and came out as a cough. George got quiet. As I said, he was like that lately, good for a few flyweight one-liners that were enough to exhaust what was left of his good spirits. I got the kinks out of my throat and led into the stock questions to fill the silence. How was he doing? Any interesting action? Plans for the weekend? The Division was having a barbecue.

"I was gonna ask you if you felt like lunch," he said finally. "But you probably wanna sleep it off."

I didn't have to think about it to realize this was the first time he'd ever asked me to do anything aside from play poker. If we got together, it was always my idea. By nature, he was a shy man. You can be a loner and not be shy—that's me. George was shy. He wouldn't seek people out . . . unless he was in trouble.

"No, no. I'm fine," I told him. "Where to?"

"How about Pink's?"

"Fine."

I decided to save recounting my prowl from the previous night so we'd have something to talk about. He needed a lift, not that I was relying on the stale tidbits I'd gathered to do it; still, it wouldn't hurt to exercise him on something other than himself. He was so self-absorbed, I doubted his mind was much on the missing reporter or any police work. My hunch was that he was using the investigation as an excuse to hide the real problem of him and his wife.

If I was right, he was doing an awfully good job, because once we got together at Pink's outdoor counter and ordered our two chili dogs apiece, and once I warmed him up with my amateur sleuthing, then tried to get to the meat of what was going on with him, George would have nothing to do with it. He had Elise Reilly on the brain. The more he asked me, the better he seemed to be feeling; getting into the case seemed to be bringing him out of his angst, that is, temporarily, until it got worse because he wasn't being honest with himself.

I got fed up. "You know what's wrong with you, Steifer? You're a goddamn workaholic. You think talking about this case of yours is going to solve all your problems. Why don't you admit you're depressed?"

"And what good's that going to do me?"

"Get in touch."

He laughed at me with chili in his mouth and told me to go join a sensitivity group, then he went back to grilling me on the previous evening. I didn't know what to make out of him, but at least he was laughing. I couldn't argue with that. We were sitting inside, sharing one of the tiny tables with a family of flies. The walls were jammed with the standard eight-by-ten glossies of the eager-looking local talent. A guy at a table by the wall looked familiar. I'd seen him on some show. He was sitting by himself. My eye caught his picture. It was on the wall just above his head. I wondered why he had to do that. I wouldn't want to look at myself while I was eating. Some of these guys, the more popular ones, have pictures of themselves to greet them everywhere they go. They like it that way. This guy was a small-fry who had a long way to go before his optometrist put him in the window, but he was ready to shoot for it.

George was telling me about the kid I'd found in the Starwood bathroom with Jimbo's body. They hadn't gotten anything out of him; he didn't seem to be involved. Steifer picked up on what I was looking at and we traded grins over it. It turned out that he hadn't heard of any of the punk groups I'd been fooling around with. He liked the angle and wanted to talk to all of them himself, especially Darby of the Bad Boys.

"This Darby punk, it's just like an informant," he said. "He decides to give you some information, but for what reason? Out of the goodness of his heart? I doubt it. The first thing you learn is not to trust something you get for nothing. You're an outsider. Why should he want to help you? He knows you're gonna go to the police. It'll get around he's a snitch, and why would he want that?"

"I'm not arguing," I said. "Maybe he wants to fuck over these other kids."

"But, you know, it's pointless to call him on it. He wouldn't admit to it."

"So you take it with a grain of salt."

"Young Hitlers. What the fuck are these kids trying to prove anyway?"

"Hell if I know."

"They got some other one called Dead Kennedys. Heard of them?"

"No."

"You haven't missed anything."

"They're the new protest generation, like mine was. You're too old to understand, Steif."

"I'm forty-three."

"That's old. Keats died at twenty-six, Shelley at thirty. Fitzgerald was forty-four."

The humor was lost on him. "Yeah," he agreed. "You had civil rights, the war. These kids don't know what they're protesting. They just think they're supposed to."

"They can't help it. The neutron bomb makes them nervous."

"The media reinforces them and big business can make money off them so they're pandered to—that's what it is."

"Maybe."

"I gotta hear why they call themselves that."

"Young Hitlers."

"Yeah."

"I'm sure they'll tell you it's because you're a fascist pig. What'll you say to that?"

"Watch it, Crandel."

"They will."

"They don't know what fascism is."

"Maybe."

"What's that mean?"

"Take it easy, George, OK?"

Steifer looked hurt. "You're getting soft," he said.

"Yeah, it's my new nickname, Softie, Softie Crandel."

Steifer frowned. "Somebody's gotta do it."

"Protect and serve? But why you?"

"It was in the family. Some kids come from doctors, lawyers, dentists. I happen to come from a family of cops."

"You chose it though."

"When you're a kid, you gotta do what you're not supposed to."

"Tell me about it."

"And in my family that meant deciding to go into law enforcement. Nobody wanted me to—*they* knew what it was like."

"So therefore you had to."

"Exactly. And know something?"

"What?"

"They were right."

"Why don't you call it quits and do something else?"

"Like what?"

"Something you could enjoy."

"A job's a job. You do something for a certain amount of time, it's hard to imagine doing something else."

"It's been done."

"This isn't the sort of job you just stop at or switch with."

"Once a cop, always a cop."

"It becomes part of you. You can't take it away. It's what you are. Yes."

"Well, then that settles it. I won't suggest you sell real estate or open a shoe store."

That tickled his funny bone. He laughed hard, too hard, then he changed the subject. We shot the breeze about Pete, my house at the beach. I wasn't bored, but the rhythm of the conversation was so slow and meandering. I reminded George that he should be getting back to work. With some embarrassment, he admitted that, starting yesterday, he was on his summer vacation; in which case, I wondered why he was sitting here in his brown-and-white seersucker suit instead of lying on the beach somewhere and soaking up some rays. But before I could start lecturing him some more, he told me not to. He didn't feel like traveling or beachcombing at the moment; maybe once he cleared up a few details, he'd think differently. For now, it was enough to be out of the office. From my side, it appeared that he'd taken the office with him.

He didn't want to discuss it. He wanted to go downtown and talk to that punk Darby and he wanted me to go with him to help break the ice. I told him he was crazy, but he said it was important, so I went along. He had a maniacal air about him just as he'd had the other night. Darby wasn't the sort of captivating character you needed to experience more than once, and I wasn't dying to see him, but, on the other hand, he was harmless enough and I didn't think he deserved to be kicked around when there would be nothing to prove by it. George had a quiet anger building in him. It wouldn't have surprised me if he'd shot out a stoplight for changing on him.

Conversation was sporadic on the way. We talked about new restaurants, read the personalized license plates and billboards. Steifer's air-conditioning was out. All of the car windows were rolled down. Smog went to town on you on a day like this, a hundred degrees with no wind. My eyes smarted behind my shades. It was blanketed thick, like

smoke. You could see the tips of tall buildings in the downtown skyline and that was about it. I unbuttoned my short
sleeve shirt. Steifer loosened his tie. It was a long drive that
set us both on edge and, by the time we pulled up to the old
factory building, I knew it wasn't going to be easy.

It wasn't. Darby wasn't such a Bad Boy once George got
to working on him. To give Steifer his due, he didn't lay a
hand on the kid. He didn't have to. It was scary. It scared
me, the kid, and everybody who heard him; and all he did
was play it straight, excessively, being obsequious, ingratiat-
ing, polite, like one of those shy mass murderers you hear
about that no one can ever explain. Darby saw the badge,
but I wasn't sure he was convinced, although once things
got going, that didn't keep him from being careful, very
careful.

At first, it was rocky. Darby didn't want to answer any
questions.

"Take your friend and fuck off," he told George.

The gang liked that. A few of them backed him up. I
looked for the pretty skinny lady, but she wasn't there.
Plumbers and carpenters were walking around, working on
finishing the conversion.

George gave the boy a hurt little smile. "You don't want
to say that."

He kept saying things like that. I don't think they would
have worked if I'd said them. There was that crazy, scary,
mad something in George's delivery, his eyes, his sweaty
face, the baggy suit, nervous hands that moved choppily,
jerking in and out of feigned stations of repose.

Darby stuck to his story, even when Steifer accused him of
wanting to smear somebody.

"I don't even know them," he claimed.

"Then why do you wanna drag them through the dirt?"

Darby pointed to me. "He asked me. I was helping out
your friend."

"You're not tellin' me anything. I don't see why you had
to tell him."

"Forget it then. Forget I said it."

George donated a pained smile. "We can't do that. I'd like to know why."

"Why's there have to be a reason?"

"There's always a reason."

"We were high. We were talking."

"Jealous of the band. Is that why?"

"Young Hitlers? Are you kidding?"

George raised his brow, inviting Darby to elaborate.

"I told you all I know," the kid said, trying not to sound as if he was pleading. But he did. There were snickers.

George got a card out of his wallet and handed it to him. "Think about it and call me. Nobody wants you to get into trouble."

Darby took the card and glared at me like he was going to break into tears. "Thanks a lot," he said.

"For what?" I turned to Darby's buddies. "Darby's worried. He thinks you think he's a snitch. Tell him something to reassure him."

They didn't tell Darby a thing; there were choice words for me, though. They knew Steifer was finished, so they called his bluff to show they weren't worried. Fair enough. These punks were probably raking it in so fast they couldn't count it. They could do whatever they wanted and get away with it, for awhile, until the next hairstyle.

Outside, we grabbed a beer and drank it in the car on our way back to Hollywood. Steifer dropped me off in the parking lot at Pink's.

"What are you gonna do now?" I asked him.

"I'm gonna go find somebody to call me a fascist pig."

"I hear it's nice up at Yosemite this time of year."

He shook his head, dismissing the possibility. "No, not right now."

"Listen, I'm between assignments at the moment. What d'ya say we go fishing for a few days after you clean up the details?"

"Thanks," said Steifer. "I might take you up on that."

Not too likely, but that was all right. George would do what he wanted, no matter what might be good for him.

Didn't matter what you said, he had to ride it out his way, the long way.

"Relax, George. Sometimes you've just gotta make up your mind you're going to stop what you're doing and take it easy. For Christ's sake, this is California."

He gave me a quick grin and patted my shoulder. "See ya, Crandel. Thanks."

"Don't crawl into a hole," I called after him. "Keep in touch."

I didn't get an answer. He was too busy speeding away.

• THIRTEEN •

B ack at my place, it was ten degrees cooler. I got out of my shirt, collected my mail, and took it with me down to the edge of the sand in order to reap the full benefit of the offshore breeze. After the monthly bank statement, I came across something with Pete's handwriting, an envelope, no return address, addressed to me. I knew what it was even before I opened it, and I shouldn't have been surprised, but, still, I was. I'd been rehearsing this moment for a long time—having it happen was another story. Like the difference between the first draft and the movie or the book, the dry run and the real thing, you can pretend you're made out of iron and concrete, but you aren't. It all depends on how bad you need to deceive yourself. Some of us never find out; we don't let ourselves know. It's too much for us, too hot to handle. And some of us try to keep the wool down over the rose-colored glasses, but the ugly truth of how we really feel tricks us and comes in by the back door without so much as a knock before we know it's there.

I walked across the boardwalk and sat down on a bench. Then I opened the envelope and removed the three-hole-punched, lined paper, notebook paper. It had been a long time since I'd seen a piece of school paper, and it added a touch of irony to the contents.

"Terrible handwriting," I told no one. "Spelling," I said further on. "Tense!" I exclaimed still further.

It wasn't till I read through it a half-dozen times that it finished me. My stomach knotted, then it dropped to my feet and held me there like a buoy; my substance was drained out of me. The kid had finally done it. He was leaving home, hitting the road. He appreciated everything I done, as he'd written, but he didn't give a shit about school anymore. He had an offer to travel and perform with another band and, since he'd been sure I'd disapprove, he'd decided the note was the best way to say goodbye for now. He'd write again soon, see me in a couple months maybe.

That was it. The school paper, the childish scrawl, and bad grammar threw a wrench in my heart.

"Petey."

I folded the paper carefully and stuck it back in the envelope. He was so young, still a boy. He didn't know anything. He couldn't spell or even explain himself without losing his temper—over anything. The world was going to flatten him with its first sucker punch, roll right over him, run him down, chew him up, spit him out. He didn't stand a chance, that's what hurt me. My ego was a little bruised, sure, but what made it much worse was that my gut instinct told me Pete wasn't savvy enough to make it, not yet. Christ, he was only fifteen.

I carried on a debate with myself over whether or not I should try to stop him, and it took me ten minutes or so to realize that it didn't matter. I didn't know his friends anymore. He'd gotten so far away from me over the last year, I wouldn't have known how to try. And if I hung out in the pop clubs, waiting till I could grab him, or got a lead on tracking him down, it would be just as bad. He'd hate me for it. He wouldn't forgive. Like anybody with something to prove, he was too headstrong to take directions.

So be it, I kept trying to tell myself. Sink or swim, the

eternal game, and nobody wants a life jacket. Everybody's got to show they have balls. That's the way it is; otherwise, god forbid, the edge is off, damaged goods.

I couldn't accept what I had to accept. I didn't want to see anybody, talk to anybody, I didn't want to drink. I sat, got up, and sat down and sat. After a half hour or so, I walked back to my house. I felt like I had to figure out what to do, and the exasperating thing was that there was nothing to be done. Stanley, my basset hound, not knowing any better, was full of good-natured howls and tail wags. I gave him an early dinner and sat quiet as a monk. I didn't know what to do with myself. The bottom had dropped out. And I'd asked for it all along, adopting a kid who was just like me. At least Pete had had someone who liked him and stuck by him for five years, more by a long shot than my experience, though he hadn't had such a hard time pulling up stakes and cutting out. Just scribbled a sloppy little note. No sweat off his back. He couldn't miss me if he hadn't appreciated me.

"No. I will not be bitter."

I said it to myself, told the dog. He thought I was funny, wagged his tail and barked.

I had a few drinks, after all. An hour later, after more whiskey and a shower, I was on my way out the door to grab some dinner. The phone rang. I came back into the living room and activated the answer machine, then I just stood there and waited to hear who it was, if they didn't hang up.

"Ben?"

Steifer's voice. Just what I needed, the other pack mule in my life who would rather heap himself with burdens than take my advice. Both of them, him and Pete, what did they want from me? Was I supposed to pat them on the back, tell them it was all right when it wasn't, when I'd be lying, outright lying?!

"I found something."

He was there still. I'd thought he'd hung up. His voice was strange, disembodied, like the dreamt echo of a dead man. I picked up the phone.

"What?"

He was breathing like a bull, not saying anything.

"George, are you all right?"

"Ya oughta see this," he said.

"What? Where are you?"

He told me to hold on, then he came back and gave me an address. I asked him if he was all right again, but he wouldn't answer me.

I stared at the piece of scratch paper I'd scribbled the address on. "This is just a street," I said. "Where is it?"

"Van Nuys," he said.

"You want me to come out there?"

No answer.

"Are you going to stay and wait for me?"

"Ya oughta see this."

He wasn't coherent. I'd heard him bad, but I'd never heard him like this. I knew better than to ask him what he was talking about again.

"It'll take me about twenty-five minutes."

"Don't call the police."

"I'll be right there."

I held on a minute to see if he'd say something else. When I put the phone down, I could hear him all the way to the receiver, huffing like a small overworked steam engine pulling too long a train.

• FOURTEEN •

I made with the internal combustion, hopping from freeway to freeway like some freak-size mechanical bunny: Santa Monica Freeway to the San Diego North to the Ventura East and I was on Van Nuys Boulevard, the nerve center or pit of the San Fernando Valley in less than fifteen minutes. The Valley, as it's called, was conceived in sin nearly a hundred years ago by a cutthroat land development syndicate which bought up its hundred thousand dusty acres for pennies, then screwed a little farm community by the Sierra Nevadas out of their water and, because the syndicate controlled the L.A. water board and owned L.A.'s newspapers, suckered the taxpayers into footing the bill for a $25,000,000 aqueduct that never brought water to Los Angeles. Amazing bullshit. That water hasn't irrigated anything but swimming pools for thirty years now. It's only poetic justice that the whole damn place, at its peak of development, is a concrete wasteland with all the dignity of a used car lot, which is all you see on Van Nuys Boulevard. Car on the brain. Drive in your car and look at the traffic and the car lots for your scenery. A pit, the place is a pit, hot as hell, too, an easy fifteen degrees hotter than the beach. It boggles the mind why anybody with money would want to live here. But they do. It makes you wonder what they see in it.

I got sick of wondering before I even started, found the street I was looking for, and turned off the main drag into one of the older and poorer pockets, weak on the streamlined chi-chi and conspicuously lacking the mandatory L or kidney-shaped swimming pool. There were short, crowded blocks of no-nonsense, sun-scorched, faded, chipped little two-bedroom stucco houses. They were perched side by side on narrow lots separated by strips of asphalt driveway decorated with trailered motorboats and RVs. Poodles, shepherds, and collies barked from within or without. Anybody who didn't have air-conditioning, had their sprinklers on and their front doors open behind the screens. Children, Mexican and white, played on the patchy lawns in their swimsuits, running in and out of the sprinklers. It was a respectable neighborhood, a little washed-out and run-down, but clean and lower middle-class; working families who lived for their vacations.

I found the address and pulled into the driveway behind Steifer's car. A hose was hooked up to a revolving sprinkler on the small lawn next door on the right, and that was it aside from a couple of small boys wearing cut-off jeans and

Little League caps who were playing serious catch in the middle of the street up at the corner.

The revolving sprinkler hissed and the ball popped from mitt to mitt. I got out of my car and walked up a short winding cement path to a cement porch. I pressed a bell that had a three-chime register. A dusty window to my right was covered with a shade; the door was dusty, too, and nobody answered, but it was open.

I went in. The living room was to the left. The evening sun cast a yellowish light over the back wall. The room was neatly furnished: thick white carpet, a beige couch with matching armchairs on either side of a glass coffee table, a large TV console by the white brick fireplace, porcelain duckies atop the mantle with hunt prints and my worried face reflected in the marble mirror above.

"George?"

I walked down the short hall looking for him. The bedroom doors were open, but Steifer wasn't in them. I came to a small den at the rear of the house. Its walls and floor were cork. Wooden crucifixes and religious pictures had been tacked up above a wood and vinyl couch. The back wall was glass. I looked out onto the backyard: brown grass, a big dead walnut tree, a bright blue inflatable rubber pool about eight feet round and three feet high, and Steifer, with his back to me, sitting before it, slouched forward in a plastic beach chair. His elbows were on his knees, his face was in his hands. Some clothes were strewn about his feet.

"George?"

He sat without moving. I opened the sliding glass door, walked across the small patio, and went down the short stairs to the yard. He waited till I was right behind him before he spoke.

"See what I was talkin' about?"

I tried to get a look at him, but his chair was up against the little pool and he was staring at the murky water. I took the chair by its aluminum arms and turned it around. George lifted his head and showed me his eyes. I couldn't make out what it was, but there was something about them I didn't like, something that made me instantly frightened for George. Sensing that he was being scrutinized, he turned away quickly.

I looked down at the clothes: a white cotton blouse and a light blue skirt, high heels, and a small bag with an abstract Oriental design—bamboo trees. I bent down to pick up the purse.

"Don't touch that," Steifer said. "It's Elise Reilly's."

"Are you kidding me? Pay dirt!"

"Pay dirt," parroted Steifer.

I couldn't understand. "What the fuck's the matter with you? You got a lead, you should be excited. But you're a basket case. What is it?"

"I'm thinking about the rest," he said slowly.

He got up. "I'll show you," he said, moving back toward the house.

I followed him back into the den and into the kitchen.

"What's for dinner?"

Before I could ask him what the hell he meant, he opened the cupboard doors above the sink. There was half a shelf for dishes and glasses and the rest of the cupboard was filled with books. George pulled one out of a stack of a half-dozen or so and handed it to me.

"Open it," he said. "It's a bible."

I opened it while George yanked open the rest of the cupboard doors. It was a bible, all right. Something was stamped on one of the front flyleaves: the outline of a fish with the initials CCRS inside it.

"So?"

George handed me a leaflet out of a large stack from another cupboard. It had a larger version of the same logo from the bible across the top. In the right-hand margin was a list of names and titles: pres, vice pres, treasurer, etc. Centered underneath, the acronym was spelled out: Christian Citizens for a Respectable Society. What followed was in a newsletter format.

"Looks like one of these new right yo-yo organizations: 'In The Name Of God, Stop The Baby Killers Now!'"

I started in on the high-octane text that followed, giving it a proper prairie preacher inflection which didn't amuse Steifer in the slightest. He grabbed the paper out of my hands and jerked his head for me to follow. We went back across the den, through the small hall, and into the rear bedroom.

To my eye, it looked excessively ordinary: neat twin beds with plain spreads centered by a nightstand and a shaded lamp. There was an off-white dresser with an antiqued finish, on top of which was a glass top and a few clean ashtrays. It could have been a room in a motel. George swung the right-hand sliding door of the clothes closet to the left. A full rack of suits, slacks, and dress shirts was hanging inside. Steifer pulled a suit off the rack and threw it at me.

"Nobody paints a closet with the clothes still in it—unless they're in a hurry."

I looked at the suit, a blue on blue pinstripe. Tiny white speckles showed across the shoulders. One of the jacket sleeves had a streaky white blotch. Steifer swept the clothes down toward the other end, then he moved into the closet and began tinkering with the rear wall. A moment later, he'd removed it.

"Shew."

It was a small arsenal of handguns and rifles, too many to count. Steifer reached behind the second wall panel behind the closed half of the closet and removed a piece of cloth. He handed it to me: a Nazi flag. Boxes filled with Nazi war medals, swastikas, Maltese crosses, uniforms, jackboots, and helmets followed.

"These must be their pet favorites," Steifer said. "The garage is ceiling high with the stuff. Hand grenades, bazookas, you name it." George picked up one of the rifles and showed it to me. It had a polished walnut stock, a large scope, and looked like it had never been used. "Three hundred Weatherby Magnum. This could stop a train—around twenty-five so far. I've found thirty–forty other shotguns and open-country rifles. The Weatherbys retail out at close to a thousand dollars, if I'm not mistaken."

"How did you find this place?"

"I went back to Jimbo's apartment and picked it over some more. He had some addresses written inside his phone book." Steifer showed me the page he'd torn out. "The way he kept circling it, I figured it must have been important."

Steifer took me out to the garage. He'd jimmied a side door and gotten in without disturbing anything. Inside, you had to be careful where you stepped. There was everything from land mines to silencer-equipped machine guns stashed in briefcases; or if that wasn't good enough, you could pick and choose from World War Two vintage machine guns, Soviet AK-47s, or MAC-10s. George showed me all of it and rambled at length about the capability of some of the weapons. The MAC-10s, for instance, fired twelve hundred rounds of .45 caliber ammo per minute; the silencers were handmade. I stopped him finally as he was going on about some powerful thirty millimeter, armor-piercing, anti-tank ammunition.

"Our cars are in the driveway," I said. "I don't think we should be standing around shooting the breeze."

Without answering me, Steifer rummaged through a number of boxes, coming up with a cartridge which he clipped into one of the machine guns. "We don't have to worry now," he said blandly.

"Let's get out of here."

"Wait."

Steifer put the machine gun down and continued his rummaging. He wouldn't budge until he'd been through most of the stuff, putting each item neatly back in place as soon as it had been identified. This went on for over a half hour.

"What are you looking for?" I asked him many times.

"Clues," he said once or twice.

At one point, he turned toward me and tossed me a heavy cardboard box. "Here."

"No!" I screamed, afraid the carton was going to explode in my arms.

I made sure I caught it, knelt down and placed it on the floor, then pulled back the box flaps, expecting to find a nest of live grenades. It was live, all right, even explosive, but of the paper tiger variety: more extremist literature, though not from the same unfamiliar organization we'd discovered on the kitchen shelves. This junk was someone's personal collection or library, if you will, and with the exception of a mailing list for World War Two memorabilia, there were few duplicated materials. Most of them were dated, going back to the late fifties and early sixties. A number of the groups were as unfamiliar to me as Christian Citizens for a Respectable Society, but, in taking in a paragraph here, a paragraph there, the common thread was unabashedly conservative far right: gun control, defense, communism, abortion, busing, school prayer, corporal and capital punishment, the Equal Rights Amendment, school textbooks, sex education, coed sports, God and the divine mission of America. Some of it was pretty highly polished and surprisingly literate if you could turn off the background noise of hysteria threatening to engulf one and all with impending doomsday if the holy message, as delivered by the Almighty, were not heeded and acted upon *immediately*. The biggies were in evidence, old-timers like the John Birch Society and the American Nazi Party, new ones like Californians for Biblical Morality, the National Christian Action Coalition.

There was a vast accumulation of printed material. George kept coming up with more of the same. He sat next to me on the garage floor, turned over a large box of pamphlets and papers and started going through them with careful deliberation.

"There's no pattern to this," I told him. "It's some kink's prized collection."

George wasn't listening. He kept sorting through the material. I started straightening my stuff up and putting it back away.

"Christian Citizens for a Respectable Society is who you're after," I said.

"I want to be sure," George said quietly. "It's maybe just a front for somebody else."

"Why don't you look 'em up and go out to see 'em?"

"I called and got a recording. They'll be back in the morning."

"We can't just sit here."

"Why not?"

"So you loaded the machine gun. It's not going to do jack shit if somebody surprises us."

"I talked to the neighbor on the corner," Steifer said slowly. "Their kid saw the arsenal yesterday when the door was up. They called it in."

"Did you check with the police?"

Steifer nodded.

"They flew the coop."

Steifer nodded. He went back to studying the propaganda rags.

"Did the police in North Hollywood know about Elise Reilly?"

"No."

"Didn't they find her clothes?"

"They haven't had time to go through everything."

I leaned against a workbench to the side and watched George for a few minutes, wondering why he'd bothered to call me or encourage me to come out here. Something was off about him, something he wasn't allowing himself to tell me. I doubted I was ever going to inspire him to spill his guts to me. Men, especially cops, don't do that sort of thing with each other. Letting your hair down is like holding hands—you do it with mother. Still, after watching the poor bastard for what seemed like a long time, I knew he was in trouble. He wasn't reading a goddamn thing. He was staring into deep, deep space, out there lost in a weird orbit.

"George," I said. "George."

He looked up. His eyes were obscured in the shadow cast by the naked overhead bulb.

"Where are you, partner?"

He did nothing but shrug.

"We gotta have a talk."

"About what?"

"You called me up and said you had something I ought to see. Is that all you called me for?"

"I thought you'd be interested."

"I am interested—in you."

"What's that supposed to mean?"

"You've been acting strange, for months. *Now,* I can't understand you at all."

"Then shove off."

"Hold it. Listen a minute. Let me give you a picture: I see a guy, a very good friend of mine who's holding something in that's eating him up. But he doesn't want to talk about it. Fine. Lately, he's been depressed over a case. His marital break-up has nothing to do with it. Fine. I'll accept it that way, at face value, if he insists. Then, now, he gets a huge break in that case of his and, I ask you, what does he do? Whoop, holler, smile, nod, take encouragement—voice *any* degree of enthusiasm? No. He sits like a goddamn zombie whose goldfish has just eaten all the guppies."

"It's too soon to know what it means."

"The lead? But you're not neutral. You're already depressed about it."

"No, I'm not."

"George, believe me, you're turning into a basket case."

He stood up holding a sheaf of papers in one hand and clenching the other. "Where do you get off telling me—"

"You've been staring into space half the time I've been here."

"I don't have the time right now to put up with your bullshit," he said bitterly, spitting out the words, practically hollering them. "So why don't you—"

I put up a hand as I interrupted him. "Right, George. I'm not gonna argue with you. I will get out of here. And I'm only being blunt because I'd really like to know what's on your mind and, whether or not you admit it, I can tell you're hurting. That's all."

I walked over to the side door to the garage and stopped before I walked out. Steifer had turned away. When I spoke

again, he kept his back to me. "I'll stock up at my local liquor store. Stop by whenever you like. I'll be waiting for
you—if you want to talk, or even if you don't."

• FIFTEEN •

It was 11:30 and I was sitting in my hot tub, drinking a
Carta Blanca out of the bottle and watching an old *Honey-
mooners* rerun on the portable boob tube that was perched on
the redwood decking around the edge. Stanley was asleep
inside on my bed. When the knock came, all of a sudden I
thought maybe it was Pete and he'd lost his key again. I got
out of the tub, wrapped a towel around my middle, and
trudged through the house in my wet bare feet to open the
door. My heart sank a little, which made me all the gladder
it was George and not somebody else.

"Hey," said he.

"Hey," said I, motioning for him to come in.

"If you're busy—"

"Nah. Just trying to unwind a little. What's your poison?"

"One of those, I guess."

I went to the kitchen for the beer.

"Pete out?"

"And how," I said into the refrigerator.

"Maybe he knows something about these jerks."

Steifer gave me a manila envelope. I opened the bottle
and handed it over. "I wish I could ask him," I said as I
opened the envelope and looked at a grainy black-and-white
eight-by-ten of five young men up on a stage, three of whom
held electric guitars, while one held a mike stand above his
head and the other sat behind a drum set. The whole picture
was slightly out of focus and the flash had washed out most
of the detail, but you could make out the Hitler moustaches
and swastika armbands on all of them; one was heavyset and

pie-faced, the rest were nondescript figures on the thin side. They wore dark trousers, white shirts, and skinny dark ties.

"You aren't talking again?" George was asking me.

I went into the bedroom, got Pete's note, and came back into the living room and handed it to George.

He read it and shook his head and looked very sad. "Why didn't you tell me?" he said, moving toward the phone.

"I don't want to run after him. It was coming for a long time."

Steifer looked away from the telephone. "Whatever you say."

"He'll get by. It's better that way than having him hate me."

Steifer stiffened. "What do you care whether he hates you. You want to do what's best for him."

"I am. Trust me. Think you can hold that kid down or, in the first place, even find him if he doesn't want you to?"

"Maybe."

"I know you're fond of him."

"I am."

"You should have heard what he's been saying about cops lately."

"Even me?"

"Even you."

"It's a phase."

"Ain't that the truth. Very adult of us to think so, too, considering it never stops."

"What phase are you in?"

"I don't know. I'll let you know when I know. What about you?"

"I couldn't tell you."

"You're in your blue period, maybe. I'm in my red period." I went into the kitchen, poured myself a long straight shot of J.D. over ice, and came back.

Steifer lifted his bottle and took a long chug, then he walked out the small French doors at the back of the living room out onto the rear deck. I followed him outside and got back into the tub. I was still holding the photo and he snatched it out of my hand.

"It's not much, but it's all I've got," he said, staring at the thing.

I thought I could almost feel how obsessed he was. It was awesome and dumbfounding, that strange out-of-synch manner he'd been displaying. George had always felt things in a quiet intense way, but never so that it seemed to be burning him up, eating out his insides. This thing was controlling him. He wasn't in the driver's seat, he was a passenger on this one. I couldn't stop thinking that he was on his vacation, carrying on like this when he should have been out of town somewhere trying, at least making an attempt at enjoying himself.

"I'm gonna get these bastards," he told himself.

I just sat there, looking at him and trying to understand what it was about this case or his life, for that matter, that was pushing him off the deep end. He felt me staring at him.

"What?" he snapped.

"That's my question."

"Huh?"

"What's wrong with you?"

"Nothing's wrong with me. What's wrong with you?"

"Lots of things. But I asked you first."

"Newspaper people are on my back. There's pressure."

"Your buddies in the department'll take care of business. You only get one vacation a year, don't you? What good's it going to do if you sit and worry?"

Steifer had been shaking his head against everything I said. "They're bimbos. They won't do any-fucking-thing about it."

"Then go back to work. It's driving you crazy not being there and worrying about whether or not they're doing what they should be doing."

"I don't want to go back there."

"You've got to do one thing or the other, George. Work or play. You can't do both at the same time, at least in your line."

That got a short, lopsided grin out of him that instantly disappeared. He paced nervously back and forth across the small deck. He stopped after a minute or so and chugged his beer. "I don't want any part of 'em. I'm sick of 'em," he barked at me.

I reached over to the TV and turned it off. "Yeah, OK," I said, just to encourage him.

He swiped the flat of his hand across his throat. "I'm up to here with it," he said bitterly. "I'm so sick of cops I can taste it. They don't do anything. They don't care about anybody. They're just putting in their time."

"That's not what you used to say," I suggested.

"Then maybe it's just me, my temperament. Do you have any idea how hard it is to B.S. daily with people you have nothing in common with? Let me tell you something: I hate football, basketball, baseball, you name it. It's a job for me to read the sports section, watch or listen to a game—it just does not interest me—but if I didn't, what would we talk about? There's sports, nookie, time in, and department politics."

"They're human like everybody else."

"They're inefficient and incompetent."

"They're tired and overworked."

"That's their problem."

"Not really."

"Let me explain something. I've got a bead on this thing. A reporter for the *L. A. Times* starts out doing a piece on punks. In the middle of her background research, she disappears. We walk through the jungle talking to every Manny, Moe, and Jack, and stumble upon a group of five clowns who are supposed to be punk rockers, but who aren't. They're clowns, all right, but they're serious clowns, and what they're up to, ultimately, from what we saw this evening, has nothing to do with music. She found out about it, which is why we can't find her."

"You're saying this Young Hitlers group was a cover for something else."

"Yeah, but what, we don't know as yet."

"Why would an extremist group want to advertise themselves as Nazis?"

"These punk kids aren't really Nazis—you know that. We've talked about it. They've got a half-dozen or so half-baked ideas about how this country is secretly a fascist regime that's oppressing them. So they wear the Nazi gear in protest, but they don't *do* anything."

"So?"

"The point is that *these* jokers are different. They're working on something, they're *going* to hurt some people, but they'd like their efforts to be blamed on somebody else, a bunch of wild kids. They want to hide the fact that they're highly organized."

"I think you're just paranoid of the new far right."

"They're something to be afraid of."

"But they're not Nazis."

"How do we know that?"

"I guess you're going to find out."

"We."

"What do you mean, we?"

"I can't do this through the department."

"Why not?"

"They think I'm crazy."

Finally, after too long of a pause: "How's that?"

"I've got a thing for the reporter, Elise Reilly."

"I'd wondered about that."

"They've put me on a leave of absence, Crandel—don't you see?"

"Not exactly."

"I've been obsessed about this case, I admit it. I met Elise Reilly when she started her article. She wanted to interview the police about their relationship with the punks in Hollywood. She was nice. I asked her out."

"And somebody blew the whistle on you for getting too personally involved once she disappeared."

"You can't run a department and have a one-track mind about one case and one case only. Everybody got on my back."

"You're too close to it."

"That was before. I'm talking now, and this is way too subtle for them. I know how they operate."

"I'm not sure you're thinking straight."

"I know what I'm doing."

"Your emotions are leading you by the tail, George. Think rashly, you'll act rashly. You don't want to make mistakes, fatal ones with somebody's life."

"Mark my words, I'm gonna break this thing—and I don't need a pack of lazy, good-for-nothing bimbos to criticize my every move."

"So they came down on you. You're not going to help yourself by being totally defensive."

"I told you. They don't want me and I don't need them anyway. What do you think any cop would say if I announced I was organizing a task force for a crackdown on the moral majority, just to find a missing person? Sure, she's a reporter and the *Times* wants her back right away—oh, and gosh, that means a real lot to these guys. They don't even know what a *Times* looks like 'cause the *Examiner*'s got the primo sports section. Well, know what they'd say? Exactly what *you're* thinking, which is, Steifer's a basket case over this poor gal he met on the rebound from his divorce."

"The only thing *I'd* say is that you're setting yourself up to be disappointed again. First, you admit you did meet this woman on the rebound, which doesn't speak well for your chances for a relationship; then, I hate to say this, but in the intellectual locker-rooms of the world there's a theorem that says that desirability is inversely proportional to availability, meaning that since she's literally out of reach right now, she's probably never seemed so attractive to you. You've got to realize all this, plus the distressing thing at this point, seeing that she's been gone over two weeks already, is that you know it's more than possible you're not going to see her again."

"I don't have to be in love with her—I like her," Steifer insisted with a shrug, "which is enough to make me bust my ass for her or anybody if they're in trouble."

"It's a lot easier when it's just a job."

"Then you don't have to care. You're trained not to, officially and unofficially."

"I guess we're going to try to find Elise Reilly."

• SIXTEEN •

I t took some doing, but I finally got Steifer to loosen up a bit and shed his coat, holster, and handcuffs. I had a drawerful of good knockwursts in the frig and, without being asked, I got out of the tub again and went into the kitchen to throw a couple into some boiling water. Then I got out the hot dog buns and spread some mustard on them; when the dogs were plump, I put sauerkraut on top. Steifer made them disappear inside of a few minutes. I fed him another beer with a whiskey chaser. Then we sat in the tub and Steifer got me talking about some of the women in my life. It was embarrassing to me to discuss Jodie or anybody else, and I wasn't very sure why until the next day when I was on my way to meet Steifer for breakfast. The thing was that he was involved with somebody. He'd been giving me a crock of shit to say he'd take trouble for Elise Reilly just because he liked her. Rebound or no rebound, infatuation or the real item, he was in love with this woman whether he said so or not. He believed in her as he'd once believed in his wife, Shirley. He was the sort of guy who had to believe in somebody. I admired him for this quality—it showed a touching, if somewhat antiquated romantic faith in the potential of love, and it made me self-conscious about my own strivings. I was doing everything within my power to avoid involvement in my life, yet, in my heart of hearts, I thought of myself as being very much like George. It made me wonder whether I was fooling myself. Like the mythical vestal virgin, was I really saving my finer sentiments for Ms. Right, or was I merely donating excuses to my conscience so I

could carry on at my leisure? Getting involved just wasn't
worth the effort. It never worked out, which, I thought, was
probably the combined fault of my personality and the
times. How long, though, does it take before you can't turn
back and change your mind? The sad, disquieting truth was
that I found it difficult to imagine feeling as intensely about
anybody as George did. For his sake, because I both admired and pitied him, I hoped it worked out. But I never expected him to talk turkey on Elise Reilly and what she meant
to him. Perhaps, he didn't know himself; and, anyway, you
can't put that sort of thing into words. Steifer would never
even try—it wasn't his style—which still did nothing to ob-
scure my awareness that every atom of him was living and
breathing Elise Reilly. It was too late for him to fool me by
soft-pedaling what I knew he felt. Something in him was so
naked it gave me a clear window into his soul—and mine. If
he couldn't talk about what was really going on, it was all
right by me. I would have given the guy my right arm. A
few years ago, he'd helped save my kid's life. If he wanted
me with him, I was ready to go and glad to be of some use;
this willingness to serve, I think, was largely the result of
Pete's cutting out. I knew all the reasons why it had to be,
but I couldn't help it bothering me; in short, I had the feeling it was my fault, that I was some sort of moral failure and
that was why my son had come to the point of having to
leave home. This may have been partly true, which was all
the more reason to appreciate George's need of my support.
I wasn't all wrong; somebody believed in me—which meant
a lot.

When I saw Steifer in Ship's coffee shop, I could have
kissed his feet. It nearly made me cry with laughter. Suddenly, for totally different reasons, the two of us were kin,
emotional cripples using each other for a crutch.

As good friends do, George picked up on something about
me and asked about Pete right away, wanting to know
whether I'd heard from him.

"No."

"Let me call it in," he said as before.

"No. I can't do that," I said, sifting through the jumble of conflicting considerations.

"Tell me if you change your mind."

"I appreciate it," I told him.

I ordered a stack of buttermilk pancakes. George had eggs and toast. As a timesaving device, they had toasters on the table here. When the waitress brought Steifer's wheat bread, it didn't pop up after he put it in the toaster. Our waitress rushed over and got the charred bread out with a fork, then waved her hands about above her head to swipe the smoke away. She brought over another plate of bread and put it in our toaster herself. She stood there with her little arms crossed and waited for the toast to come up, which it did, nice and even, two minutes later.

"There," she said proudly, as if that explained everything.

And, in a way, it did. Rules for the most simple operations shift suddenly for unexplained but simple reasons, and, impossibly, in order to adjust, we have to be able to anticipate the changes before they take place; otherwise, we lose our wives, girlfriends, kids, the job—we get burned. It's not pleasant. We like to avoid thinking this sort of thing can happen. When it does, we're never prepared. It's embarrassing, especially when we find out it could have been avoided.

Everybody seemed to be burning their toast this morning. Food for thought. It was going to be that sort of day, full of false moves that wouldn't make anything right. George grabbed the check before we got up from the table, and I went outside to move my car from the restaurant parking lot to the street. It was only 8:30, but Westwood Village was already congested. I found a spot a block and a half away, put the top up and locked the car, then walked back and met George at his Dodge. We made the short trip to Century City with the repaired air-conditioning going full blast. It wasn't really that hot yet. I rolled down my window and stared at the tall buildings that came at you out of nowhere between West L.A. and Beverly Hills on some acreage once owned by Twentieth Century Fox. People find the place exciting, but the architecture is a small collage of boring block buildings and uninspired towers that show about as much imagination as the street names: Avenue of the Stars, Century Park East.

George found the place we wanted and headed down a ramp into a subterranean garage, taking his ticket from the automatic machine, then passing under the turnstile. We took the escalator up to ground level and went in through the glass-paneled doors. George pushed the button for the twentieth floor in the elevator. We rode up with a carload of gents, all in suits and attachés, most of whom got out with us on the twentieth. They turned right and we, after George hesitated a moment to get his bearings, went in the opposite direction.

We came to a corner suite at the end of the short hall. Thick brass letters in a buff finish stood out from the door: CHRIST WORLD U.S.A.

I didn't get it. "Christian neighbors? I thought it was Christian Citizens for a Respectable Society."

"Maybe they changed their name."

Steifer scratched his head, then ran a hand through his straight jet black hair, smoothing it down. The flourescent lighting overhead didn't do much for him. His complexion was pasty, almost sickly, and his dark eyes had leaden, grayish bags under them. He straightened slightly, shrugged his summer-weight navy blue coat into a better fit, and turned the handle on the door, ushering me in. Before I'd taken two steps, he was ahead of me.

Unlike most reception areas, this one was anything but colorless and neutral. It had a message which, I supposed, was intended to bring the average God-fearing fella down to his knees in humble supplication to the greater glory of Christ Worldly aims. The wall to our left was covered with a mural depicting the crucifixion. It was all in earth tones, and there were lots of Roman soldiers in leggings and tufted helmets. Across the top of the wall in fancy script: *I will come again and will take you to myself.* The right-hand wall had another mural showing a hilly pasture dotted with many sheep and a lone shepherd at the top of the highest rise and was

headed in the same florid calligraphy: *The Lord is my shepherd.*
Betwixt these, at a pioneer bench-table centered before the
rear wall, sat a slight fragile little man in a black suit. The
one thing that made him go with the rag rug, colonial
couches, and sewing spindle heirloom was that he didn't
move, his body, that is. His eyes were blinking rapidly and,
as we came up on him, I saw that he was engrossed in the
Good Book. A photo portrait gallery filled the wall above his
head, avuncular business magnate types and the pious
clergy in robes of royal blue and deep purple; among them,
I noticed Senator Jesse Helms and Reverend Jerry Falwell,
the bully tough front line of the moral majority.

George cleared his throat deliberately and the little man
jerked his head back with a start, looking up his nose as he
squinted to get us into focus. His hair was slicked down and
greased so thoroughly you could make out the comb tracks
across his head; a neat part showed a line of scalp on the left
side of his skull. Except for the deep creases laddered on his
forehead, his face was unlined. He could have been anywhere between thirty and forty-five years old.

"Goodness, I didn't hear you."

"I'm sorry to bother you," George began.

"No bother, no bother," the little man insisted, pursing
his mouth into a prim, pious smile. "I've just got to catch
up. I've been ill, you see, and our bible study group meets
today. Our leader's Tom McGivern. You don't know him,
do you?"

"No, sir. We—"

"He's the best we've had, but it's *so* demanding. He asks
us questions to be sure we've done our homework. It can be
embarrassing if you draw a blank. Sometimes, people
laugh, you know. Ralph Lawson says religion's competitive
just like everything else, but Tom says if he keeps thinking
skeptical like that he'll grow horns and a tail. You've got to
take the Lord at face value."

The guy had a high little squirrelly voice that gushed and
hammered at you simultaneously. It was so shrilly sincere
you half-believed he was ready to shut up if you nodded

enough to convince him you were in complete agreement.
But he didn't. He kept going without breathing, it seemed,
and his weird pale blue eyes jumped and blinked alarmingly.
I was almost curious to see what he'd do if we let him go on,
but George's threshold had been reached.

"Police," George said. "Police."

It brought the little guy down a notch. He stopped and
took a breath. "Excuse me?"

George showed him his ID. "Los Angeles Police Department. I'd like to speak to your head honcho."

"You don't need an appointment," I wisecracked, gesturing toward the murals.

George didn't go for the horseplay. He gave me a look.
The aging choirboy hadn't even heard me.

"Why, yes, certainly," he said. "I'll see to it." He grabbed
at the phone in a panic and punched out an extension to one
of the inner offices. "Mrs. Scott, very sorry to bother you,
but there are police here in the reception area. . . . No. I'm
so flustered, it altogether slipped my mind. . . . Yes, certainly. One moment." He cupped his hand over the mouthpiece and looked up at Steifer. "Mrs. Scott is as busy as a
bee, she says. We've never had problems before. She just
asked me to make sure there isn't some mistake, because
I'm sure your time is just as valuable, too."

George nodded and opened his mouth, but the little man
sputtered onward.

"I hope you understand me. There are so many religious
foundations. Most of them mean well, but some of them are
profiteers. We've had our name borrowed because *we* have
such a fine reputation. Have you heard of the World of
Christ? They're not us. They just reversed our name. They
should be ashamed of themselves. There should be an investigation because I've heard the minister draws an astronom-
ical salary. He should be ashamed of himself. On the other
hand, Reverend Dailey—that's his picture, third from the
left—he's giving us our own new Jerusalem. I've been there.
You should see it: four hundred acres in Wyoming. He's a
man of God, a true man of God. He preaches and gives food

to the poor. He's a humble man. Do you know this whole wall behind me was supposed to be a mural of him, but he wouldn't stand for it. He—"

George had caught on. He was going to let this fruitcake spill his guts and see if anything valuable might come of it. But the connecting door leading into the office suite had opened quietly a moment before. A youngish woman stepped into the room. She was a tall, statuesque solid pole of a thing, hiding her youth behind a carefully upswept coif of frosted hair and wearing a collarless Nancy Reagan suit, ivory with black trim running down the center and circling the cuffs. A big red paper carnation was pinned to her breast. Her short-heeled pumps had bows on them.

She folded her palms together and held them just above her stomach. "Henry," she drawled sweetly.

Henry turned around from the rear wall where he'd been gesturing at the wide expanse that had been planned for Reverend Dailey's ill-fated mural. He was still holding the telephone which he regarded with surprise now, blushing noticeably and hanging it up as he met the young lady's beneficent gaze with a sheepish, hangdog look.

"Mrs. Scott," he said. "I was trying to explain. You know how I—"

"You did right, Henry," she said, glancing quickly at him, then turning her attention strictly to us. "I don't know what I'd do without this wonderful staff I got. Now, gentlemen, please, please follow me."

We followed her. She walked straight-backed with a quick, short knock-kneed stride, hardly lifting her feet. Her nylons rustled against each other. The secretaries buried their noses in their typewriters as our procession moved past. I noticed that large and small cans were stacked in artful displays on the tops of tables and file cabinets. It was freeze-dried survival food, from chocolate ice cream to shrimp creole. The labels read: MANNA FOODS. Placards and posters went for the jugular: "What will *you* do when the earthquake strikes? Are you prepared for the inevitable? Do you have food insurance? Is your family worth saving?" The slogan seemed to be: "Be smart. Be prepared. Buy Manna Now!" There were charts graphing skyrocketing inflation and pictures of contented families eating the stuff for dinner. It didn't look very appetizing. My stomach felt a touch queasy by the time we entered Mrs. Scott's office, the walls of which were permaplaqued with honor scrolls, diplomas and special awards from a number of churches, bible schools and community groups. Among these, framed under glass, were a dozen or so quaint homilies stitched in needlepoint, some Robert Frost, the Lord's Prayer, touching snippets.

Mrs. Scott went directly to her antique oak desk and sat in an uncomfortable-looking ladderback chair.

"Make yourselves comfortable, please," she urged us.

Considering the undersized matching ladderback chairs arranged side by side before her, it seemed like a better idea to remain standing. George reached over the desk to show her his ID.

"Thank you, but that's unnecessary, Mister—?" she said without looking at it.

"Steifer. George Steifer. My partner, Ben Crandel."

I nodded and said hello.

"Mister Steifer, Mister Crandel. You look like good men. What can we do for you?"

"Is it possible to speak to Reverend Dailey?" George asked her.

"He's in Wyoming now, I'm afraid. We have no way of reaching him, although he does call every afternoon at exactly five. We're in the middle of building our new home."

"Henry was telling us about it," I said.

"Henry," she said, smiling with prim absentmindedness as she shook her head, then returned with, "Yes, it's to be a community for all ten thousand of us."

"Who is *us* exactly?" George inquired.

Mrs. Scott folded her hands together and furrowed her high forehead with convincing puzzlement. "Could you explain?" she asked with touching eagerness to please.

"Have you heard of an organization called Christian Citizens for a Respectable Society?"

"Why, yes, certainly. They're one of our affiliate groups, our political arm, I guess you might say."

"Who runs them?"

"They operate under our direction."

"In other words, CCRS is another name for Christ World, is that what you're saying?"

"Not exactly, and to tell you the God's honest, I'm not completely sure about it. But I can promise you this: As soon as Reverend Dailey's in touch, I *will* ask him to tell me. If *he's* not sure, I don't know who will be. But if it's important that you know, we *will* find out."

Steifer wasn't satisfied. "On your door, it says you're executive director."

"Yes," she said with a proud but prim chin nod.

"You're not going to tell me you're not sure whether this group is separate from your operation or belongs."

"It's rather involved."

"Why don't you stop beating around the bush."

"I assure you—"

"Are you going to cooperate or not?"

The lady paled a bit and looked so sensitive, I felt like handing her a handkerchief.

"I'm doing my very best to cooperate," she said in a quavery voice that went beautifully with the poutish mouth and soulful eyes. "But there are certain things which I truly do not know. These are privileged areas which Reverend Dailey handles himself personally. I'm afraid that you will have to ask him yourself."

George smirked. "But he's in Wyoming. And after he gets back from there, we'll *just* miss him probably before he hops off to someplace else."

She didn't like that. Her cute pout turned slightly prunish. "I don't think it's fair to presume," she said.

The phone rang and she picked it up. "Yes, why Reverend Dailey," she said with happy surprise. "There are some policemen here right at this minute who are very anxious to talk to you. . . . It's about CCRS. They have some questions and they're becoming very impatient with me. . . . Yes, certainly."

"Good morning, gentlemen. I hope we have a good connection."

Coming from the squawk box on the desk, the voice was full and resonant, with a solemn, cloyingly sincere and martyr-weary lilt to it that made me feel I should have been wearing my Sunday best.

"We hear you, Reverend Dailey," George told him. "I'm George Steifer."

"Ben Crandel," I told the airwaves, feeling, by now, that there was no need for my presence.

"Is there anything wrong?"

"We need some information about CCRS," George told him. "Can you tell us who we should speak to?"

"CCRS is a separate independent organization which, in the recent past, has contributed generously to our church," the Reverend said, choosing his words carefully and reciting as if he were preaching to an assembly of kindergartners. "They are located in the nation's capital, in Washington D.C. When they first formed a few years ago, they shared offices with us for a very short while. This is why you were referred to this address. Mrs. Scott probably told you."

"No, Reverend Dailey. I wasn't sure."

"Of course, dear. I forget you haven't been with us but a year. Excuse me."

George got to his feet and paced the carpet. "Is there someone I could talk to in Washington?"

"They've changed hands. I hardly know them myself. Please tell me what you need to know and I will see if I can find out for you."

"A reporter for the *Los Angeles Times* has disappeared. She was doing an article on the local punk rock music scene. We found her clothes and purse at the home of one of these bands who, we have reason to believe, may have been infiltrating the punk music scene to create a cover for extremist or terrorist activities."

"I'm not quite sure I fully understand."

Either did I. I left the room to go take a leak, took a few wrong turns in the hall and ended up passing by what, at first, I thought was the same room I'd just walked out of. But George's voice, raised in complaint, was soft, and the Reverend sounded like he was standing on the other side of the closed door. I looked around, got my bearings, and hurried back to Mrs. Scott's office.

"How's the weather in Wyoming?" I asked, coming back into the room.

Steifer glared at me, demanding silence.

"I comprehend what you are thinking," the Reverend was saying. "But I am sure the CC would never sponsor such violence or extremism. God has blessed America and its government and, even though they may have moved and changed their directorship, I know that I may speak for them when I say they are God-fearing men and law-abiding moral people."

"Is it as hot as it is here?" I asked louder.

"Excuse me?" both Mrs. Scott and the Right Reverend asked together.

"Wyoming."

"Shut up, Crandel."

I grabbed Steifer by his shoulder and yanked him out into the hall as a tall spare figure in a light gray suit came rushing out of the door I'd passed and started away at a fast stroll.

"Why, if it isn't Reverend Dailey," I guess I must have yelled.

"Freeze!" George screamed at him.

The guy froze. As we came up to him, he turned around, slowly.

"Simon says hands on your head," I said, anticipating Steifer's next directive.

He put his hands on his head. If I hadn't seen him once or twice while passing the channels on the Sunday evening evangelical shows, I would have thought the guy was something slick like an insurance exec or a money market man. He was slick, all right, a picture of health, and he looked a hell of a lot younger than that martyred world-weary voice of his: a full head of rich gray-blond hair, a nice short dimpled square at the base of his chin, delicate hands, good tailoring, and bushy eyebrows that probably made him a heart throb with the God set.

"I hope you have a good reason for this," he said with impressive composure bordering on quiet indignation.

"Where'd you think you were going?" Steifer asked him, patting him down, finding nothing, then pocketing the gun.

To my eyes, since I was the least involved, the whole thing was really very funny. "You were in Wyoming just about as much as your CC group's in Washington, huh?"

"You can't speak to the Reverend like that."

I looked for the voice. It was the receptionist, Henry, who was surprising himself by sounding so forceful, and most of the office crew, along with Mrs. Scott, were gathering in the hallway. Well, there's no way you can assemble a crowd without inspiring a clergyman, I suppose, and the Right Reverend seemed to take the assemblage as his cue that now was the time for his daily Sermon on the Mount. He spread his delicate fingers and raised his hands high above his head. His light tan darkened as his face colored with the fiery emotion of his high spirit.

"Anger is the evil servant of the devil," he said, shifting down into a fuller, more commanding preacher voice as he towered over us, and singled out poor Henry, addressing him with his intense slate gray eyes. "Resist him and he will flee from thee in fright."

Henry nodded and trembled, looking fit to pass out or away at any second. Christ World incarnate spread his arms wingedly in a gesture that swept over all our heads; his gaze, however, centered on George and me, giving us the evil eye even as he harped on against it.

"Take pity on these men, for we cannot expect the restless mind of the sour skeptic to comprehend the ways of *God* in heaven. The *God*-fearing shall speak the truth, though who shall hear it? Certainly not the blasphemer who would crack and crumble the pious pillars of the *holy* temple of truth. And why, *why* other than that they might seek to fulfill their self-ish cynical aim which is to destroy the one and only *King* and his *king*dom. These—"

"Are you done?" Steifer said futilely in an effort to throw off his surging rhythm and stop the claptrap.

"*These*," he said, pointing toward us with both his index fingers, "are men with bitter bile and black hearts."

He paused a second, half-expecting George to butt in again, but I could see Steifer was content to let him go on a little. He had his arms crossed across his chest and he was shaking his head like he couldn't believe the guy was for real. I was sick of his stare-down technique myself and took one step to the left and leaned against a wall to let the two of them have their showdown.

"See, that ye may fully comprehend," Rev Dailey went on, laying into George with repeated pointing down the barrels of both his forefingers. "They know not how to receive from the Lord who is always giving of the boundless bounty of his glory. But *they* cannot re*ceive* it, for let not that man think that he shall re*ceive* anything of the Lord unless he asks in faith, nothing wavering. For he that wavereth is like a wave of the sea, wind-driven, tossed, and swallowed up by the salt-bitter blasphemous bile of sinning cynicism!"

"The salt-bitter blasphemous bile of sinning cynicism. Shew!" Handsome, spiffy Reverend Dailey took a breath and revitalized himself as I marveled over his gift of gab. "You gotta hand it to him," I told Steifer. "This is off the cuff."

"Now you finished?" Steifer asked with cold fury.

Rev Dailey ignored us. He had more to say for the benefit of his brethren. "Hence, these men, men who abandon the good and joyful home of truth and become as *spiritual* vagrants. They *believe* not, for they *know* not. Know not how to listen to *His* silence; *know* not how to watch the *in-vis-ible* wonder of His ways. Who can tell them so that they may understand: *God* does *not* operate in the *vis-ible* realm."

George stepped forward. Reverend Dailey was a head taller, which placed him at about six-five. "Hold it. Shut up."

"If you would just read the bible, you—"

"*Keep* talking down to me all you want, friend. It's not going to make me go away—not till I'm good and ready. You wanna talk privately or out here in the hall?"

Many of the ten to fifteen brethren tried to butt in and protest on the Reverend's behalf. He raised a hand and it silenced them immediately.

"In the loving company of my congregation and, with *God's* will, *always*, you will never succeed in your sordid scheme. Yes, oh yes, you may try—and try you will, I am sure—but with our faith and the Lord's will in *heaven*—hear me *God* almighty—you will never taint our wholesome efforts by spreading slanderous and libelous innuendo. We are not Nazis as you might like to think, and we would never meddle with an innocent young woman's life. We know nothing about this, and if you expect me to dignify your outrageous insinuation by any further inquiry, you are profoundly mistaken."

"You'll do anything I like if I tell you," said Steifer. "Just you wait and see. You and your *God* squad. I'm gonna break you wide open, buddy, and you'll squeal like a stuck pig, just like any other common criminal, which is what you are."

Mrs. Scott came forward to stand by her Reverend. As she spoke, her long, large right hand fussed about her neck so nervously, she almost looked as if she were trying to choke herself. "Please," she told George in a quavery voice, "I'm afraid I'm going to have to ask that you leave."

George made a show of laughing throatily in her face. "You don't just ask the Los Angeles Police Department to leave—that is, unless you want to leave with me. Just say the word and we'll all go downtown together—the whole congregation—because the next time I come back here I'm bringing a warrant."

"Dear God, pardon these poor sinners," Reverend Dailey intoned, looking heavenward toward the ceiling. "They know not what they speak."

George raised his voice in competition. "And why, why,

why? as the Reverend would say. It's not because I'm any Antichrist. Anybody who wants religion is entitled to it. But something smells around here. Maybe it's that special canned food of yours. You know, all you had to say was something simple like some of your church literature must have been confiscated or placed into the wrong hands; that would have accounted for it. But instead, you're lying and covering up when you didn't even have to. I don't think you people are too smart. That's why you have to get these sharpie fund-raisers to work up the computer mailing lists for you. They collect the dough for all of your great causes, and some of the money goes to them for expenses before a nice big chunk comes back and weighs down your pockets. I bet you make a bundle with that dough before you get around to finishing the retreat in Wyoming."

"You're very rude," said the indignant Mrs. Scott, who was still fussing over herself.

George tore a poster off the wall. It was an advertisement for Manna brand survival food, a long holiday table with Christmas wreaths and Styrofoam snowmen topping a can pyramid centerpiece with twenty or thirty plates of various samplings of the stuff all around. In large print, some corny slogan like, BE READY WITH MANNA. George shook it in the Reverend's face.

"Half the world's starving and you're stockpiling food. That's really Christ-loving, Reverend. The third world'll give you a big fat kiss now, won't they?"

"You're not proving anything," I told Steifer in a low voice.

"Maybe not," George said loudly for everybody's benefit, "but this is just the beginning."

• SEVENTEEN •

They didn't like that, not the Reverend, Mrs. Scott, Henry, or any of the others, but luckily, George seemed to feel he had spoken his piece and we got out quickly as Henry and a few of them called after us with squirrelly threats of hell and damnation and Reverend Dailey quoted some scripture jibberish at us with his booming phony preacher voice. To me, it was a relief to see that George was getting himself under control. Sure, he'd been angry, but it had been easy to tell he knew what he was doing. He hadn't come close to losing it. He was back on track, or so I thought.

In the car, he asked my opinion.

"They're a bunch of harmless cranks," I told him. "This reverend's probably just a natural snoop who likes to get the lay of the land before he commits himself to anything. Mrs. Scott knew he was eavesdropping on the conversation. All of these zealots got a persecution complex. He thinks you're trying to pin something on him, which, to me, means he and this CC group probably don't know a thing about any extremist offshoot."

"I wouldn't be so sure about that," George mused on our way out of the underground garage.

"If you're right, which I doubt, you're going to have a hell of a time proving it."

"Not if we catch these punks, I won't," Steifer insisted.

"You really think some neo-Nazi group could be affiliated with the moral majority?"

We were going up the exit ramp and there was a car behind us. Steifer ignored it as he braked to a halt and turned to me. "I'm not joking around. These are people who want to control the books and newspapers you read, the TV programs and films you watch, your body, your children, your religion. They're all connected, they're in conspiracy to overtake the democratic political process and they'll do it any way they can. If that doesn't sound like fascism and Nazism, you tell me what does?"

I didn't know what to say.

Steifer went on: "I used to think these fuckers were a joke, but I'm telling you, they're serious."

"You're grasping at straws."

"No, I don't think so."

"To keep yourself going, you're imposing order on what may be a hopeless situation."

The car behind us was honking. George continued up the ramp to the tollbooth, paid for the parking, and exited onto Santa Monica Boulevard.

He had a point, but I didn't see how he could possibly confirm his hunches, and, more important, even if he did, it still didn't mean he was going to be rewarded with an alive Elise Reilly. His bullheaded insistence about a new right conspiracy reminded me of my boy Pete and the kiddie punk party line about American fascism and repression that George had dismissed quickly as utter hogwash just the other day. Well, there was a reactionary wave, but, as George had said in a more conservative frame of mind, it was possible that the only thing that was making it stronger was the exhaustive overkill in the media. And then, again, there could be more to it. In some respects, the tie-up George was looking for would tell us something. If he got to the bottom of the Elise Reilly affair and found connections that led in a number of interesting directions, it might make me a believer. Otherwise, he was dealing with bad seeds, a rotten batch of white trash kids with a lot of confused ideas, who possibly, in their confusion, somehow felt it was incumbent upon them to become fascists in order to battle fascism.

Political malarkey. It gives you a headache. And as that shifty decoy of a reverend had said, God does not operate in the visible realm, meaning that, politically speaking, you can find out whatever you want, but when it comes to big scale stuff, you're not going to be able to pin anything on anybody, usually.

George was on his way to Laguna Beach, Orange County headquarters for the Robert Oak Society. We'd unearthed a box of a thousand membership applications in that Van Nuys garage and Steifer was determined to find a reason for it. Along with a little green chapbook which summarized the Oak Society's theories of international communist conspiracy operating behind the sham of so-called democracy, there were letters and handouts which admonished one and all to be forewarned and to band together to fight off the cancerous blob of atheistic Marxism and save God and free enterprise before it became too late.

Myself, I had no doubt there was a reason: we'd stumbled onto a crackpot splinter group, a small bunch of young kooks who had taken it upon themselves to assist every organized fanatical reactionary cause in existence. Overlooking the reluctance of any of these organizations to cooperate in a police investigation which would, at the very least, reveal their extremist sympathies, Steifer had only a lousy blurry black-and-white photo of five nondescript young Caucasians in somber suits, slick short hair, and Hitler moustaches, and no names to go by. Even assuming the outrageous possibility that CCRS, Robert Oak, or any of the others might want to help out, Steifer could give them nothing to go on.

The whole thing was absurd. He couldn't deny it, but he had other ideas, notions which, while not being reactionary or impossible, were, well, extreme. He'd already advanced his theory of conspiracy among the new far right; more particularly, he had come to believe that many of these allied groups were using undercover agents to infiltrate for intelligence purposes or to camouflage their most controversial acts of reactionary insurrection. This Young Hitlers group, then, was a cover for the militant arm of a strong new right organization that wanted to disrupt or eradicate certain foes with impunity. In other words, they wanted to do a shitload of dirty work and not get caught holding the bag.

"What do they want to do?" I asked.

"That's what we're trying to find out."

The "we" bit made me look around and realize Steifer

had just passed Westwood and was heading for the San Diego Freeway South on-ramp.

"You just passed Westwood," I told him.

"I thought you were coming with me," he said blankly.

"I don't see that there's anything for me to do," I told him. "I don't see that there's anything for you to do either, but that's your business. I can understand that you've got to try to do something. All I'm going to do is try to discourage you."

George's shoulders narrowed and hunched up higher, knotting, as his hands tensed on the wheel; then he seemed to shrug it off. "Friend of mine's got a place on the beach there. We'll drop by, sit in the sun, have a beer. He's always home. Beautiful house right on the beach."

"Who?"

"Jonathan Polansky."

"The big cop writer?"

"Yeah. I knew him when he was just Jon."

"What's he like?"

"He's a nice guy who wasn't cut out to be a cop."

"What do you think of his books?"

"They read real nice."

"Meaning?"

Keeping one hand on the wheel, George turned towards me. "Maybe I wasn't cut out to be one either," he said stonily, "but I can fit in with them, OK? I know 'em, I understand 'em. Jon never fit in. He was always on the outside, he didn't spend much time on the street or ever get real involved, except maybe with a few people he could feel comfortable with. Now, he's made himself a millionaire writing these sensitive stories about what policemen are really like. But he doesn't know the first thing what they're about."

"He gets great reviews."

"He tells people what they want to hear, that cops are normal guys who get screwed up by the incredible stress of their jobs, just like everybody else does. That's how Jon is maybe, but most cops aren't quite like that."

"How's he wrong?"

Steifer looked back at the road. "It's hard to put into words, but some people do things from compulsion—an artist, a writer like you, a criminal, cops. Everybody has a different reason for it, but it's not a normal impulse, that's all I can tell you. It's either in the family, for sadistic reasons, power tripping, leadership, a moral or religious obsession. A cop doesn't start out normal. I can't explain it well, but Jon, he's a sweet guy, but he's got a lot of simplistic notions that don't wash. I kind of feel sorry for him."

"Why?"

"He's got a beautiful wife, three super kids, money in the bank, and every time I see him he's more depressed. I wouldn't tell him exactly, but I think he knows he doesn't know what he's talking about. He's got a great imagination. He should write science fiction, something like that, I told him."

I made no effort to protest as George turned onto the south entrance to the San Diego Freeway. He was lonely and I didn't have anything else to do, besides which I'd never been to Laguna Beach and was curious about it. It was going to be a scorcher today. It might be fun to catch a few rays civilized by a nice offshore breeze, and have a beer with Jonathan Polansky and see if he was really the way Steifer described him. More than anything else, I was glad that George was talking. He was still tense and oversolemn, but somehow seemed even-keeled about it all now. He hadn't blown it with the Jesus freaks and he wasn't brooding deep into himself. He was in touch again. I wanted to encourage him to stay that way. So I kept him talking. The monolithic facades of the federal building and the Mormon temple faded away into the smog, and we passed the big fountain shrine to Al Jolson on the top hill of an adjacent cemetery near the airport, and headed past the creaking oil derricks of corrupt Signal Hill and the sewage stench of Long Beach toward the Disneyland Matterhorn of our fair land's heartbeat, the pulse and guiding light of tomorrow's America, Orange County, the fastest growing foothold of ultraconservative suburbia in the U.S.—birthplace of Richard

Milhous Nixon, West Coast headquarters of the Robert Oak Society and the maverick Libertarian Party, home of the legendary John Wayne, setting for the historic San Clemente White House, this is the last frontier of the unyoung, unpoor, and unblack. Not too old, actually, and not too young either; not too rich, and definitely not poor; not too white, though never more than golden brown. Orange County people. I'd been reading about them and hearing about them for a long time. I'd even met a few and hadn't been struck by anything spectacular. They were just regular folks who preferred the company of regular folks, like the majority of American voters, and one I remembered had seemed a little too worried about something he'd referred to vaguely as social conditions, which could have meant a lot of things, all as boring as his defense industry job. Rev Dailey would be sure to know about Orange County. A large number of his followers probably lived there.

We got off the freeway at Newport and turned down to the coast. What impressed me about the place was that it was too clean. The streets, residential and business, were laid out carefully, landscaped methodically, as if they belonged to a model built to scale. It gave me the feeling of being on a military base, like you'd get slapped with KP duty if you dropped anything on the sidewalk or turned into the wrong driveway by mistake. There were lots of new high-rises, most of them as sterile as I expected.

Laguna Beach was just as predictable. It was self-consciously rustic and quaint, with a careful, overscrubbed quality, the sort of place that has chain ice cream parlors and real estate companies in the antiqued shells of handsome new-old Spanish colonial buildings that have been gutted out and modernized on the inside. Somehow, movie sets seem a hell of a lot more honest—after all, they don't pretend they're not trying to fool everybody. As advertised in the local travel books, L.A.'s "historic artist's colony" had plenty of small galleries, and artist easels and unframed canvases decorated much of the sidewalk. The never ending sequence of serene and tempestuous seascapes made me feel like popping a handful of Dramamine. And the people looked just about as wild. You had to blink your eyes to stay awake when you looked at them. Young and old wore something with an alligator label, and none of the ladies moved their hips. It was enough to make you shiver, even though the temperature was in the low nineties already.

The Robert Oak Society was housed in its own building, a two-story antiqued brick and plaster Tudor smack-dab in the center of the shopping district. The Society had its own library and public reading room downstairs, with book displays in the front window. Two tomes that figured most prominently caught my eye on the way in through the office entrance: *None Dare Call It Conspiracy* and *America: Home Of The Brave—Red*.

Inspiring stuff. At least they were out in the open, which, depending on your point of view, was a first step for either their success or their demise. There was no directory by the elevator. We got in and went up to the next floor. The elevator doors opened directly into an air-conditioned bustling office complex packed with desks and open cubicles, most of which were occupied by earnest-looking types of both sexes scribbling, typing, or hawking on the telephone.

George walked up to the closest desk and faced a young fellow in shirtsleeves and a wide striped tie. He had a pencil in his mouth and was looking up, staring into space, trying to think of something.

"Who's in charge here?" Steifer asked him.

The young man dropped his head a notch and his eyebrows flittered with a start as his concentration broke. "Excuse me?"

"Who's in charge?"

"You mean the editor in chief?"

"Whatever."

"The third office on your left."

I followed as George walked in the indicated direction. The door to the third office was open. Steifer walked in without knocking. In contrast to the supermarket lighting in the main room, it was dark. A dim diffused square halo seeped out of the molding around the ceiling and a small crane-styled lamp glowed meekly through the center of a glass desk. A blond man was sitting behind the desk. The light caught the hair over his forehead and left the rest of him in shadow.

"Yours truly," he said quietly and stopped.

Switches clicked. A bank of lights came on overhead, and the room turned bright. He put down his Dictaphone and squinted at us with disinterest like a turtle who had just come out of his shell. He had the hawk beak, too, but the rest of him was ivy smooth: striped tie, blue blazer, light gray slacks, and brown penny loafers with the pennies. His Kennedy haircut had gray highlights and so did his light blue eyes until he picked up a pair of owl-eyed horn-rims and parked them on that aggressive nose. His lips were so tightly pursed, he looked as if he were puckering up for a big fat kiss. Contented birdies sucking up a good worm in the morning grass look just like that, too. I couldn't make up my mind if the guy reminded me more of a big turtle or some type of rare bird. He even had muscles under that blazer and his tan complexion had a certain outdoor athletic look; ditto for the cords in his neck, the hard chin, and the big wrists showing outside his pale blue Oxford shirt cuffs.

"Sorry," he said, keeping his mouth tight and small. "With all the close work, one rather needs to rest the eyeballs. Are you the chaps from graphics?"

George told him who we were and why we were there.

"Indeed," he kept saying.

His English accent may have been the real thing, but he poured it on so thick it made you want to puke. I had the feeling he thought it made him sound educated and convincing; to me, it had the opposite effect. I kept wondering what sort of game he was playing and looked around the office as George presented him with some of the Robert Oak literature we'd dug up in the garage, showed the Young Hitlers picture, then recited the tale of Elise Reilly's disappearance on remote control, flatly, without emotion. Tinted windows faced the street; the rest of the room was paneled with rich mahogany. A modular couch set-up sat across from the desk in the corner facing the window. It was white, the carpet was dark gray. A round glass table sat on a thick chrome cube base in front of the couch. The walls in this area were decorated with two large oil portraits. Cap in hand, standing straight as a rod, and looking dwarfed in perspective before a looming red-and-white background field of the American flag, a young Army lieutenant-colonel saluted a graying man in blue pinstripes who stood before a stately desk and faced the young officer thoughtfully, puffing on a pipe. I wasn't sure who they were, but one of them had to be Robert Oak and the other was probably Matthew Holt, the founding father of the Oak Society. Holt was supposed to be a very rich man and Robert Oak, a veteran of the second World War, had received the death sentence for murdering a reputed Russian spy. It had been in the papers a long time ago. That was all I knew about either of them. Above the Englishman's glass desk was an enlargement of a magazine cover. Done up with the red, white, and blue motif, it was called *American Digest*. Beneath the logo was a photograph of a thin graying man with a mean hard look that came from the stern disbelieving turn of his brows and how he smiled with his teeth clenched against his pipe stem. Next to the photo: *Exclusive interview with Matthew Holt*. The painting advertised the mild-mannered philanthropist; the photo dramatised a no-nonsense man of action. He knew how to handle his poses. You could see that about him right away.

So did this odd-looking English gentleman. "My dear fellow, you must think we're absolute savages," he was telling George, his bugle lips splitting into a thin flat wry smile that served public notice he was at his leisure and amusing himself thoroughly with this foolish trifle Steifer was trying to pin on him. "We have three-quarters of a million active members and a twelve million dollar yearly budget—we even run summer camps for children—and you want to know whether we've abducted a journalist from one of the nation's leading newspapers. Indeed, we could hardly afford to. Think of the bad press."

"What if she found something you'd been hiding?"

"Preposterous, considering that I can think of nothing whatsoever we have to be secretive about. It's the bureaucratic elitists of Washington and Wall Street who, I'm afraid, excel in that area."

"What are the secrets of Washington and Wall Street?"

"It's very simple, actually. They mean to keep the common man—the regular fellow who totes a lunch pail—down. They mean to keep him as small as a fly—in the name of democracy, of course."

"And Matthew Holt and Robert Oak and you and your magazine, you guys are gonna bust your buns just so the average dog can have his day."

"Why, yes, of course," said the Lord of *American Digest*, crinkling his eyes approvingly as he gave a little nod, then set his lips back on the invisible bugle. He took an unsharpened pencil, tapped his bottom lip with it, and it made him speak some more: "We care and we care *tremendously* about the deteriorating state of government, business, and society. It's all an interrelationship. If there's too much of the first one, government, it sullies the others, encumbers them. We simply want to free America from its Bolshevik influences and give it back to the people to whom it belongs. America is for Americans, I think we can agree on that, can we not?"

"The Commies are taking over, is that it?"

His lips puckered. George was pushing him to tackle the high hard one. "I'm not going to shout and argue so that you may both leave here telling each other that Oakers, Oakies, or Oakites—whatever—talk about the quote-unquote Commies just like unidentified flying objects, but they *are* among us and have been for such a long time that they are hardly noticed. Foreign influence is rampant and, I hate to say it, but, yes, it controls us. Our government has been wrested out from under us."

I'd been staring at his name plaque, DAVID SEARING III, and couldn't restrain myself any longer. "But you supported Ronald Reagan, didn't you Mister Searing?"

"He is much more fond of government and its attendant evils than we had thought."

"You must be brave," I said.

"How is that?" he asked with the wide flat smile.

"Here you are, an Englishman rooting for America to prevail against the evils of foreign influence."

"I'm hardly English. London School of Economics. I may have stayed a touch too long."

"Then you're well-bred. That doesn't exactly align you with the common man either."

"I cannot tell you how intent I am to make myself a touch more—how shall we say?—uncomplex. I was once very much a moderate, unfortunately, very much an Eastern party man, and I'm trying, as they say, to unlearn the awful process of it all. I want to pull my blinders off," he said, taking his horn-rims off his beak with a little flourish that made me look away at George and smile. But he was too busy marveling at David Searing III.

"You're full of horseshit," he decided, after snorting a little nasal laugh. "You didn't go to the London School of Economics for nothing."

David Searing III puckered and squinted and didn't say anything. He parked his glasses back on his beak.

George leaned across the guy's desk. "You love the common man as much as your mother, don't ya, pal? You wouldn't give the common man the time of day, unless, of course, he pays you for the privilege. You wouldn't happen to know a Reverend Dailey, the TV evangelist? No? Of course not. He's got his turf, you got your turf. But you share the same suckers."

"I'll thank you to—" Sir David started.

"Save your breath," George said, backing off and heading for the door. "We're leaving. Just remember that if you know anything, or even if you don't, when we get the lid off this thing and find out some bimbo worked for you or knew you, you're gonna be up shit creek with no paddle for your leaky canoe."

"I am quite sure you have no idea what you are talking about," David Searing III said politely.

• EIGHTEEN •

Indeed. I couldn't disagree with him. George seemed to be developing a special penchant for hopeless situations; if that wasn't bad enough, the whole thing was embarrassing, putting every other crackpot and his brother on the spot with nothing to hold them there. I wasn't just starting to wonder if it took one to know one. We seemed to be as flaky as they were. We and they, us and them, him and her, everybody seemed to be dreaming up theories of conspiracy. Maybe we were all nuts.

George took us over to Jonathan Polansky's, where after a few beers and some amiable conversation in the breezy sunshine on the famous cop writer's beautiful beachside terrace, it didn't seem quite so bad. I almost got the feeling that Polansky had been eavesdropping on the critique of him that George had recited on the way down, because he seemed to take up right where Steifer had left off, saying that he had no business writing about cops and was sick of it; and he was funny about it, too, as he drew Steifer into reminiscing with him about some of their more amusing experiences. Every time Polansky poked Steifer or slapped him on the back or knee, I could see it working on George, loosening him up. It wasn't long before he was laughing a little, except when Polansky asked what had brought us down to Laguna, all Steifer would tell him was that it was involved. Which was all right by me. I was up to here with it. Polansky and I talked shop about the movie and book biz and I told him how I had written two novels first before I came to California. It was only after the words were out of my mouth that I realized I was both apologizing for myself and trying to get the guy to understand that there was more to me than met the eye. Steifer picked up on it. He looked over at me and I could have crawled into a hole. He'd been doing that to me. Something in the guy was wired up to a sensitive mechanism that zeroed in on the deficiencies in my character. It was getting to be a little too much.

I was glad when we headed for home. Neither of us had anything pressing on our minds that needed to be said, so I leaned against the window and drifted in and out of a catnap thinking about whether I should go back to writing books or continue being a screenwriter. I was making good money as a screenwriter, whereas I hadn't even made poverty wages as a novelist; I'd gotten a few good reviews for my two books, but, actually, they hadn't been very good. I'd had this youthful notion of literature as something precious and transcendent and set apart from regular life, which was because I'd had both bad and humble beginnings, and language had always done something to me. Cynically awed by the claptrap blarney of grammar-school teachers, prairie preachers, and juvenile court judges from earliest memory, I had felt it was the one ticket out of the drab and ordinary, and I'd worshipped words too much perhaps, thinking they could be owned and not knowing that what made them so grand was that they belonged to everybody. I'd been more caught up by style and effect than having something to say. What was good about my work had slipped in, in spite of me. So, taking myself very seriously and yet less seriously now, I felt the next book might be better. But it was like the silence between George and me. There was nothing pressing that I felt I had to say. I couldn't just concoct something, trump up some silly adventure. You could do that in the movies, especially when you could take the money and run; but with a book, you had to live with what you were doing for a much longer time. It took longer to produce and you were the only one responsible. You couldn't blame its crassness or stupidity on the producer, the studio, or the director. If you didn't do the right thing, it could haunt you.

I was really a guilt-prone bastard about the few things I valued. It was nothing to be ashamed of. The only real problem was that I needed the exercise of writing a novel for my well-being and self-esteem, but there was no room for the workout without a story or theme that seemed important to me. It would come. I couldn't push it. It was too rich here on the West Coast for things not to happen to you. I'd heard more than one lily-livered Easterner wax eloquent on the civilized virtues of home versus the cultural wasteland on that faulted seaboard so far away. Some of them could even get strange about it and tell you that California was the place where people came to die. From what I'd been seeing, I wasn't sure they weren't right either, but since death is at least half of life, you couldn't help but feel the pulse or rumble of the Ultimate Mystery if you kept your eyes open and your ear to the ground. It was a hell of a lot better than growing mold on yourself like some people I could think of, and the far right liked it fine here, you could see that right away. There were so many of them and they were only growing. It was as far away as you could get from Washington without freezing your butt in Alaska. Kind of scary, though, with all these nuts all in one place.

George put the radio on and we listened to Bill Evans' piano and a Grover Washington Jr. sax solo on the jazz station as we came back into town. I asked him what he was going to do next.

"I'm going to look into that Reverend Dailey, see if I can find anything. Few other things," he said in a bored voice.

"Like what?"

"Couple of the other leaflets."

I was going to tell him again that he was wasting his time, but there wasn't any point in it. He was going to do what he had to do and couldn't have cared less what I thought about it. At least he was calm. He didn't seem to be tottering on the brink of a nervous breakdown anymore. I couldn't help thinking that this might be the calm before the storm. He knew he wasn't fooling me or anybody else. He wasn't trying to. He had an idea of the shape he was in, but I wasn't sure what he intended to do about it. His friend Jonathan Polansky had sensed something, which explained his pronounced jolliness. Early on, he had asked me if George was OK when Steifer had gone looking for the children.

"You still think there's a conspiracy?" I asked him.

"Yes, I do. Does that mean I'm crazy?" he said, picking up on what I was thinking.

"Did I say that?"

He shrugged.

"You may be a hundred percent right, but that still doesn't mean you're going to either be able to break it or find Elise Reilly."

He nodded.

"I know I've told you a million times already, but you're under a lot of strain, George, and you're going to heap on more. You're frustrated already. You're just going to make it worse."

"That's your opinion," he said, flashing a sudden smile.

"OK."

Steifer pulled into Ship's Restaurant in Westwood, where we'd had breakfast. I got out and looked back down into the car.

"Thanks for the company, Crandel. I mean it. OK?"

"OK."

As I'd told myself a number of times already, if Steifer wanted to drive himself crazy, it was his own business. There was nothing I could do about it. He was forty-three years old, a big boy. He'd been through crises before. He didn't need me to hold his hand every minute. You could go bug-eyed worrying over other people's problems.

I went into Ship's and had an early dinner at the counter. My waitress ruined it by asking me to watch the guy on my left who she claimed was sitting over a cup of coffee and stealing her tips. I looked at the guy. He was wearing a UCLA sweatshirt. He looked perfectly normal, except he smelled a little and he couldn't sit still. He kept tapping his heel. You couldn't hear it in there, but it went up his leg to his knee and from there to his trunk and shoulders, shaking him all up. He was definitely suspicious, but I figured that if he was desperate enough to resort to pinching nickels and dimes at a coffee counter, he probably needed it more than the waitress. I'd leave it up to them. I wasn't going to worry about it.

But I didn't enjoy my dinner. The waitress kept coming by to give my neighbor dirty looks and me meaningful ones. I felt like she was standing over me even when she wasn't and I couldn't stop stealing side-glances over at the guy. It's hard to mind your own business; sometimes it's the hardest thing in the world. You can never quite figure out if you should or not or if other people want you to or if you're acting in your best interest or theirs or both of yours. It's enough to give you indigestion, which is exactly what I got. I didn't leave a tip.

Outside, I bought the troubles of the day for a quarter. Anxious to see if the negotiations were progressing in the baseball strike, I turned directly to the Sports section to get disappointed. Sorry, folks, game called on account of greed. I folded the paper back up, put the top down on my car, and drove home, thinking about Pete and how he wouldn't be there the whole way. I didn't want to rush back so I could hurry up and get depressed, but Stanley was waiting for his dinner and I'd had enough of humanity for one day, too, and couldn't think of any other place I'd rather be. I stopped off at a supermarket and bought a basket of strawberries, two bottles of rum, light and dark, and a package of ice. After I got home and fed the dog, I threw the stuff in my blender and started drinking. I knew I was just going to get tanked and then make the rounds on past and present girlfriends, so I welcomed a 7:00 call from Jodie while I was still fresh. She sounded strange, distant. I could tell she was up to something right away. That didn't stop me from asking her if we could get together that evening. She wanted to know if I remembered two nights ago, then she wanted to know why I wasn't mad at her. It took me a few minutes to catch on, but by then it was too late.

"You mean you aren't jealous?" she asked quietly.

"Of what?"

She hung up on me, which prompted my hindsight. I was

supposed to be jealous of having discovered another man in her apartment. That was it. It was some game she was playing, but it touched me. Under ordinary circumstances, perhaps in bygone times long, long ago, it would have been enough for a girl to mention the word marriage to give a fella the only hint he'd need, but things were so different today. The women I'd been dealing with were either so desperately intense they scared you off or they were more numb than novocaine. Jodie had fallen into the second category—nice, very nice, but I hadn't felt she was doing anything but marking time with me until something better came along. Now, I got a different story. She hadn't done much to show it, but I couldn't have hurt her unless she'd felt involved.

I called her back, but her line was busy and stayed that way for over a half hour. I felt real bad, so I went out and bought some flowers and drove over to her apartment. My heart was racing. I felt young and excited, like something good might come of this. Romance may be out, but my desire for it certainly isn't. I was hoping Jodie might feel the same way. I took the elevator up and navigated the maze of passageways to her door. She opened it before I knocked. She wore a tunic-styled thin white silk shift. It had small pearly buttons running its length from shoulder to hem and it deepened her light tan into something rich and appetizing that, instinctively, you'd want to sink your teeth into ASAP. Her blonde mane had been teased wild. She was all done up and ready to go somewhere. She held a flat little handbag against her tummy and took a deep breath.

"I'm busy," she said.

Then she slammed the door on me.

"Now, come on, Jodie," I tried. "The truth is I was so out of it, I don't even remember being here. Come on, open the door."

"I'm expecting somebody else. I have other plans."

"Let's just talk a minute."

"We have nothing to talk about."

"Oh, come on, now."

She went away. A moment later, some rock music boomed

my way. I couldn't argue above that. On the way home again, I thought it over. She was being infantile, sure, but there was more to it than that. If she hadn't had to pretend to be so cool and disinterested, she might have been able to confront me in passion instead of withdrawing in hysteria. These seesaw emotions, from one extreme to another, were tied into each other. It was a lousy deal, this shallow pretense of cool gift-wrapping the desperation and gloom. Jodie was a little young, but just about everybody I knew was the same way. It was too bad, but we had to be that way today because nobody seemed to be dependable. Everybody dumped on everybody else. We think we're more inclined to lose than to gain, though, consequently, everybody plays it cool, signals get crossed, and nobody gets what they want. And the desperation grows.

Blending myself a few more strawberry daiquiris didn't prime me up for the world again and put me into a festive spirit as I might have expected. I felt listless and spent, and the more I drank, the more I thought about Jodie. I was hot for her, all of a sudden, like I'd never been before. She had such a good body and she sounded sexy when she was angry. She'd be a screamer if she could let go of some of that in the hay. Fuck. Doesn't matter whether it's pussy or patrimony—you always want what you can't have. Another campaign slogan to add to my list of givens.

I tidied up the house, took all of Pete's things and put them in his room, made his bed, and closed his door; then I took Stanley for a long walk on the beach. I refused to jerk myself off over Jodie. She wasn't worth it. I waited till it was dark before I turned back toward the house. There were too many stars in the sky. The night was hot and sticky. No breeze. I hated it but I liked it. I felt like the last man alive, lonely but heroic in a melancholy pissed-off sort of way. I didn't give a shit about anybody or anything. I was all used up. When I got home, I gave Stanley a Milkbone and went right to bed. It was 9:30. I should have known I wouldn't get away with it. It couldn't have been more than an hour later that I was awakened with what, under the circumstances, I least needed: an obscene call from a *woman*—really a singularly unique occurrence, though not at all amusing when you're slightly drunk and depressed. I said hello a few times before I picked up on the labored breathing. Then, huskily, she asked me what I was wearing.

"Shit," I groaned. "This is a first."

"A woman, yes," she panted. "I'm doing myself. You don't mind, do you?"

"Do whatever you have to do, lady."

"Would you like to *come* help me?"

I hung up on her and got up and found myself a beer. I realized that, in another mood, this sort of thing might have amused me. Now, it just made me sick. America had sex on the brain and L.A. was the capital sin city. It was enough, at the moment, to make me envy the life of a eunuch. It wouldn't be so bad to be out of commission, at least for a while. Hold off on the slam, bam, thank you, ma'am. It was high time I sought quieter pleasures, experiences more fully savored, less quickly spent.

Yes. I found a dusty selection of Mozart piano concertos, put it on my stereo, and pretended to enjoy myself.

The phone rang again. I let it ring about twenty times before I answered it.

"Lady, I'm tired. Why don't you pick another number?"

"Ben Crandel?"

A man's voice. "Uh, yeah, sorry. I thought you were somebody else."

"This is Bob Armstead. I work under George Steifer."

"Yeah, sure. What's up?"

A loud indistinguishable voice in the background.

"I'm over at George's apartment. I just stopped by to see how he was doing."

"Is that George yelling?"

"Yeah. He's been carrying on a little. Says you'd understand what he's talking about. I wouldn't 'cause I'm a policeman."

"I thought he was settling down. I was with him all day today."

"I don't think so."

"What's he so upset about?"

"His missing reporter case. You know he—"

"I know all about it. Anything in particular?"

"Get out of here! Who said you could use my phone? Who you talking to?!" Steifer yelled within range.

"Your buddy, Ben," Armstead told him.

"You guys have no right. Can't you leave me be? I'm working on my own time. You can disobey me, but you can't stop me. Tell that to Maculvey, why don't you?"

Terence Maculvey was an assistant chief of police. Steifer had *kvetched* about him to me. "I'm talking to your friend," Armstead insisted.

"I think I better come over," I told Armstead.

"Thanks," said Armstead.

The receiver knocked against something on the other end. "I'm serving up my resignation, Maculvey," George told me.

"George, it's me, Ben," I tried.

"You give me back my free reign in this or you're finished," Steifer screamed in my ear. "I'll talk to the press. The PD sucks and I'm gonna tell the taxpayers all about it."

"Steifer!"

"Won't help much when you run for governor, now, will it?"

I hung up again, gave Stanley another Milkbone, then I locked up the house and drove back to Hollywood.

• NINETEEN •

For close to a year now, through his separation and divorce, Steifer had been living in a garage apartment on Curson above Hollywood Boulevard. Like the front house, it was a boxy stucco structure that had been covered over with plain wood shingles to achieve a rustic effect. It wasn't much, but it was away from the traffic and clean, with varnished floors, fresh trim work outside and in, and a few good-sized ponderosa pines taking up most of the view from the side window in the living room. Furnished by Budget Rentals, cheery but spartan, the sort of low-maintenance burrow tailor-made for a typical walking wounded casualty of modern day marriage to sort out the pieces and try to put them back together again.

I parked on the street in front and walked down the driveway to the back. Lights were on in the front house, but no one was home. It was Friday night. Whoever lived there was probably out trying to have a good time, dancing on ludes, eating the nose candy, watching some simulated killing, having some good old all-American fun. Armstead was standing at the foot of the side staircase that led up to the apartment. He was around my height but his trim build gave him an extra two or three inches. He was wearing a light wool blend suit that was turning his shirt into a wet washcloth; still, his tie was up all the way. He gave me a sweaty handshake and kept pushing his wire-rimmed glasses back up onto the slippery bridge of his nose.

"Am I glad to see you," he said.

"What's wrong?"

"He went into the station and said he wanted to form a task force, a special investigative unit. They pulled the plug on him already—he knows that. He threw a tantrum and stormed out when they gave him the stall. I was there the whole time. They sent me over to see how he was doing. I would have come anyway. George broke me in."

"I know."

"I owe him an awful lot. He's good people. Serious, sure, but one of a kind."

"You can say that again."

Armstead looked up the stairs. "Well, you couldn't ask for a nicer guy or a better cop."

"Loosen up. You don't have to sell him to me."

"We better get back up. I just wanted to fill you in."

We went up the stairs. Halfway, Armstead turned

around. "He's just gotta get his head together, that's all," he said meekly, obviously out of his depth now that the father figure of Steifer the invincible supercop was toppling from the highest mountain.

"Just don't treat him like a piece of china, OK? If you do, he won't trust you."

"Yeah," nodded the young cop.

"He needs to trust somebody. We can't lie to him."

We went up the rest of the way and walked in. The place had a bad odor, like sour milk or rotten cabbage. Newspapers, food containers, milk cartons, and soft drink cans covered the floor and furniture. It was about two or three weeks worth of neglect, deterioration, despair made visible. Living like this, it was a small wonder that George was still getting his clothes pressed and shaving; though from the looks of him sitting before me on his rented couch, it wouldn't be much longer. He'd just gotten out of the shower. His hair was dripping wet and he was wearing an old pair of jeans.

"George."

He looked up from the newspaper in his lap. "What are you doing here?"

"Bob called me."

He folded the paper neatly and laid it next to him on the couch, then he shot to his feet, his nostrils flaring, as he pointed an accusing finger at Bob Armstead.

"Didn't I tell you to get out of here?"

Armstead stepped forward and tried to clasp Steifer by the arms, but got shrugged off. "I'm on your side, George," Armstead insisted. "All the way."

Steifer spit on the floor as he turned from Armstead and spoke to me. "They wanna commit me. This is the first step."

"Calm down," I told him. "Just because they don't agree with you doesn't mean they're gonna put you away."

"He took my gun."

I looked toward Armstead. "Give him back his gun."

Armstead loosened his tie and pushed his glasses back up on his nose. "I don't know," he said.

"Look how you're living," I told Steifer, gesturing at the mess.

"I let things go," Steifer said. "I was cleaning up."

"Bob's concerned."

"He sneaks into my bedroom and takes my gun behind my back. Some concern."

"George, I—"

George pointed a finger at himself and tapped his head. "You've got to have an imagination to think—I've always told you. You can't tow the line and memorize procedure. Follow their orders."

"But I wasn't. I—"

"Don't give me that. They told you to get my gun, so you did what you were told."

"There must have been a reason for it," I interjected.

"They think I'm crazy."

"You have done something to suggest it."

"I want a unit. I'm an assistant commander. I know what I need. They say, 'You already have one. We'll take care of it,' they say. Do you think I'm a moron?!"

"I'm on the unit, George. I know what's being done," Armstead whined. "We're doing everything we can."

"I need more men!"

I stared hard at Steifer till I got his attention. "And you wonder why they think you're crazy."

Steifer picked up his newspaper and shoved it at me. "Look at this, would you? If that doesn't drop it in our laps, what will?"

A fine-tipped black pen had traveled round and round the article, setting it off with scores of overlapping circles. The heading, ANTI-SEMITIC VANDALS HIT FAIRFAX AREA, had been boxed in in the same fashion:

Vandals spray painted Nazi slogans and posted anti-Semitic handbills on Jewish-owned businesses and apartment buildings in the Fairfax Avenue area early Thursday.

Police recovered copies of crudely lettered handbills

and posters from the walls of buildings in the 500 block of North Fairfax Avenue, which threatened Jewish residents with "death and destruction" by the National Socialist Caucasians Party.

One of the hand-printed posters marked with swastikas and headlined ATTENTION JEWS, said the party is planning a march in the Fairfax area. No date was mentioned.

"If any members (of NSCP) are assaulted in any way, death and destruction will come to you," the poster said. "Your stores will burn and your churches will be blown up and then your people will die! Beware!"

The handbills were signed by the "new führer of the new reich" in hand-lettered German. Building walls were marred with painted swastikas and slogans written in German and signed by the NSCP. One slogan read "das ist ur der anfang," which translates as "this is only the beginning," and was marked by a black circle with a crossed-out red Star of David in the center.

Assistant Chief Terence Maculvey, spokesman for the Los Angeles Police Department, said stepped-up efforts are being made to halt the anti-Semitic vandalism that has plagued the area for several weeks. However, no arrests have been made.

"Why didn't anybody tell me about it?!" Steifer was demanding of Armstead.

"We did. You were, uh, preoccupied or something."

"How many occurrences before this one?"

"Oh, two, three. It's not like it hasn't happened before," Armstead whined.

"Yeah. I seem to recall Nazi Germany," Steifer sassed.

"Not that. I mean in L.A. In my opinion, drawing everybody's attention to just a handful of crazies, the only thing it can do is make it worse."

"You're stupid, Bob," Steifer told him. "I hate to say it, but that is *stupid* thinking of exactly the same kind that gave the world the Holocaust. Sweep it under the rug."

Armstead pushed his glasses back and scratched at his messy mop of banged blond hair. "I wish you wouldn't put words in my mouth," he said quietly.

As I looked up from the article, I could see that George didn't feel sorry for him. On the contrary, he was coiled up like an angry cat about to pounce, standing in front of Armstead with his arms nailed across his chest, his face beading with sweat. "Then what are you trying to say?"

Armstead had to get a little angry to defend himself or at least get a few words out. He took a step back and made helpless gestures with his outspread hands. "All I'm saying's that the press will do anything for a story. They'll make a mountain out of a molehill, distort everything out of proportion. You wanna give the limelight to a couple of psychopaths and make 'em seem like an army, that's up to you, George. But I'm not going to."

"It's not just a couple psychos with spray cans," Steifer countered. "It's a hell of a lot more than that, huh, Ben?"

The tone of his voice, the look in his eyes, I can't explain it, but under the circumstances, the last thing I intended to do was to contradict my good buddy and embarrass him. I didn't trust Armstead myself either. He was out snooping for the police and I wasn't about to contribute to fucking George over.

"Could be," I hedged.

"This is a lot more involved, Bobby," George said condescendingly. "I've been doin' my homework on this. Crandel's been helping me out." He stopped and looked Armstead in the eye, hesitating. "This is strictly between me and you, but we found Elise Reilly's clothes, some ID, and right now we're smack-dab in the middle of a conspiracy of political extremists. All I can say is that there are lots of possibilities. These neo-Nazis may not be as far out as you think."

Armstead shook his head, despairing. "George."

"Oh, they're loony, all right, but the point is that they're building up to something. This desecration is not random or small scale. It means something."

Armstead kept shaking his head and scratching it and shoving his glasses up on his nose.

"That's right," I felt I had to say.

Armstead's mouth dropped open. "You mean you agree with him?"

"I'm not saying I agree or disagree. But from what we've been finding, it's not entirely impossible."

"And neither are ghosts. But that doesn't mean you have to believe in them."

"We're talking about something real."

"Wise up, would you?" George said, dishing out the bravado now that I was behind him.

We had a difficult time bringing him around, but Armstead finally allowed that we might know something he didn't, and not that I believed him, but he agreed to take a favorable report back and keep his mouth shut for the time being. He even offered to see if he could find anything current on police investigations into neo-Nazi groups. And his family had a cabin up at Tahoe. He offered it to Steifer after getting tongue-tied at trying to tactfully explain how George should enjoy his leave of absence and not look at it as punishment.

"You are crazy," I told Steifer once I heard Armstead start his car.

"What?"

I pointed at him. "Nuts, psycho, crazy. Out of your mind. You." I slapped the paper I was still holding. "You think this tripe is your big lead? You're so desperate. I didn't want to embarrass you in front of your buddy—so I agreed with you. And you know, maybe he was looking into your mental condition. I wouldn't put it past them. Sure they are. They're very worried about you. But not half as much as I am."

Steifer sat down on the couch. His gun was on his knee and his right hand held onto it and squeezed it like a prized toy that was giving him incalculable solace. I kept talking at him, trying to drum some common sense back into his head.

"You have no reason to believe that this anti-Semitic episode has anything to do with your case. The city is filled with crackpots. We didn't find any materials or mention relating to this group; there's no reason to conjecture that some relationship exists. Again, even if we could tie them together, there were no arrests or identification, and this group, whose grand total membership probably numbers one or two, I'm sure changes the party name and line daily and operates out of some other garage somewhere. It doesn't mean anything, believe me."

"I think it does," Steifer said numbly.

"All I can see is that you're gonna get yourself so low there's going to be no way back up."

"That's your opinion."

"When are you going to stop?"

"When I'm satisfied."

"With what?"

"That I've done all I can."

"You're not going to kill yourself or anything, are you?"

"I don't believe in that."

"That doesn't mean you're not going to do it."

Steifer looked down at the gun.

"It's not pretty to look at. Put it away or something," I told him.

He got up and walked into the bedroom, carrying the gun. Immediately, I regretted my suggestion. He took his time in there. When he came out, I let out a big breath.

"Nervous?" he inquired.

"Fuck you."

I think the gun was what did it, the way he'd cradled it on his lap, that and the weird little trick he'd just played on me, wanting to both alarm and defuse me at the same time. I made up my mind to stick to him like glue. If I left the guy alone now and something happened, I'd never forgive myself. And, no doubt, something was going to happen. He was covered with sweat. It was hot, sure, but not that hot. He was like a sick man with a fever, sweating it out. And it would get worse before it broke. I didn't think he was up to handling it by himself; therefore, since the truth was bound to be far from pleasant, I felt I should be there.

• TWENTY •

H e didn't make it easy on me, but I was glad I stuck around. I went to his refrigerator and helped myself to a Pepsi, then I came back into the living room and sat in the armchair and put my feet up over the debris on the coffee table. He ignored me and walked around picking up the trash. After a while I got up and helped him.

"What are you doing?" he asked me.

"What does it look like?"

"I'm not lonely. I don't need you to hang around."

"That's your opinion, as you'd say."

"What do you think I'm gonna do, off myself the second you step out the door?"

"Did I say that?"

"What's the idea?"

"Not much, really."

"You going to hang around all night?"

"Longer than that."

"What?"

"I'm sticking with you till you're done with this investigation."

"You're kidding."

I shook my head to the contrary.

"Then I'll leave."

"And I'll go with you. What's wrong, Steif? Before you said you needed a partner."

"You're not a partner. You're an attendant."

"Look on the bright side. We can have a lot of fun together."

I smiled coyly and batted my eyebrows, but it didn't seem to give him a charge. He got his vacuum cleaner out of the closet and went back to work. I did feel a little ridiculous being unwanted and all, but I thought I was doing the right thing. I went into the kitchen and did the dishes. The phone rang as I was finishing up. Steifer kept letting it ring.

"Are you going to get that?"

I'm an urban animal. I can't ignore a ringing phone. It's torture to me. Finally, I had to pick it up.

"George?"

Nice voice. Very soft and sensitive. "One second." I put my hand over the phone and called to Steifer over the sound of the vacuum cleaner. "Telephone, George. Don't keep her waiting."

He showed he wasn't interested by disappearing into the hallway and making a racket there as he crashed the contraption headlong into the baseboards.

"He's busy," I had to tell the lady. "Would you like to leave a message?"

"This is Elise," she said. "Elise Reilly."

"You're shitting me."

"May I speak to George?"

"Yes, yes, you may. Hold on."

I took the phone to him, kicking the vacuum cord out of the socket on the way.

"It's Elise," I told him.

He stood there, angry, wincing sourly.

"Elise Reilly."

He dropped the vacuum and grabbed the phone away.

"Elise?"

She said something that lit his face up like I'd never seen it.

"Are you sure you're all right?"

They went on like that, exchanging rapid-fire small talk. From George's side, I gathered that they had let her go, she was home, and she wanted him to come over. He asked her if there was anything she needed.

"That's no problem," he told her.

Then he hung up. We exchanged looks. I knew Steifer was too pumped up to say anything, so I just said, "That's good news," and went back to the kitchen.

He came out a moment later, patting his pockets to check if he had his keys. He'd combed his hair and he was wearing a colorful flower print Hawaiian shirt with the same jeans and had stepped into a pair of Topsiders.

"I'll see you later," he said. "Call you tomorrow."

"Great."

He was out the door before I opened my mouth. The whole place shook as he flew down the stairs. I stood there with a soapy dish in my hand, like a frumpy housewife gawking at nothing as the big big world spun by at a speed more startling than any day or nighttime soap opera. I was having one of those slow motion flashes you get when you're suddenly in the middle of an accident. A certain special phone call, George's tense and weary face shedding its gloom, George leaving. I'd never seen him in public without a suit and tie. Well, he wasn't going out in public and he was in a big hurry. You could tell from the way he peeled out the driveway. I should have been happy for the guy. He'd bucked the bad odds and come up with a little luck. Elise Reilly was alive and she wanted him and he wanted her . . . too much. Or maybe not. Maybe he was just caught up in the liberating spirit of the moment, and maybe the reason the particular moment wasn't so liberating for me was because I couldn't share in it. Maybe George's previous paranoia had rubbed off on me and I had gotten overly familiar with entertaining doubts and suspicions. But there was something about it that was too ideal. Whatever had happened, it was certain that Elise Reilly had been through an unpleasant ordeal. Wouldn't she want to rest before she saw anybody? Or—this was it—if she was free, nervous and restless, if George was the one she wanted to see, wouldn't she have come to him instead of calling from her place? Wouldn't she be afraid to be alone?

It was a trap. Somebody was playing off George's weak spot. The voice could have been Elise Reilly or somebody else. They knew he wanted to believe she was safe. They knew he'd do anything. I found his calendar book with Elise

Reilly's address and phone number on a page from two
months ago. I picked up the phone and dialed the number.
"George?"

Why not hello? Hadn't she called anybody else? I hung
up and started for the door, then something occurred to me.
I turned around and tracked back to Steifer's bedroom and
went at it like a cyclone, turning everything upside down. I
knocked things out of the closet, swung open the tall doors of
an armoire and tilted it, dumping out the drawers and contents. When I flipped over his top mattress, it slipped out
from underneath his pillow and fell to the carpet with a little
thud. Cozy place for a gun. Maybe George had started to
believe you were supposed to sleep over them with a little
prayer. Maybe. There were lots of maybes. And no time.

• TWENTY-ONE •

Elise Reilly lived in the Los Feliz area, not far from the
Planetarium and Greek theater in Griffith Park, up
high on the bulge of a short curlicue of a street that had a
view toward downtown which romanced you with a crazy
quilt of dazzling lights and dim stars, like a lovely aging lady
given to theatrics, showing herself to best advantage by
night. By day, you knew she'd have to hide behind a killer
smog screen to punish anybody rude enough to scrutinize
her blotchy sallow pallor. The house was a handsome narrow two-story Spanish mission-styled job with an arched
front door and a glassed-in veranda covering the length of
the second floor. Rough-hewn beams protruded in regular
intervals across the top, supporting the flat platform for the
overhanging tile roof. It had a thick rough plaster finish and
was painted plain white. Lights were on all over, outside
and in.

I parked across the street behind George and walked up

four steep flights of cement stairs railed with steel piping and bordered with a thick waist-high hedge. A few ferns and lemon trees decorated the small rise at the top where it was flat; the rest of the hill was covered with an ugly prickle of ice plant.

I was all embarrassed suddenly, afraid that I was about to break in on something private. But I hadn't whizzed over here, holding my breath and skirting a half-dozen near miss head-on collisions for nothing. I might be half-cocked, but I wasn't going to go away carrying a dangerous quandary on my shoulders just because I should have consulted Emily Post.

Still, my confidence was at such a low ebb I rang the door-bell and waited all of about ten seconds before I was face-to-face with an angry sight.

"What the fuck are you—"

"Now, George, wait a minute."

"Go to hell."

He started to close the door, but I pushed against it and squeezed into the small front hall. I slipped on the Spanish tile and George tried to shove me back out, but I caught hold of the door and slammed it shut with my back to it.

"I apologize if I'm interrupting you," I began.

Steifer walked away from me into a dark wood-paneled room with a high ceiling that went way above the top of the arch forming the entry. I saw a note on a library table in the hall:

George,
  Feel very nervous. Went for short walk. Please wait.
                                                  Elise

I took the note and walked up to George in the living room. He was standing with his back to me, next to a baby grand that took up most of the room, looking over a floor-to-ceiling bookcase that covered the front wall on either side of a rock and mortar fireplace.

"Don't get mad, but are you positive this is her handwriting?"

He whipped around and grabbed the paper out of my

hand. Then he turned around again. "I know you have good intentions," he said slowly, speaking between clenched teeth as he fought for control, "but I'll kill you if you aren't out of here the next time I turn around."

That pissed me off. I wouldn't have minded if the guy had been your average run-of-the-mill psychopathic dark stranger—you know, an ax murderer you'd never seen before, that would have scared me shitless—but this guy was my best friend. It pissed me off.

"I'm plenty sick of you, too," I told him. "I'm up to here with the crazy people I got to deal with day in and day out. And now you gotta be one of them." I tapped him on the shoulder. "I just want you to know it's not my fault you're so fucking crazy."

He whipped around again and swung at me. I ducked it and started to come up on his midsection, which was just what he wanted so we could tear each other apart like a couple of crazed animals. I had to keep my wits about me, especially if he couldn't. I backed off quick and walked away.

"We're sitting here and begging for it. That's all I know," I told him. "Somebody's going to come through that door, climb in a window, if they haven't already, and it's not gonna be Elise."

Steifer had turned back to the wall of books. He put his arms up against the highest shelf he could reach and stretched out like a man on a rack being tortured by forces beyond his control. I thought of something and walked around the house, upstairs and down, testing the sinks and faucets. None of them had been used. There was dust over everything. The water ran rusty. The water level in the toilets hadn't changed. Nobody had been here for months. I wouldn't have expected Elise Reilly to return home and set to cleaning house immediately, but she would have gone to the bathroom, taken a bath or shower, or washed her face and hands. Somebody had come here, all right, but nobody had come home, not in my book.

I went back to the living room. George was standing

where I'd left him, in the same position, riding that torturous long shot all the way. At this late stage, nothing could stop him. I wasn't about to argue with him. Not again. I took his police revolver out of the back of my pants and conked him with it on the back of his head, at the base of the skull. He fell back into my arms. I slung him over my shoulder and headed for the door. Going down the steep stairs, I held onto the steel pipe rail and looked around, expecting people to jump me. I set the passenger seat back all the way and put him in my car.

Nothing happened until we were two blocks down the hill. I heard an explosion, then another, then another, five or six in all, at intervals of ten to twenty seconds. The sky behind us lit up like a ball of fire. I backed up a ways until I was absolutely sure. Flames were hissing out of the broken windows of the upstairs veranda. People were out on the street.

George opened his eyes.

"Look behind you," I told him.

He turned around and looked. Then he buried his face in his hands and sobbed loudly without restraint.

It's an awful thing to see a grown man cry, but I was too stunned to be very sympathetic, which was just as good. George didn't want me fussing over him. I kept thinking about the two of us in that deathtrap and how we'd sneaked out by the skin of our teeth. Another minute of haggling or dilly-dallying and . . .

I put the car back in gear and got out of there. Five minutes later, we were down to Franklin Avenue, between Western and Vermont, and George was still crying with all the stops out. By the time I pulled over and parked, he had stopped.

"Why'd you stop?" he asked me.

"I wanted to make sure you were all right."

He wiped his eyes with the back of his hand. "I'm OK," he said.

"Good."

"Where you going?"

"I was just driving."

"Let's go to Sarno's." He rubbed the back of his neck. "What'd you hit me with?"

I showed him his gun. "This."

"I should of left it with Armstead," he frowned, watching as I shoved the gun into my glove box.

"It was either that or a marble bookend."

"Ow," he said, wincing with the imagined pain. "You sure know how to hurt a guy."

I looked at him. He was trying his damnedest to make it light and yet he was still on the verge of tears. You could tell by his voice. It made me feel for him, the effort he was making to be appreciative, to say thanks when his gut told him there was too little to be thankful for to say anything, but something in him couldn't forget I'd just saved his life. I wasn't sure whether this vague urge toward everyday civility meant he was thinking about giving up or just coming back down to earth in order to levelheadedly pursue an extremely complex investigation.

• TWENTY-TWO •

Sarno's was this cute kitschy Italian place on Vermont above Hollywood Boulevard. It was next door to an art theater and a bookstore that advertised poetry readings on the weekends in its front window. An odd combination of small shops and supermarkets lined both sides of the street. I'd never been there before, so I was surprised when we walked in and some little old guy was standing before an upright piano, belting out an aria from some opera. He was on his second pair of teeth but his voice was loud enough to rattle the coffee cups. People were packed in there like sardines, everybody from children in funny-looking formal dresses and suits, to college kids in sandals, and plenty of middle-aged folks and old people. It was a jolly joint. I didn't mind the gondola mural or the Formica tables or the waitresses' homely uniforms. I'd never been to an opera in my life, but I liked it when the old geezer hit his final high note and the crowd standing and sitting broke into applause, and another volunteer popped up to take his place as he was finishing his bows. All of the regulars knew Steifer. The hostess wanted to know where he'd been and whisked us directly from the waiting area to a choice table. George smiled graciously and mumbled "Good to see you" and "Busy, busy, busy" to everybody who asked.

"It makes you feel good to hear music," he said once we were left alone with our menus. "Opera is pure emotion."

The new performer was clenching his fists and exulting in song, gesturing expansively and putting his whole heart into it, but he couldn't help coming off sounding like he was gargling a malted. I smiled.

"If not in execution, in intent," Steifer corrected himself.

"Yeah, he's got spirit."

"It's Verdi," Steifer told me. "Alfredo's love song from *La Traviata.*"

The new singer was walking around the restaurant, bellowing joyfully at everybody.

"Must be nifty to let it all hang out like that."

"The great ones spill their guts totally, but with control. They push every emotion beyond its limit."

"Sounds a little frightening," I suggested.

George was caught up in verbalizing his passion. "They feel more than we can imagine."

"Scary."

"That's what makes it so good."

"The risk?"

Steifer nodded in acknowledgement. "And what you get for it . . . sometimes," he added, looking over at the big-hearted crooner.

He turned back to me and put his hands neatly before him on top of the table, nodding up and down with a blank face. "She's dead," he said.

"It's a possibility. You're coming to grips with it."

"I keep hearing that voice. It wasn't hers, but it was close enough so that I let it convince me."

"Maybe it was."

"I don't think so."

"If she were alive, what you're thinking is they would have used her."

"Yeah."

"So if it wasn't her, you're probably right. But we can't be a hundred percent sure."

"Except that we must have hit pay dirt with one of those crackpots."

"We really inspired 'em."

"But we got nothing to build a case on."

"Maybe she's one of them."

"Who?"

"Elise Reilly. Maybe it was her and she tried to set you up."

Steifer looked away again. "I hate to disappoint you, but you can't make this into the bonehead plot of some lousy B movie."

"I beg to differ."

"Life may have the same quality, true, but it seldom works as neat." He leaned forward. "She was never one of them. Believe me. I'm not as wigged out as you think."

I raised my hands in surrender. "OK."

There didn't seem to be anything else that needed saying. The waitress returned and George ordered the first of three liters of the house red wine. Neither of us was hungry. We drank and listened to the opera aficionados. George told me what they were singing. I don't remember anything he said. The tension coiled up in me sort of sprung out and left me feeling quietly giddy and empty-headed as soon as I drank my first glass. I couldn't make much of what the hell the singers were hollering about, but my mood responded to all of the different nuances of the music. A big-breasted, dark-haired girl impressed me the most. She was on the chubby side, with a big bottom and love handles on her hips that spread out around her colorful peasant skirt, but when she belted out her song it made my nostrils flare. Her pale neck flushed every time she held a note. I was mesmerized, that is until her parents gave me a dirty look when she sat down, a reminder that she was probably only fifteen. George said he thought she might have a future and I agreed with him right away and didn't look at her again. None of the others inspired me with any feeling of romance, which was just as well. I needed a rest, some quiet time to myself to think over what it was going to be like to be alone again without Pete. I needed a new girlfriend, some new friends too. First, though, there was George, who had to go for the payoff now that his obsession had led him into a life-threatening predicament. We were going to be spending some time together. Tonight, for instance, I knew he was either going to crash in a motel or sleep at my house. There wasn't any way he could go home, not after almost being blown up and barbecued.

He didn't put up an argument and his common sense had returned to the extent that he didn't want to go back and pick up his car for the fear that someone might have rigged it with explosives. I got up to leave when my peasant goddess started in on another aria. I just couldn't take it.

"I have enough problems already without falling in love with fifteen-year-old girls," I told no one in particular.

I must have said it kind of loud. The waitress looked up from adding up the check.

"She wouldn't understand you," she said.

"Either would you," George told her.

She was good-looking, a slightly older version of the peasant girl and carried herself with a lot more assurance. I was surprised I hadn't noticed her until now. Her eyes were lively, almost saucy, but her mouth had a prim little pout to it that made up for her manners. I suggested that I wasn't entirely hopeless and managed to wangle her phone number out of her.

"She's a nice girl," Steifer told me once we were out the door. "Be on your best behavior."

"What's wrong with her?"

"Nothing."

"She's either new in town or crazy. This city doesn't specialize in *nice* girls."

"It's not as if the menfolk are such a prize."

"I'm very suspicious of nice girls or, for that matter, nice people. They can stick it to ya bad, you know." I gave Steif a rib poke for emphasis. "Nasty is up-front. Nasty is sexy. Nasty turns me on. I'm a corrupt personality."

"Just treat her good. She's a friend of Elise's."

That made it work, not fun. I was going to throw away her number, except I decided to be responsible and hold on to it, put it in the case file. Oh, well. I got us back to Venice and we crashed out till noon the next day, went out for lunch to the Sidewalk Cafe, and both got headaches on top of our hangovers, sitting out in the strong sun. Picking up the day's paper, George saw that another incident of anti-Semitic vandalism had taken place, this one bigger. Out toward west L.A., a Jewish studies center and a synagogue had been desecrated to the tune of an estimated $100,000 worth of damage with the same slogans and graffiti as in the Fairfax area, which made it the work of the same mindless little gang; but, having investigated only two far right groups thus far, Christian Citizens for a Respectable Society and the Robert Oak Society, we had all but eliminated the neo-Nazi fringe as a result of the previous evening's scare. Somebody had to be thinking we knew a lot more than we were letting on. Somebody had something to hide. The chap at Robert Oak had been a reasonable sort for an extremist, a genteel highway robber not unlike the prez himself or one of his phony budget men; but that evangelical character, with his long-distance disappearing act and defensive fire-and-brimstone sermonizing, had been more into the fancy footwork and slippery shenanigans. For now, he was our man.

I drove us to Century City. By way of Main Street in Venice and Lincoln Boulevard, we had no trouble picking up a couple of hitchhikers. The first was too stoned out to follow what George tried to tell him, but the second was just fine once he took the stereo cassette headphones off his head. He was a straight nondescript college kid from Chicago, tall and skinny, with longish red hair and freckles, out here for summer vacation and on his way to take a first gander at the Sunset Strip. I could have told him that there's not a hell of a lot to do for entertainment once you've had somebody take your picture in front of the Whiskey a Go Go, but I didn't want to bring him down before he got started. Besides, maybe he'd never seen a real honest-to-goodness out of work TV actor or stand-up comic or a lady of the evening in broad daylight. There was no way of telling what exciting things lay in store for him. George said we'd get him more than half the way there and twenty bucks the richer for a certain simple errand which entailed merely opening a door or knocking so we could find out if a good friend of ours was in his office. It was his birthday, George said, and we were organizing a big surprise. All the kid had to do was to find out if anyone was there. I hammed it up, babbling some nonsense about what a lot of fun this was, but the kid couldn't have cared less. He wanted that twenty bucks and he wasn't asking a single question. George put the radio on a rock station to keep him pacified.

When we got there, the kid unscrunched himself from the cramped space behind the seats and went up after George gave him the name of the concern and the floor number and told him which way to go once he got off the elevator. He went up and we waited on the street, parked in the red. He was back three or four minutes later.

"I don't think anybody's there," he said.

"You knocked a bunch of times?" I asked him.

"Loud?" George added.

"I pounded."

"Good," George told him, handing over the twenty he'd been holding out folded lengthwise and laced in between his fingers.

We gave him directions for getting up to Sunset and then we got out of the car and went into the building and took the elevator up to the twentieth floor. We each turned the doorknob and George knocked a bunch of times, then we tried to pick the lock, but to our mutual embarrassment, neither of us could open it. We'd come prepared, too, having hand-picked a little jimmying tool set of small screwdrivers, pieces of wire, and flat bits of metal and plastic out of my garage. We gave up after about fifteen to twenty minutes when some bony-legged, gray-haired conscientious fool working on Saturday in matching madras shorts and shirt passed us in the hall on his way to the executive washroom and furrowed his brow a little too quizzically. It took us another half hour to find a maintenance man vacuuming a rear corridor on one of the upper floors. George flashed him ID and acted stern enough so that the guy, a large muscular middle-aged black fellow in a hair net with curlers, thought we had come to arrest him. He put out his hands and said, "I was there, man. I didn't do nothin'."

Steifer had to explain himself and, once he did, the guy was more than happy to take us down and open up our office, though Steifer, being the perennial cop that he is, still wanted to know what the poor fellow had on his mind, why he was so guilt-ridden. He gave us a song and dance about not reporting a hit-and-run he'd witnessed. I didn't believe him for a second, but at the moment I didn't care either. George took his name and address off his driver's license, then told the poor fucker he could go. He walked away grumbling to himself, probably cursing the both of us and the lousy taste of his own shoe leather.

I followed Steifer inside and got greeted by those two lovely murals of the crucifixion and the lone shepherd. The only thing that was missing was the furniture: the rag rug, the colonial couches, the reception desk, and sewing spindle were all gone. Steifer went for the connecting door to the inner sanctum, flung it back and went in.

At first glance, the place didn't appear to be completely cleaned out. The walls were covered with faded squares and rectangles from where the posters and pictures had hung, and the desks and countertops were bare, but nearly all the furniture was still there. You could have almost thought they

were in the middle of a little late spring-cleaning, painting
and redecorating, that is, until we started going through the
drawers, cupboards, and closets. The framed needlepoint
sayings had disappeared off the walls of that Mrs. Scott's office. The empty space outlined in the carpet had been occupied by a big antique desk. Everything with a personal touch
had been removed; the remnants were office rental junk.
Nothing in writing, not one bit of paper, no stationery, none
of the advertising copy for their Manna survival food, nothing at all had been left behind. After ten minutes of going in
and out of all the offices, we had nothing left to do.

"Nothing," sighed George.

"Definitely—though I seem to feel a presence. What
about you?"

"The only presence I feel is a hangover from cheap wine."

I closed my eyes and held up my hands and felt the air.
"It's the Right Reverend. Remember: '*God* does not operate in the *visible* realm.'"

"Tell me about it."

• TWENTY-THREE •

It was hard for him to do, but Steifer knew he couldn't get
any further by himself. He called Armstead from my
house about an hour later and started in on giving him everything he had. After a while, he hung up and asked me if
he could borrow my car. I didn't see him until eight o'clock
that night, though by 6:30 I had visitors, four uniformed
boys who heralded his anticipated arrival with the formal
announcement that they were to serve as my palace guard. I
served iced tea to celebrate, then I went into my bedroom to
take a nap and left them to their duty. I called the pretty
plump waitress from Sarno's and talked to her for close to an
hour. She had the highest regard for George and, while
nothing she said entirely surprised me, still it was slightly

awesome to hear him described with such scintillating effusiveness. She said he was "so unobtrusively handsome," a fascinating and sincere conversationalist, but what she loved the most was how he played the piano while Elise sang opera. This was all news to me, of course. I had just been introduced to Steifer's passion for opera; now, it seemed like he was being described as a lapsed child prodigy. It didn't take me long to gather that the young lady was half in love with him herself. Aside from the gushing sentiment, I got the picture that Elise Reilly felt the same way. She and George had become nearly inseparable after just a few weeks. They had been meant for each other and that was why the plump young lady had been taken aback and rendered nearly speechless at seeing George in the restaurant the previous evening, as she knew what he had to be feeling. I couldn't make with the come-on and ask her if she wanted to get together because I couldn't imagine we'd be able to think or talk about a damn thing else but George and Elise Reilly. The thought of it made me very tired, a touch ill, like tasting a bad meal on the return trip. I promised her she'd be one of the first to know as soon as we found Elise or had something to go on.

Steifer came home disappointed, but I could tell he was back on his feet again. It had to do with his cronies, who seemed to have welcomed him back into the fold, though the irony of it wasn't lost on him either, considering that the only way he had convinced them to pursue the case with renewed dedication was by coming close to getting himself killed, which didn't say much for the integrity of his colleagues. But then Steifer had been more than ordinarily involved; he had been obsessed, strung out, a poor way of convincing anybody of his objectivity.

The only difference now was that he had both his feet on the ground again. He was still obsessed, but soberly. He listened, he talked, he surveyed his surroundings with a discerning eye, and when he looked at you, you didn't doubt for a moment that he was all there.

The cops around the house were in an up mood. It

seemed like a simple game of pin the tail on the Reverend, with all state, county, and federal agencies determined to stick it to him.

They didn't have to look far. They found him in public on Sunday morning, on stage before a predominantly black congregation of five hundred in east L.A., doing his fire-and-brimstone act in front of four live action cameras. They stopped him in midstream and yanked him right out of there and nearly started a riot, but he was released after questioning when nobody could come up with a proper charge for him. The church had simply moved its office to another location, so it was said, and vehemently denied any contact with Elise Reilly or association with violent extremist groups. The story was that they didn't deny being extremist, but being true Christians by nature, they could not be violent. An interesting theory that seemed to overlook the course of history.

Whatever George or I or the police might think, the only thing it added up to was one big fat zero—that is, until Monday morning. It was kind of like the day after New Year's when you have a hard time remembering what you were so wild to celebrate. The command post had pulled up stakes and bid me adieu with many thanks for the fruit bowl, soft drinks, and cold cuts, and now, as they weren't returning, it was back to business as usual. The Elise Reilly investigation hadn't been totally quashed again, though George and I both knew it would just be a matter of time, a week at most, before they turned the pilot out on the back burner. George was returning to work in good standing, at least, if that counted to him, and I was driving him back to his apartment, where his car—which had been detailed by the bomb squad—was waiting for him. From there, Steifer was going downtown to drop in on an arraignment. The clowns who had been raising havoc in the Jewish community had been arrested the day before, Sunday at two AM, when they had been caught off guard by a vigilante force of twenty newly deputized members of the Jewish Defense League who had been patrolling the area and stopped to investigate when they observed that a few of the exterior windows of a neighborhood synagogue had been shattered. The L.A. chapter of the National Socialist Caucasians Party was said to be composed of two men, Ed and Earl Tully, brothers in their mid and late forties, who, once apprehended, had confessed to this and the other recent misdoings. A box of Polaroids of the Young Hitlers group had been found in the house in Van Nuys. Armed with this blank ammunition, George was going to follow through on the job, look these men over, show them the pictures, and ask questions. By now, even George had to admit that there didn't seem to be much point to it. He was surprised when I asked him if I could come along, then he gave me a little tight-lipped smile as if the answer had just dawned on him.

"I'm OK now," he said. "You're the best nursemaid a man ever had, but I'm not going to drive off a cliff."

"I appreciate that you appreciate my concern." I stopped while we both smiled big and sheepish like ten-year-olds. "But this is on my own. I'm just curious about these guys. What do you think they'll have to say for themselves?"

"What makes them tick, the roots of their prejudice, that sort of thing, I doubt we'll hear about whether they hated a Jewish teacher in grade school or how it was inherited as a hallowed tradition from their forebears."

"There's such a lot of them and so many varieties, you'd think it would tell us something."

"You've seen the kind of people we've been dealing with. Stupidity's not interesting. It's boring."

"But how can there be so much of it?"

"Sign of the times."

"What type of sign?"

"Stop, Yield, Detour, Road Divided. Nobody knows which end is up, what's good or bad, and the haves and have-nots are digging in for the final face-off."

"People are desperate."

"People have always been desperate; maybe now they're more desperate. There's more to be made off it and the market's ripe for a good scapegoat. A kike or a nigger, the cops,

Russia, Democrats, Republicans—we need somebody to lay the blame on."

"Why?"

"It's soothing. Relaxes a man, gives him something to work on and live for."

The minutes flew as we philosophized all the way to George's, but he hadn't warmed up to the idea of having me along.

"Don't waste your time," he told me.

"I'm not," I said. "I'm trying to understand some cultural phenomena."

"Somehow that doesn't sound like you."

"You never know. I might end up pitching it as an idea that would be good for an outline for a treatment for a screenplay."

"That's the Ben I know."

"Really?"

"Nah. Don't worry. By my book, your reputation's not bad."

"Then let's get going."

Steifer gave a big sigh. "Suit yourself."

• TWENTY-FOUR •

On the surface, if you were looking for excitement and intrigue and faced the extraordinary challenge of entertaining some dim-witted producer with an attention span as long as a yawn, the courtroom scene would have been deadweight in a story conference. Ten men and three women were sitting together in the jury box when we came in. We didn't have a bit of trouble picking out the prez and vice prez of the L.A. chapter of the National Socialist Caucasians Party, and they were sitting side by side to highlight the family resemblance, as if that was necessary. They looked so alike they could have been twins. There was no way of telling which was older. Ed and Earl Tully was a double vision of a modernized hillbilly, the kind who drops the transmission passing through in his cross-country rig and strands himself and stays because he can't afford a bus ticket or because he gets ahold of a sweet young thing and can't let her go. Sitting down, they looked tall, with square, thick faces topped by full heads of darkened slick hair swept across and set to the side in the standard razor sharp part that showed a straight fine line of scalp. They had thickish reddened necks foreshortened by double chins, sunken chests behind pot-bellies, reddened thin arms attached to long-fingered hands, plenty of forehead around small, dark, deep-set eyes, spongy bulbous beer snouts, and, finally, big beautiful even teeth that showed all the way to the top molars in a huge oafish grin. The smiles would have been pleasantly mischievous on a young boy, but for no reason looked menacing, potentially vicious, a little bit insane on guys who were middle-aged, especially two guys who looked alike and sat there showing off the same expression at the same time. For the life of me, I couldn't tell if they were itching to spit or shake hands, though once I looked them over awhile, they impressed me as silent types, regular down-home folks who would make with those big smiles to welcome a new next-door neighbor, then turn around and get up a hooded posse to burn down his home. Never up-front, forever unpredictable, they're the most dangerous; forever astounding and confounding with ever darker ignorance. They both wore short sleeve shirts that had seen lots of washings; one was white with thick dull red vertical stripes, the other pale yellow. They had ink-marked vinyl penholders in their breast pockets. Their pens and pencils had been taken away, probably so they wouldn't commit hari-kari before their day in court or mess up the jail walls with some of their inspired sayings.

George opened his briefcase and took out his pictures of the Young Hitlers. Four out of five of them couldn't have weighed in at over 130 or been over twenty-five, and the other was short and squat in comparison. They resembled ol' Ed and Earl about as well as a tadpole does a frog, meaning they were similar fish by nature, but you certainly couldn't match them up, physically speaking.

I started to stand up. "Shall we?"

George put a firm hand over my knee. "Wait a few minutes."

I thought it was going to be all day, so I picked the prettiest prisoner and stared her down until I caught her eye. She had jet black hair with blond roots, a little heart-shaped face with wide Spanish cheekbones and a cleft in her chin that was matched only by the line of her cleavage leading down into a scooped-out, pink Angora sweater. She looked like she was fifteen going on fifty when she made her glossy mouth crooked and twitched her small wide nose to give me a good short sneer. She turned away, but when she looked back I had her. She licked her lips. I licked mine back. She leaned forward. I kept licking my lips. The saliva ran in my mouth and I had to swallow a few times. Thinking that I'd soon hear her name and get privy to a little obvious background info, I started to plot an approach, hoping she'd come up before the Tully boys; but as luck would have it, they were the first called.

Earl stood up and approached the bench with his attorney, a dumpy young guy with an egg-shaped shaved head, wearing an ill-fitting blue-gray suit with big bell-bottoms and wide lapels. Earl was an inch or two over six feet and an easy two hundred and fifty pounds. He'd been sitting with a bible in his hand, which he clutched as hard as a peasant woman wringing the neck of a chicken as he came out of the jury box. Judge Cohen was presiding, which might have made things cheaply interesting if the guy hadn't been such a cold-blooded pro. He went through both of the goons like clockwork, treating them like a couple sticks of furniture, and they used their secret weapon, smiling at the dirty Jew with all they had, and grunting, "Yes, sir," with the pursed lips of yokels whenever possible. Their attorney had a nervous cough that cut off his voice. More than once, Cohen had to ask the man to repeat himself. Earl and Ed were TV repairmen. According to their attorney, this and the claim that they had no previous criminal record, made these "family men and solid citizens" great assets to their community and insured that they wouldn't miss their trial. Cohen's face tightened through this standard bit, but that was all. There were two charges; trespass to real property and malicious mischief or injury to property, bailable at $1,000 apiece, which equaled a paltry two grand per man, small potatoes considering the damage they'd done. After finishing with Ed, the judge raised his chin at the attorney who was waiting for him to say that the bail would be posted as set without being reduced. The judge was a small man with thinning light gray hair. A brushy white moustache stood out from the loose folds of his serious leathery face.

"Your honor?" asked the Tullys' attorney.

Cohen leaned forward, smiling perfunctorily. "Will these '*family* men and *solid* citizens' be able to restrain themselves from desecrating other synagogues, at least until their trial?"

"Surely your honor doesn't suppose that—"

"Please save it," said Cohen. "They never done it before and they ain't gonna do it again, huh, boys?"

"Yes, sir," smiled Tully one and two.

"Everybody makes mistakes," said the one named Ed.

"Excuse me?" said the judge.

"Nothing, your honor, nothing," urged the frazzled attorney.

"For the record, please, what did you say?" the judge asked Ed Tully.

"Your honor, I said we all make mistakes, yes, sir, your honor," Ed Tully said with his shit-faced grin.

Cohen opened his mouth, then he picked up a glass of water and took a sip to compose himself and cut off the pointless bantering.

Steifer got up and walked over to the bailiff as Cohen stared blankly at the slick assistant DA who keyed into the judge's wry aside, adding a little burst of gusto as he repeated his menace to society charge for the second time and advised that the suggested bail according to code was more than lenient as this malicious and willful disrespect and slight to an entire people was a hell of a lot more than a little harmless fun. He ended with a clipped little flourish, saying that perhaps an altogether new statute was needed to cover cases such as these. It was obvious the guy was jockeying around, trying to kiss the judge's ass and tell him what he thought he'd like to hear. Judge Cohen didn't go for it. He set the bail straight to the max as he had before without so much as a nod to anything the DA had said.

After the next case was called, Steifer and the bailiff walked over toward a couple of deputy sheriff transports who were standing to the side of the jury box, leaning up against the wood-paneled wall and talking in hushed voices. The defendant's name was Stephen something. He was a skinny kid about twenty-one, very nervous, and he had a long fair face that was burned as red as a berry and his nose was white with zinc oxide. He wore hiking boots with white socks and a pair of suede Swiss yodeler's shorts with suspenders, no shirt, and his shoulders were tannish, freckled, and peeled. He had been arrested for trespass and indecent exposure on the beach in Malibu Colony and for assaulting a private security policeman.

"Be brief," Judge Cohen chastised the slick DA before they got started.

George came back. "They're gonna meet us in a conference room upstairs," he told me.

We went up there. It was a windowless jury room with a long clean table of blond wood and twelve matching straight armchairs with vinyl-padded seats and backs. There was acoustical tile on the ceiling, the mushroom-colored walls were blank, and the beige-and-white linoleum had the same swirly cumulus pattern they use for decorating bowling balls. The deputy sheriff transport was standing there, smoking. The Tully brothers had pulled out a few chairs from the middle of the table. The one named Ed straddled his backwards and looked at us with that big, dumb, vicious idiot smile. The other guy, Earl, had been searching for some inspiration out of the good book. He looked up at us

with a finger holding his place, and his big brown eyes had
the wholesome native intelligence of a cud-chewing cow. He
took his cue from Ed and came up with the shiteater's grin
on tape delay.

Dirty Mr. Clean, Esquire, needed a shave over cheeks
and skull. He had Phillip Morris over his uneven teeth and
bitten-to-the-quick fingernails and you would have thought
the leaf he was inhaling was some pretty precious hemp from
the way he was toking on it and holding his breath. He
talked faster and acted even more nervous up close and out
of the courtroom. In between puffs, he chewed on the dregs
of his thumbnails on either hand and drummed his fingers
over the hard top of his battered briefcase which he had
placed on top of the left-side head of the table.

George walked right up to him and put out his hand.
"George Steifer, Captain of Detectives, Hollywood Division. I just have a few questions, nothing specific."

"Glen Schultz," the bald eagle said by way of greeting,
quickly extending his paw, then withdrawing it upon contact
and going back to his tom-tom act on the briefcase. "I don't
have to tell you that my clients have no obligation to you
whatsoever."

"Of course not."

"I've already advised them against answering any
questions."

"I'm sorry to hear that," Steifer said, putting on a disappointed look.

"After all, you'll have plenty of time during the course of
the trial."

"This is another case. I don't think it can hurt them."

"That, of course, is rather debatable, wouldn't you say?"

"Anything is rather debatable when you come right down
to it, huh, counsel?"

Schultz unsnapped the briefcase and took out a bent card
which he handed Steifer with a choppy attempt at an offi-
cious nod. "I'm sorry, but why don't you call me and—"

Steifer took the card and flicked it back and forth against
his thumbnail. "I can see you want to be cooperative, and

that's admirable, but it's just gonna cost your clients here *so* much money."

This got Ed and Earl's rapt attention. You could tell because the manic light dimmed out of their eyes, even though the grins stayed just as they were.

"Legal fees up the kazoo," George told them. "Prelims and continuances, all kinds of motions and witness statements. Shit, I'm tellin' ya, God knows, we play this by the absolute letter of the law, it could drag on, well, I'd say an easy six months, maybe a year. Boy, an' all I want can't harm you guys no way."

Steifer opened his briefcase and took out the pics.

"I just want you to look at some pictures. If you know who these guys are—and even if you boys done wrong—I'll guarantee you complete immunity, that is, unless you killed somebody."

"We ain't killed anybody," they both said. "No, sir."

"Then have a look."

"Ed, Earl, I must warn you," said Schultzy.

"This is costin' us as is," Ed said strongly.

"You of anybody oughta know what kinda shape the treasury's in," Earl chastised, holding up his bible with his finger wedged in between the pages as a bookmark.

"You a member?" I asked the attorney.

"I don't see what bearing that has," he said between coughs, beating on his tom-tom again.

"You the treasurer?" George asked him.

"What if I am. It's a free country, isn't it?"

"With no thanks to you," I told him.

Ed and Earl reignited those smiles. Schultzy turned to the transport. "We'll go now," he said.

"Sorry, forget that," George told him. "We're all a little tense. Let's save ourselves a whole lot of time and money."

Earl tightened his grip on the good book. "We ain't done nothin' wrong," he said. "So we tore up one a them Jew dens. So what."

"We just wanted to see what they was hidin'," Ed added.

"I know, sure," George mollified. "How about these here?"

They looked over the pictures, ten to fifteen individual Polaroids—before and after the Hitler moustaches and with and without the dark gear and swastika armbands—the hazy group picture, and two or three group snaps, jackboots and all, including whips and bayonets. They got a genuine kick out of it, you could tell, the crazed smiles got calm and peaceful and the three of them nodded to each other with pride as if they were acknowledging one of their own.

"Know them?" Steifer asked.

"Who are they?" asked Ed, licking his lips.

"That one bears a strong resemblance," said Earl, putting an admiring finger on one of the young men in a group snap, the one who most resembled a real live young Hitler.

"You know him?" George asked Earl.

"He sure resembles the *führer* good, don't he?"

"That's all?"

"Yeah."

"I never seen any of these guys," Ed chipped in. "Must be some kind of independent admiration society."

"What about you?" Steifer asked Schultz.

"Of course not," said the indignant Schultzy.

"Of course not," George smiled. "You'd contact me, of course, if you came across them."

"Sure," Ed told him. "They criminals or somethin'?"

George gave him a big apple-cheeked, close-mouthed shiteater yokel grin. "How'd ya guess?" he said.

"We'll let ya know."

George collected his pics. "Sure. Well, I bet you gentlemen are anxious to get your walking papers. I won't bother you again unless I have something more definite."

Steifer thanked the deputy sheriff for his cooperation and we all walked out into the hall. I couldn't stand looking at those goddamned grinning jackasses another second, that's how I ended up walking behind them, bringing up the rear. George was ahead of me, walking in between the brothers Tully and jawing with the transport. Schultzy had gone off to the restroom after assuring Mutt 'n' Jeff that he'd have them out on bail before noon. He really should have hung around,

because all of a sudden, very unexpectedly, and without saying a word, the boys got themselves in a terrible pinch. You
see, I was right behind Earl, who was the one carrying the
good book. He was swinging his arms like a carefree country
boy walkin' barefoot down a dirt road and totin' his fishin'
pole and worm box, except he had the good book instead,
swinging back and forth, towards me, then forward and
away, his arm a cadenced pendulum, keeping time with each
step. Maybe it was because my head was just chock-full of too
much bogus good-time religion these days, but I got mesmerized by that bible, I couldn't take my eye off it. Finally, close
to the elevator and after about a block of corridor, without
fully knowing why, I grabbed it out of his hand.

"What?"

He stopped in his tracks and whirled about to face me.
His brother Ed, George, and the transport all whipped
around.

I flipped it open and looked at the inside of the pasteboard
cover. At the top, toward the left-hand corner of the plain
white paper facing the first blank flyleaf, there it was: the blue
stamp of the CCRS logo, the four bold letters filling up the
rounded belly of an outline of a fish that had a little triangle of
a tail. This wasn't one of your plain old ordinary bibles. This
baby was wired up with a direct line to the Almighty. It told
you all the tallest tales before you got to the first page. I
clapped it shut before the apocalypse set my hair on fire and
juggled it between my hands like it was too hot to handle.

"Praise the Lord," I said.

• TWENTY-FIVE •

I handed the bible to Steifer and told him to take a look.
Earl stood there confused, not sure what I was carrying
on about. His brows spooned together and his mouth got
tight.

"Gimme my bible back," he said.

Ed was the one who jumped between us and tried to get his hands on it. The transport grabbed him by the collar and ripped most the buttons off his faded shirt, which exposed his solidly fat and pale belly.

"I told you leave that!" he yelled at his brother.

George took a peek and came up smiling with his incisors. "Well, well. A few more questions."

The brothers Tully were handcuffed to each other. We chaperoned them back to the jury room and wasted some more time. Steifer played it just this side of legal and dished out all the threats he could think of as he tried to get the hicks to talk. The transport told him that they had a right to have their attorney present, but he didn't care much either when George said the attorney couldn't stop him from arresting anybody on charges ranging from kidnapping to murder, arson, and attempted murder and assault.

But, again, he got nothing from them he could hold in his hand. Neither had any recollection of where the bible had come from. They hadn't bought it, it hadn't been given to them. It was just there.

"Picked it up at some church," Earl explained with many serious nods.

Steifer tried to badger him. "What happened to that stupid grin? You worried now?"

"You're makin' some serious accusations."

"So you're white as a dove, aren't you?"

"Yeah, sure."

George gave him the yokel smile. "Then why's this gettin' ta ya?"

"We're tired, mister. We'd like to go home to our families," whined the bible thumper.

"Ah, gee, I feel for you fellas. I really do."

"We don't know about this group or the other," Ed insisted.

"Just a couple of dumb yokels."

"Yeah."

"What church was it?"

"We go to lots of churches, huh, Earl?"

"That's right."

"Earl collects the holy book. He got 'em from all over. You can't expect him to remember where he picked each one up."

"Swear on the bible."

"So help me God," said Earl, lifting his right hand.

Ed's grin started working its way into a comeback. "That's the God's honest truth," he said, raising his lip over his nice uppers.

Steifer ignored him. "Thanks again," he told the transport.

We left the Tully brothers sitting there and walked out. We hadn't gotten anywhere on the new information, and I expected Steifer to be at least a little down about it, but he wasn't.

"Do you know what this means?" he said.

"Tell me."

"Fuck those guys. We don't need them to confess anything. We have this. He held up the bible. "This is all we need."

"You working on a sermon?"

"This tells us there's a link between two apparently disparate, unrelated entities, both of which have repeatedly denied having anything to do with each other."

"You can't prove it."

"There's a pattern. We've got to find it and break it. It's this anti-Semitism thing. They're building up to something."

"The Fourth Reich maybe. Their dream."

"Don't laugh. If there's a connection between these neo-Nazis and the moral majority, they're a hell of a lot bigger than we think. They've got power, these zealots, and they're wheeling and dealing at the political table like there's no tomorrow."

"You don't see me arguing, but if you can't prove anything, why all the bother?"

"I'm gonna find Elise. Whoever, whatever they are, they're out to hurt somebody in particular, maybe a few people of importance, and I aim to stop them."

I could appreciate George's earnestness and dedication, and I could see some of the pattern as he saw it, but still I wasn't convinced, not until we paid a visit to the Jewish Federation. Located on Wilshire Boulevard, between Fairfax and La Cienega, I'd driven by the building a million times without noticing it. Since the Federation serves as a sort of grand central station for most Jewish agencies, charities, and community groups, George was familiar with the organization, having fielded numerous complaints, inquiries, and requests, many of which dealt with protecting the safety of the large elderly population in the Fairfax area, geographically the center, and culturally the heartbeat or core of West Hollywood. We went through the regular screening system to enter the building, both of us showing ID and George asking to speak to a Mrs. Finestein, an executive director he had dealt with in the past. We went up to Mrs. Finestein's office, and before Steifer could give his name to the secretary, Mrs. Finestein herself had popped out of an inner office to greet him.

"There he is: Mister Small, Dark, and Handsome. *Where* have you been?"

She was like that: a little too old, a little too round, a little too loud. The gold bangles dangling all over her, the bright orange hair, the long, blood-red nails, and high-heeled stilts, excessive, all of her squeezed you like the girdle perched on her thick thighs, but somehow the effervescence, vivacity, and impish candor won you over so you didn't care. She was George's height. As he came up to her, she pinched both his cheeks and kissed him full on the mouth, leaving a big smear of shocking pink lipstick.

"If he were only Jewish," she said.

"I wouldn't be exotic," Steifer told her, catching it and batting his eyebrows.

A little more mischief, an intro for me, and they settled down to very serious business once we sat down inside the lady exec's small office. Within three or four minutes, Finestein was slamming her desk, breaking off a long vampish artificial fingernail as payment for the momentary burst of passion.

"You're not in. You're not in, they tell me. You're on leave. These vermin are ruining the community, scaring everybody half to death, and *you're* not in."

"I'm sorry," George said meekly.

"What, you were sick?"

"Yes."

"The rest of them, the clock could stop and they wouldn't know it. They've never learned how to *move*. You let these imbeciles, two stupid men, run amuck like they're some kind of geniuses. It takes three weeks, twenty-one days from the first incident to the last, just to get your hands on them, and now you come over to apologize when it's just going to happen all over again."

"Those two men are under surveillance. You don't have to worry about them."

"Well, la-de-da. You don't really believe that. You're just saying it."

"They're not the problem anymore. Somebody else will take up where they left off."

"What are you saying?"

"It's something more than a couple crackpots."

George laid out what he had, quickly summarizing the details of the case, then ending with the recent rash of anti-Semitic incidents. Possessing only what he'd gleaned from the newspapers and a few police reports, he wanted to know if Finestein or anyone else knew of other recent occurrences.

"Psychos and fanatics have their own set of rules," Steifer told her. "They've got a sense of drama or pageantry sometimes. I think they're sending out signals, setting the stage for something big."

Finestein had a list of the occurrences and articles from the *B'nai B'rith Messenger.* Steifer skimmed through the material and leaned over the desk. "I think there's a pattern here, a movement from the general to the particular, but I can't quite see it. Help me. What about this, the Eric Weiss Center. They've hit it twice. What is it?"

"You don't know who he was?"

"I'm a goy, remember. Tell me."

"Eric Weiss was a survivor of Auschwitz who dedicated his life to tracking down Nazis all over the world. The Eric Weiss Center is an institute for Holocaust studies."

"A specialized history library."

"More than that. They keep tabs on mass behavior and study and document present social conditions here and abroad to examine the causes of past and present anti-Jewish prejudice. In two weeks, they're honoring Hyman Lachmann. He was Weiss' assistant for thirty years."

"Two weeks?"

"Yes. It's going to be a big event. They're dedicating a new wing to him."

"That's a long time away."

"So?"

"We're going to have to wait it out."

"Wait what?"

"These Nazis I told you about, they're going to try to kill this man."

Mrs. Finestein nodded her head in agreement. "Now you're thinking. I could have told you before you sat down, but I wanted *you* to say it. This way maybe we can get something accomplished. Poor Hyman. Nothing will stop him from coming. He's fearless, but this will be a disaster."

"Maybe not."

"You're a nice man, Mister Steifer, but your police are incompetent or they just don't care. Either way is a tragedy for us. We cancel and feel like cowards or Hyman comes and gets killed."

"Not necessarily. Let me explain."

Finestein picked up her phone and started to dial a number. "If you'll excuse me, please, I've got to see what I can do here."

"Who are you calling?"

"The Eric Weiss Center. We've got to hold off on this, at least. Maybe they'll wait awhile."

"Sooner or later, it's going to happen. Please, let's talk first."

Steifer stared at Mrs. Finestein and her phone until she obeyed him and hung up.

"That's better," he told her.

"What do you propose to do?" she asked a little nastily. "Talk about it until one of them shoots him with a deer rifle?"

"I'm going to stop it—personally."

"How?"

"We know what the bastards are going to try to do. That puts us way ahead of them."

"I feel they're toying with us," observed Mrs. Finestein. "They're daring us to try and stop them."

"Sure. They want the publicity, and they're going to get it, too, for the last time."

"I wish I felt your confidence." Mrs. Finestein reached for a pack of cigarettes in a carpetbag on the floor, got out a low tar C-stick and lit up, pulling at the high neck of her cotton sweater.

"Don't worry," Steifer assured her, getting to his feet.

"You men. Always telling us what we want to hear." Mrs. Finestein raised her eyebrows at me. "I'm sorry. What was your name again?"

"Ben."

"Make sure he keeps his word, will you?"

"With that," I said, "you won't have any trouble."

• TWENTY-SIX •

Mrs. Finestein should have known better than to second-guess whether George Steifer would keep his nose to the grindstone as promised. Steifer's diligence was the last thing the lady had to worry about, providing he could make it through another two weeks of limbo. But he had that air of resignation about him that convinced me. He appeared to have given up believing he was going to find Elise Reilly alive. During that period of waiting, I saw George for lunch or dinner or drinks almost every day. Although he was back on the job, he was encountering a lot of the same old problems. Nobody was listening to him cry wolf. As far as Armstead and all the others were concerned, the Elise Reilly investigation was just one of those things destined to drag on forever and a day, and there wasn't a shred of evidence to link the reporter's disappearance to the anti-Semitic scare that had been nipped in the bud. Steif was allowed to maintain his surveillance on the Tully brothers, though nobody, but nobody was taking his theories to heart. He couldn't whine because he was scared they'd boot him off on leave again, so he was always calling me. He wasn't brooding about it. He was matter of fact as he rehashed the office gossip and relayed the dead ends he'd been coming up against as he pursued the thing on his own.

My son Pete had been gone for two weeks now and I felt rotten, so it was a relief to me that something had come of the time and effort I'd put into mothering George. Christ, it's hard to admit this, but my guess is that he was mothering me now. My life didn't seem to be in such great shape all of a sudden. My agent Ronny Rosen had gotten me a classy new writing job that paid well, but I just couldn't enjoy it. The story was so decent, cute, and entertaining, it made me sick to my stomach: *Silver Lake*, a touching tale of enduring old love and the young at heart. It was so forgettable, I couldn't remember it as I was writing it down. That's real impact for ya, makes ya feel like you're doin' somethin' real important, like makin' a con*tree*bution so as Folks'll come away with somethin' more than the popcorn 'tween their teeth at the same time as they're grabbin' them hankies or belly laughin' so as they're fit to be tied. Yes, sir, order me another one a them pies in the sky to go. Thank you so much.

I sat in the old writers' building at Fox and scribbled dippy little mash notes and dirty limericks to the secretary they gave me. She was a would-be actress, of course. After we sacked out together the first time, she had the nerve to ask me if I thought there might be a part for her in the picture. Walking on to TV sets on the lot and meeting Steif on

Fairfax Avenue were my only diversions. I preferred Fairfax. George had been hanging out there, jawing with all the shopkeepers, *yentas*, and *alter kockers* on the street, covering every square inch of sidewalk between Beverly and Melrose. The whole place, in general, is a comforting counterpart to the sleaze of Santa Monica Boulevard, wholesome and invigorating when you think of the Israeli folk tunes on the outdoor speaker of the record store or imagine dropping in on a Charlie Chaplin or Buster Keaton bill at the boarded-up old Silent Movie Theater, though it's a plaintive theme, with so many of the old people looking as if they've been put out to pasture. You can see how much it hurts them just to move. Still, they hobble along, never completely lost, clinging to their small world. They live in places with names like the Shalom Retirement Hotel or the King Solomon Home For The Elderly, and when not *kibbitzing*, spend a great deal of time in the waiting rooms of the senior medical clinics in the area. Ravaged and withered by the curse of age, their stubborn yet gentle faces gazed nearsightedly into the looming presence of death.

The old people appreciated knowing that the police were looking out for them. They didn't know it was just George, and, as the saying goes, what they didn't know wouldn't hurt them. The militant Jewish Defense League had started taking an active part as well. Packs of four or five men and women dressed in jeans and t-shirts bearing the JDL logo of a clenched fist rising in a Star of David, swaggered up and down the avenue with their trained guard dogs. The charged atmosphere seemed to both vex everybody and make them proud. People were worried, but they were banding together, too, so that their normal sense of stoic resignation was shed like a bulky winter coat, and they talked excitedly, exulting in their common purpose and heightened sense of belonging. I may have been down in the dumps, but that didn't stop me from putting on a little weight just being there. Day or night, wherever Steif decided to stop and talk to somebody, we got food shoveled at us. You could take your pick of falafels, peaches and plums, the tenderest Nova

Scotia, pizza, Chinese, Hungarian, coffee cake and Dan-
ishes, what have you, it was all there, up and down one big
block, in the short-order food stands, open-air produce mar-
kets, the butchers, bakeries, and delicatessens. Fairfax has
to be the only street in Los Angeles that, for the most part, if
you can ignore the sticky smells of hair oil and nail polish re-
mover coming at you from the assorted beauty salons and
barbershops, truly smells good.

Even so, by the second week, Steifer began to feel he
wasn't doing much more than spinning his wheels. Then,
the sick shenanigans recommenced and his visibility on the
avenue brought in some valuable delayed returns. It started
when I came home one night to find a Nazi storm trooper in
my living room. I'd never had the d.t.'s, but I'd been drinking pretty heavily and I thought this might be it: cockroaches, boa constrictors, white mice, or a herd of pink
elephants; in my case, a Nazi S.T. sitting on my couch.

"Ve have vays of making you *talk!*" I told him.

"Good evening," he said, rising to his polished black jack-
booted feet, snapping his heels, and giving me the straight-
arm salute and a "Heil Hitler!"

I tried to blink him away, but he was in his early twenties,
medium height, and swaybacked even standing at attention,
with a wide, thin mouth, a pinched narrow nose job, and
wide-set small green eyes that glistened with self-absorption.
His skin was pasty with an oily sheen and pimply around the
chin. He wore an officer's cap over short dyed-blond hair
and a starched khaki shirt with a swastika armband on both
long sleeves. The points of his collar were decorated with
gold swastika pins; his tie tack was a Maltese cross. It was a
nonstandard uniform that struck me as an eclectic assemblage of all his favorite dark fetishes.

"At ease," I told him. "All you're missing is a monocle
and a bullwhip."

"I am tape-recording this conversation," he said, pointing
to a small portable unit I noticed on the coffee table before
the couch. "This is so you will have an accurate transcrip-
tion for the Jew press. My body I will leave here as proof of

the sincerity of our mission. We will maim and kill the dirty Jew swine who so feebly attempt to halt our destiny. We will kill Jew and Jew lover alike in the name of Jesus Christ, our Lord, so that we may honor and protect the future purity of the perfect white race. Death to all Jews, sham Jew democracy, the Jew press, and Jew banker economy. We shall triumph, have no doubt."

He spoke with assurance in an even natural voice, over-enunciating each word as if he were reading them individually off a list. I didn't see a gun.

"I have no doubt you're one crazy sonofabitch," I told him.

"Long live the International White Peoples Alliance!"

"Where's Elise Reilly?"

He laughed, keeping his mouth wide and thin with his lips over his teeth, cackling from the back of his throat. I walked over and grabbed him by his necktie and pulled him to my face.

"What did you come here for?"

"I told you, comrade."

I patted him down without finding a gun or knife on him.

"What makes you think I'm gonna tell anybody you were here?"

"You will."

"Yes, maybe you are right, comrade." I picked up the phone and asked the operator for the police.

"They are on their way," he told me.

I hung up. "I wouldn't be so absolutely positive you're going to get publicity out of this."

There was a knock at the door.

"Come on in!" I yelled.

In came a small aging Ivy Leaguer in wrinkled blue-and-white seersucker trousers, penny loafers, and a white button-down shirt open at the collar. He was missing most of his hair and the traditional striped necktie, but that couldn't have been what was making him so puzzled as he frowned behind thick tinted glasses and pointed at the Nazi with his Bic pen.

"Am I too late?" he asked.

"For what?"

"The press conference."

I nodded toward the Nazi. "He's running the show."

"No, comrade. Come right in. We're just starting."

"Thank you."

"Heil Hitler!" exclaimed the young fanatic by way of official greeting, making with the Nazi high sign.

The small man didn't react. He took a tiny spiral notebook out of his back pocket. "What's your statement?" he asked.

"You are with which paper?"

"Santa Monica Daily Outlook."

This touched the kid. His eyes glistened with restrained tears as he nodded up and down. His voice turned quavery as he said, "Thank Christ the Jews didn't stop you. Your paper must be the only one they don't control."

He was all choked up, then he stopped and got a grip on himself, clicking his jackboots and snapping to attention with the stooge salute. If the coffee table hadn't been in his way, I'm sure he would have goose stepped in place. He didn't hear the reporter tell him he was off base with his paranoid assessment of the press.

"We will maim and kill all the dirty Jew swine who so feebly attempt to halt our destiny. We will eliminate Jew and Jew lover alike in the name of Jesus Christ, our Lord, so that we may honor and protect the future purity of the perfect white race."

"Amen," I said. "It's his prayer," I told the reporter. "Told me the same thing."

"You aren't a member of the party?"

"No. He just decided to use my house."

The reporter was only half-listening. "Is that it?" he asked the young Nazi.

"You will hear more," the Nazi said proudly, giving one last flick with his straight-arm before letting it down.

"I have some questions," said the small bald man.

The young Nazi stared toward the door. He didn't say anything.

"Are you advocating some particular violent action?" the reporter asked.

The young Nazi didn't answer.

The reporter went on, referring to his little notebook. "The message left by you or your organization said, quote, 'Come if you wish to learn what you've never known about the American Nazi movement.' I thought there was a remote possibility you might be a defector. But you're an advocate, aren't you?"

The Nazi kept staring into space in the direction of the door.

"Nothing you tell me is new. How many are there in your organization?"

The Nazi didn't answer.

The reporter closed his notebook, but he persisted. "You call yourselves the International White Peoples Alliance. Is that because you had some falling out with the mother organization, the National Socialist Caucasians Party? Tell me about them. Why didn't you get along? What was it about them you didn't like?"

The reporter and I looked at each other. "He's taken a vow of silence all of a sudden," I said. I passed a hand in front of the young Nazi's face. He wouldn't look at us. "Come on, kid, now's your big chance," I told him. "Give some hype to the press."

He made with the straight-arm again. "Long live the International White Peoples Alliance!"

Then he opened his mouth wide as if he was going to scream. But he didn't. He shut his mouth with a loud chomp, showing off his good bite. But that wasn't it either. His jaw muscles tightened and his pallor heightened, blanching his face, whitewashing it hideously, while his wide-set little eyes sprang wider, then froze in terror. He winced and bit his bottom lip, his chalk white face flushed with color, and his legs gave out. He fell over the low table.

Either the reporter or I could have caught him, but we were stunned. We watched the Nazi fall on his head and looked at each other.

Momentarily, I turned him over and slapped at his cheeks, trying to revive him. He was pale again and though his eyes moved, he didn't see me.

"Call for an ambulance," I told the reporter. "He swallowed some poison."

"A true Nazi," observed the reporter. "Potassium cyanide, probably. He'll be a goner inside of five minutes."

He rushed to the phone anyway. I dragged the kid into the bathroom, stuck my finger down his throat and tried to make him barf. On the first few tries, he made some quiet gurgling sounds. Then he stopped. I dumped him in the tub and ran the water over his mouth, trying to get him to swallow. It didn't work. I felt his pulse. He was still alive.

The reporter came in. We lifted him up. I stuck my hand down his throat again. He didn't make a sound now. Then his pulse stopped. No heartbeat. He was dead.

"Did you know this guy?" the reporter asked me.

I shook my head. I was looking at the Nazi. His face was all pasty again now. He kept looking at me with his wide-set frightened little dead eyes, like the sight of me was going to scare him to death for eternity. I tried to close the lids, but the eye muscles were set and I didn't want to force them.

"Any particular reason why he would have chosen your house?"

"I have no idea," I lied.

"Are you sure?"

I had to pretend to be indignant. It seemed like the only way. "Do I look like a Nazi to you?" I yelled at the guy.

"You're avoiding the question," he said coolly.

I pretended like I was mad as hell and went into my bedroom and slammed the door. I picked up the phone and called George.

"Get your ass over here," I told him.

"What's up?" he asked sleepily.

"I found a dead Nazi. He looks like one of the punks."

"Where are you?"

"My house."

The reporter came in as I was hanging up.

"Who were you talking to?"

"I just called the police."

"Mind if I hang around?"

"As a matter of fact, yes, I do."

The guy smiled. "I had a feeling you'd say that."

So he waited outside. Twenty minutes later, immediately before the cops appeared, he came back inside my gate and knocked on the front door. I opened the door.

"I went to a pay phone," he told me. "Nobody at the West L.A. or Santa Monica Police Stations received a call from this address."

Two patrolmen had drawn their guns on him before all of the words were out of his mouth.

"Don't move," they told him.

"Bob Bishop, the *Santa Monica Daily Outlook*. I called you guys," he protested.

"Just stay where you are—you too," they said at me.

The two of them came in the gate and walked up. Both were in uniform, about thirty-five, with greasy brown hair and short moustaches and too much stomach. One of them held his gun on us while the other felt us up for weapons.

"I called Captain Steifer from West Hollywood," I told them. "This is his case."

"How do you know?" said the one who had just gone over me for the gun.

"There's a dead kid in my bathroom who's wearing a Nazi uniform. He came here to make a statement and called the papers and the police to tell them about it. He didn't just choose my house by accident."

"How so?"

"That's all I can tell you before Mister Steifer gets here."

The reporter started getting self-righteous. "But when I asked you, you said you had no idea."

"Sorry."

"Let's see your ID," the cop with feelers said to the reporter.

He took out his wallet and showed them.

"OK," said the same patrolman. "Nobody's got a statement yet. We're going to have to ask you to leave."

"Can't you guys just give me some idea?"

"We don't know," they both told him.

"All right, I'm not gonna argue," the reporter said spunkily, looking at their badges and taking down their names. "Mind if I call you later?"

"Fine," one of them said.

The reporter left, then a black and white rolled up, announcing itself from a mile off with its siren. I showed the two that were already there into the tiny bathroom and stood outside the bathroom door as they looked over the body.

"A real gestapo," said one of them.

"Looks like he's dressed for a movie," said the other.

"Took his role pretty serious, though, didn't he?" I chimed in.

The other cops bulldozed their way in; these two clean shaven, older, one of them taller, both fatter, with less greasy brown hair. They looked in at the Nazi in the bathtub.

"Fuck," said the taller one. "What's this, Halloween?"

"B and D nut," said the other new one. "Somebody drown him?"

"He poisoned himself. I was trying to get him to throw it up or wash it out with water," I explained for the second time. "He had a tape recorder. You can hear everything that happened."

I got the tape recorder, rewound, and played them the scene, then they patched a call to Steifer's car to check my story about calling him, and picked him up two blocks from my house. When he walked in, he went straight to the body after showing the West L.A. cops his ID. I stood at the bathroom door, watching him as he went over the young dead man's pockets, looking for ID.

"Nothing on him," the tall older cop told him.

Without saying anything, George rushed out of the house, then returned with his briefcase. He took out his pictures of the Young Hitlers punks, dropped the briefcase on the living room floor, and rushed back into the bathroom. He sat on the edge of the tub and held one of the small close-ups next to the dead man's face. The four cops and I crowded in for a close look.

"Could be," said somebody.

"Maybe," said somebody else.

"I don't think so," said another.

I didn't think so myself and George didn't seem sure either. It was close, but the picture had a smaller, squarer face and much different eyes. "We have a positive ID on this kid," he explained to his audience, indicating the snapshot. "We'll have to match the prints."

"What did he do?" asked one of them.

"One murder, maybe others. We don't know yet."

George called the coroner's office and West Hollywood, then he turned on the tape. The West L.A. cops left.

"At ease," I heard myself saying for the third time. "All you're missing is a monocle and a bullwhip."

"Wisenheimer," Steifer said without pleasure.

He listened all the way through, turning the volume up when the reporter and I got out of range, arguing inside my bedroom.

"That's it," I told him at the point I'd turned it off.

Steifer shrugged. "Maybe he recorded something else."

The blank tape played itself out, manufacturing a scratchy, breathy-sounding silence that dominated. We started to talk a couple of times, but Steifer sat on the edge of the couch, poised and anxious like he was afraid he might miss something.

We listened until it stopped at the end—nothing going nowhere at full speed—and yet, a dead Nazi was lounging in my bathtub.

• TWENTY-SEVEN •

B ut this nothing, specifically, had first and last names: Alfred Norman Tully. He was the nephew of the two country bumpkins George had taken us to see down at the county courthouse. West L.A. found his '65 Chevy convertible parked about six blocks away. It isn't every car you see that's hand painted with quaint sayings such as NIGGER GO HOME and KILL ALL JEWS. The first team of patrolmen who had stopped by my house passed it on Rose Avenue at some time later that night. Interested, they stopped. The top and tires had been slashed, but in the trunk they found a change of street clothes and a wallet with a current driver's license and other ID. George told me all about it at ten o'clock the next morning when I called him at work to see if anything was new. We decided to have lunch and he told me to meet him at Canter's Delicatessen on Fairfax.

When I got there, a crowd was blocking the sidewalk before the entrance. I stood on my tiptoes and looked over the old peoples' stooped shoulders. Swastikas, X's, and crosses had been spray painted on the sidewalk, starting at this point and going up the street a ways. Five or six bearded young men wearing skullcaps were down on their knees in the open center of the crowd, scrubbing at the cement walk with wire brushes and dipping them in buckets of strong-smelling paint thinner. There was a soft buzz of hushed voices.

I went into the restaurant and my nostrils were assaulted by the infinitely more inviting, one of a kind aroma of yeast and sugar and garlic distilled from the take-out bakery and deli counters on either side of the main entrance. George waved to me from the short line beyond the cash register where he was waiting for a table. He'd seen the commotion earlier that morning. When we sat down, he put it all together for me.

"The couple in the house in front of my apartment saw the car around eight o'clock last night, driving around the neighborhood, parked across the street. He must have given up waiting for me and decided to try you instead. He stopped on Fairfax on his way down to the freeway, about eleven."

"He wasn't hiding anything, was he?"

"He was fresh out of Camarillo. Thought he was Jesus two years ago, but he was supposed to have settled down."

"His uncles got him excited."

"If we'd swallowed a tenth the black beauties he had, we might have volunteered to be his henchmen."

"Hmm. That Nazi hunter's due here in a couple days now. Maybe this was part of the buildup."

"And maybe it wasn't."

"I'm glad you're the one saying it."

Steif and I ordered our sandwiches and ate awhile without talking. We looked up at each other at the same time.

Steifer pushed his plate to the side before he said, "I think it's all over."

"What about Elise?"

"She must have just rubbed one of them the wrong way. They got scared and ran away."

"No conspiracy?"

"That's what I'm beginning to think."

"You're probably right."

"We found her, day before yesterday. Buried in her own backyard."

"No."

"They did something terrible to her."

I couldn't look at him.

"I've given it a lot of thought. I only knew her two months. I met her on the rebound, as you've said. Who knows how long it would have lasted. I've decided I shouldn't torture myself."

"But you were in love with her," I told the top of the table.

"I still am. I probably always will be. I'm just going to have to learn to live with it."

"She would have wanted you to be happy and go on. That's what you have to remember." Saying that, I winced and looked up, smiling wearily. "I didn't mean to sound like your grandmother."

"Don't worry about it." Steifer leaned back in the booth. "It's true."

"But that still won't stop you from feeling low. You can't help but lose faith awhile. It'll seem like there's nothing to look forward to."

"I know."

"I'm real sorry."

"Yeah, well, I hope we get to them before it happens to someone else."

"They'll tip themselves sooner or later."

"It may be tomorrow, two years from now, or never at all. Once the first couple of weeks pass, there's no way of knowing. Let's put it this way: I'm finished holding my breath. I can't afford to get into a state where I'm no good to anybody, least of all myself."

I nodded my agreement, listening to him try to talk himself into something it was evident he didn't feel. He picked up on what he was doing.

He rolled his eyes. "Listen to me—well, you've listened to me enough."

He took the check and got up. The owner-manager of the outdoor produce market called to Steif as we walked past on our way to the parking lot. He was standing at the cash register and scales, a wiry little man in a soiled white apron, with wispy white-gray hair and a dark silvery stubble catching light from the overhead tube lighting filling in the warm shadows underneath the aluminum awning that shielded the precious fruits and vegetables from the hard sunshine on the edge of the sidewalk before the store. He wagged his right index finger at us as he finished ringing up a customer's order. We stepped over to him. He finished making change, slammed the battered cash drawer closed, then he smiled and stepped out of the enclosed area.

"Take over," he told a curly-haired Latin boy who was

weighing some honeydew melon. "Captain, how are you?" he asked Steifer.

"Fine, Mordecai, just fine," Steif told him.

"He doesn't eat," Mordecai told me. "Both of you, whatever you want, take."

"That's very nice of you," Steif told him. "We just had lunch."

Steifer started to step away. We smiled and nodded good-bye.

"Please, I must talk to you."

The little man buried his hands in the front pockets of his apron, did an about-face, and walked briskly ahead into the back of his store. Without even knowing the place, you could see that all of his business was in the front. The resident shoppers are quality and price comparison experts. This shop obviously wasn't known for its butcher or canned goods. The main floor of the store was empty, with nobody in the grocery aisles or waiting by the meat counter. The cans on the shelves were dusty and some of the manufacturers had changed their label art since the last time Mordecai had placed an order.

The little man turned around and nodded once he got to the back of the store. When he looked at George this time, I saw that he was blind in his left eye. It was covered with a milky film; the other was light blue.

"I know somebody who saw them," he said.

Steifer didn't get excited. "They won't be the first or the last. I have more witnesses than I need from last night."

"Not that. You were asking about what happened at the Eric Weiss Center, weren't you?"

"Right."

"This lady I know, a friend of my sister's, she was there that night. She's a little sick, just scared, but very smart. In Berlin, she used to teach at the university. She speaks five languages fluently."

"The building was closed."

"I know that. She's a rummager, not a bag lady. We like

to call her a rummager. She's clean, but very poor, with no family. You see?"

George nodded.

"I give her food, but half the time she won't take it. She rummages. There's an Oriental restaurant next door to Eric Weiss. She was in the back in the alley, going through the trash when they broke in there."

Steifer nodded eagerly. "I'd like to talk to her."

"She gets old bread almost every day from a bakery here down the street. From me, she won't take; from somebody else, she's not so proud. She doesn't realize I know. I saw one day when I was driving through the alley."

Steifer was impatient. "Which bakery is it?"

"She won't talk to you without me. If you're there waiting for her, she'll be too scared. I know the people who run the bakery. I'll call them and tell them to inform me when she comes in. Then I'll go down there and pretend to run into her. Where can I meet you?"

"What time will she come?"

"Any time in the afternoon."

"Page me in Canter's. I'll wait for you in the bar."

The old man nodded. "In the bar."

• TWENTY-EIGHT •

The bar in Canter's is called the Kibbitz Room, though it's the only quiet part of the restaurant. Decorated in early sixties swank modern, with walls of cork and rough wood, a low ceiling suspended from the old one, and dim lights like flying saucers, it's on the far end of the new wing. Four orange Naugahyde booths face the ten seat L-shaped bar. The unfinished finishing touches are modeled along the lines of what a swinging sportsman might put in his den. The shiny dark wood shelves on either side of the cash register are half-filled with fishing trophies, dull bronzes in the shape of marlin and swordfish, and a fancy scale model white-and-red cabin cruiser sits on a small shelf in between the cash register and an animated Coors beer sign with a sparkling mountain stream. To the side, chairs are stacked over the tarp-covered upright piano bar. A cheap painting of a blue moonlit sea is reflected by the long mirror on the wall behind the piano. If you sit in the second booth and look a little to the right, the picture takes up the whole mirror and you can almost imagine you're having a by-the-numbers nightmare in which the terrible blacklight of a ruptured moon has turned the entire earth ultraviolet forever.

We were the only *kibbitzers* in the Kibbitz Room. George wasn't interested in a drink either. He just knew the bar was always empty. We could hang out here all day without getting nudged from the table. For the most part, serious drinking seems to be predominantly a gentile sport. I fought my nature and ordered a chocolate roll and coffee after flagging down a waitress. Some punishment. I broached the delicate subject with Max Schulman, the bartender, while George went off to make phone calls. Max was a pleasure of a sharpie, a pastured cabbie out of Brooklyn, by way of Detroit. With his small head and loose reddish jowls, overlarge thick blue lips, and mountainous gut, he looked like a huge hunk of smoked salmon. I thought he would blow bubbles when he talked, but he didn't leave his yap open long enough to make an O. I didn't mind. *Au contraire*, I was hard up for a good yak, a carefree conversation with no ulterior motive in which the participants, in person, attempt discussing some subject other than themselves. It's a dying art. You have to practice once in awhile to get the knack or keep it.

"Jewish people have less of a need to be *shikkers*. It's because of the religion," Max asserted at one point.

"And Christianity, by its design, is escapist," I decided. "There's a better life after death."

That wasn't all. Max leaned over the counter, his small bloated face deepening in color, flushing under the pressure of heartfelt thought and emotion. "And a Jew would rather read a book or take a walk than shoot an animal. Fishing, shooting, fox hunts—to kill, is this recreation?"

Initially, having got carried away in the tipsy spirit of expansion and remodeling, the management had certainly erred in their grasp of the fundamentals. But the food was so good, the failure could be pardoned, even condoned. The empty Kibbitz Room was part of what made Canter's Canter's.

I ate and thought. "Maybe Christian man is more hostile," I suggested. "We're confused. Since life is supposed to be better after death, we drink ourselves to oblivion and shoot things in order to hurry the process."

"To each his own," Max chided me. "Every man should be able to do what he wants. Live and *let* live."

"Sure."

"Just don't tell me God won't hear my prayers or that I'm going to hell because I'm a Jew."

You couldn't get away from them these days, not around Fairfax. "The moral majority."

"They are dangerous. It's how they started in Germany—slow. The people ignored them."

"Then they became the people. Americans are smarter, though, Maxie. Ya gotta believe that."

Max lifted his left hand and showed me that he was crossing his fingers. "We hope."

George came back tense. It was contagious. In an hour, I had a headache. I went out and bought a pack of cards and walked around. When I came back, Maxie had gone off duty. I played solitaire awhile, then George took me up on a slow round of gin rummy. After another hour, I needed another breather. Outside before, I'd seen a bunch of guys playing basketball on the outdoor courts at Fairfax High. I decided to go over and see if I could get into a pick-up game. It was summertime and nice and hot out. You couldn't meditate on the moral majority every second of your waking life. Once in awhile, you had to goof around, get loose, and live. Besides, the little grocer had probably drawn a blank.

I called my bitch actress-secretary at Fox and told her I wouldn't be coming back to the office. Coldly, she reminded me I'd be missing a meeting with my moron boss, that forty-year-old idiot savant Harvard MBA who was so sickeningly suave and youthfully sensitive that he'd decided to become a tortured artist after making his first trillion in real estate. He wore designer jeans, custom safari shirts, and carried a purse. Each time we met he'd take his powder right in front of me and sniffle and tell me he was afraid I wasn't feeling the characters in their full depth. He was right and he was wrong. They were so deep to me, they might as well have been buried.

I told the bitch I felt ill and would stop by the man's office in the morning. When I hung up, I decided to finish my first draft at home. I didn't need these people. They needed me and a lot else, too, that I could never give them. They were living in a moral vacuum. Just being in the same room was enough to make you feel empty-headed. No wonder the neo-Nazis, the moral majority, and all the other assorted crank cults were doing so well. Entertainment, these days, had become so sleazy, pointless, and inept, it almost made you applaud the new right's efforts to do away with our freedoms of speech and press, even if these new messiahs were nothing but mean-spirited, tasteless, bigoted, intolerant, and small-minded—almost, but not quite, if you could still count all your fingers and tell the Pledge of Allegiance from the "Volga Boat Song." No sir.

Then, as soon as I'd returned to the bar to say good-bye, I saw the little man coming up the short center stairs dividing the old wing from the new. He had removed the apron and changed his shirt and he was steering an old decrepit woman by the elbow. She would go a few steps, then stop on him like a stubborn mule. He'd lean close, talk to her, and she'd go on only to stop on him again. I told Steifer. He stood up and waved at them from the booth. When they came into the bar, I got a better look at her. Stooped now and wasted low by arthritis, the lady had once been tall; even the way she was, with her back painfully hunched over, she towered over the little grocer. She had to be at least six feet. Her glasses magnified her blue-gray eyes and made them look as large with terror as she probably felt. Tears coursed down her long face which, like the rest of her, was far too thin, though the emaciation gave her prominent cheekbones a beautiful Asiatic quality. Her small mouth was sewed up and bitter. She was chewing at the bottom lip, and with the way the cords in her neck strained, it was like she was holding back a scream. Still, I could picture her young, which, I suppose, is what made my first impression a tragic one. She had such beautiful silver hair, pulled off her forehead and braided into a bun, and though her skin was spotted and too pale, it was hardly wrinkled. She was a pressed flower, a sepia-toned picture of exquisite youth cut short and somehow cruelly preserved. Her clothes made you want to weep: a heavy, faded blue-black skirt with a matching bolero-styled jacket that had been trimmed in something—fur, probably—that had been taken off. The ends of her sleeves and the inside edges were deeper in color and showed traces of stitching and small spots of glue. The skirt was frayed across the back edge where it dragged over the ground and shorter in front, coming half way up the ankles of heavy and unseemly dull black laced boots on short heels. The frayed and yellowed blouse under the bolero had a delicate little scalloped collar which she wore buttoned to the neck. None of the buttons matched. Some were pearly, others white or ivory.

"I'm sorry it took so long," said old Mordecai. "Missus Baum didn't like the way she was dressed. I had to take her home first."

The lady's chin wrinkled under the sour mouth. Her pride was hurt and exposed. She hadn't wanted us to know that this clean but shabby getup was the best she had to offer. She fought to straighten her shoulders and turned away.

Steifer slid out of the booth and took the old lady's hand and placed it between his palms like gentle handcuffs, urging her toward the booth. "Hello, Missus Baum. Pleased to meet you."

I handed her a cloth napkin. She took it with her free hand and dabbed at her face.

"It's alright," the grocer told her. "These are nice men. They won't hurt you."

"He's always talking," she said, glaring at the little man. "You had no right to speak for me. I told you I would tell them when I was ready. Isn't that what I said?"

She had no accent, and though her face was tight with anger, her voice was sweet.

Mordecai shrugged. "I got tired of waiting," he said gently.

"Please sit down," Steifer urged, still holding onto the tall old woman's hand.

The little old guy pleaded with her. "No one thinks you did anything wrong, Sarah. These men need your help. I told them everything."

"Then what do they need to know?"

"I just want you to look at some pictures," George said calmly.

"I hardly saw them."

She pulled away from George and slouched down on the edge of the seat across from him. He grabbed his briefcase off the table.

Mordecai shook his head. "I'm surprised at you. Tsk, tsk."

The old lady looked down at the table. "I don't remember."

"You said the outside light shined right in their faces."

"I tell you, I don't remember."

George had his pictures out. "You want some coffee? How about a Danish, anything?"

"No," she said. She wouldn't look up from the table.

Steifer put the pictures on the table in front of her. "Just look at them. Tell me if any are familiar. Nobody sees you. I won't tell anybody."

"They'll kill me," she cried into the napkin.

George tried to soothe her. "No, no," he said.

"It can happen again," the old man insisted.

She started to get up, but the grocer wouldn't let her. He

held her left arm on the table and pushed up the sleeve. I saw part of a concentration camp number.

"Young girls branded like cattle because a beautiful, intelligent, free woman cannot, even for a moment, conquer her fear. Is this what you want—more of this?"

She cried terribly and cursed the little man in an assortment of languages. I went off and got her some tea from an understanding waitress who had been standing nearby, trying to eavesdrop. As soon as I put it down in front of her, the waitress was back with a sweet roll.

"She won't take, but everybody's giving," the grocer sighed. He leaned over and spoke to her in a voice more tender. "If you can't take, you can't give, Sarah. Help yourself by trying to help us. Don't hate yourself."

She pushed the tea and sweet roll away and looked over the pictures. She went through around twenty or twenty-five, many of them decoys, then she saw one that made her gasp. She covered it with her open hand. I knew it was one of the Young Hitlers, a tall, skinny blond punk, nothing distinctive about him except a certain native ability to trigger the creeps.

"Are you sure?" George asked her.

She wouldn't take her hand off the photo. "If they had seen me, they would have killed me," she told herself, her sweet voice turning raspy now.

"We're glad they didn't," Steifer told her. "Nobody wants to live in fear. We're all proud of you."

The grocer patted Sarah Baum on the shoulder. "You've taken a big step. You should feel good for a change."

But she left without saying a word, walking slowly like a tired ghost.

The little man called out her name. She didn't seem to hear him. He apologized and went after her.

"They might listen to me now," Steifer told me.

"The cops? I doubt it," I told him.

• TWENTY-NINE •

Between George's diligence and the high-pressured arm-twisting of Mrs. Finestein and the Jewish Federation, the PD conceded on the off chance of getting caught with its pants down and at the last moment gave its begrudging consent to a follow-through with the team approach, meaning that two days later at the Eric Weiss Center, over seventy-five officers from the LAPD's Special Weapons and Tactics Team (SWAT), Detective Support Division, Public Disorder and Intelligence Divisions were either in attendance or about the general vicinity during the outdoor ceremony honoring Weiss' renowned colleague, Nazi hunter Hyman Lachmann. Undercover men were in the audience and about the canopied parking lot, on the neighboring rooftops, and sitting in parked cars.

George called me and told me the story before I heard it again on the eleven o'clock news and read it in the paper the following morning. I wasn't there. Probably at the exact moment the two punks took their medicine and checked out, I was at Fox, lying my way through a story conference with that stupid hophead from Harvard, telling him what marvelous progress I was making in learning how to *feel* his precious characters. What happened was that an Abbey Rents truck pulled up after the festivities had started, the two of them got out, opened up the back of the truck, and took out a load of extra chairs. They carried them as far as the front door before the police closed in, then they ran off down Pico Boulevard, one of them firing ʾld bursts from an Uzi submachine gun, the other brandishing a hand grenade from which he pulled the pin. The street was already barricaded for four or five blocks and nobody was worried about them getting away. They just wanted them in one piece, but that wasn't to be. The grenade went off and so did they. Seems like suicide, but Steifer says they're not sure. Maybe the kid just waited too long to heave off. Not that it matters.

The other three Young Hitlers are still at large, as they say, though their home bases have been pinned down. They have names, too, but I forget them. All I remember is that two were from L.A., the third from Houston. And one of the L.A. boys is Jewish. His folks live in the Fairfax area. There was an article on them about a month after the Hyman Lachmann affair, all about their shame and grief and consternation over the boy's clandestine betrayal and how they couldn't understand how he'd gotten that way because he'd been an honors student in physics; and they found the mother just in time about a day after the article appeared in the paper, head in the oven. That was in the paper, too. You can't keep a damn thing out of the papers these days, except what's important. It's not that we don't have a free press, but they're so afraid of having lawsuits slapped on them, they won't run anything interesting unless they can back it up with a veritable Fort Knox of proof—especially something about the moral majority. The media is running scared. The networks are so afraid of losing their sponsors due to a Bible Belt shoppers' boycott, they've warned the sitcom writers to watch their jokes and they're making the girls hold back on their jiggle.

I found out firsthand by taking the *L. A. Times* reporter who had done the piece on the Jewish Young Hitler out to lunch and telling him the whole story. It wasn't good enough for him. He liked it at the time, mind you, but when I called him two weeks later to see how it was going, he said he'd been shot down in editorial. They couldn't risk libel on my interesting theory.

"You're a reporter. Look into it. Investigate," I told him.

"I'd like to, I really would," the guy said, placating me in that overearnest voice people use to calm down the average crank.

"So it's like that."

"Excuse me?"

"I saw Jerry Falwell's picture on the wall of a TV evangelist's office and found a bible on a neo-Nazi, so I'm jumping to crazy conclusions and all you can do is put me off nicely because we had lunch and maybe you feel sorry for me because I sound like I'm a little overworked."

"Not exactly. I just need something solid as a backup."

"What I've been trying to tell you is, this sort of thing is never solid until it's too late."

"Keep in touch if anything comes up."

"Yeah, sure. See you in the gas chamber."

Click. He didn't like that. Maybe he was all or part Jewish and I'd struck a nerve. I don't have an ounce of Jewish blood in me, so apart from being agnostic and recording this insanity on paper, I'd be as safe as baby Jesus.

I tried to reach the reporter for the *Daily Outlook,* the one who had showed up at my house to stand watch on that crazy kid Nazi's Jim Jones-styled departure, but he had left town without a forwarding address. People are like that when you need them. I got the guy's address and went over to his place in Santa Monica. It was a bungalow court with tile around the flat edges of the roof. The furniture was gone.

I don't even know why I bothered, but I guess it has to do with how this all started out. My son Pete had carried on about me being an aging flower child too oblivious to be hipped that I was living in a fascist police state, and my best buddy George, the policeman, had gotten himself into something that made us agree with him.

It's been three months now, and still no sign. Steifer has run every check there is. If only the little bastard would write. I'd just like to know he's alive and well. But he's not taking any chances on my coming after him. No clues, no trace, no trail.

Nothing.

Zilch.